Is Love Enough

MARISA ADAMS

Copyright © 2012 Marisa Adams

All rights reserved.

ISBN: 1479377201
ISBN-13: 978-1479377206

DEDICATION

This book is dedicated to my husband and best friend. Without you, I would never have taken the time to explore my dreams. Thank you for being you!

CONTENTS

Acknowledgments	i
Prologue	Pg # 1
Chapter One	Pg # 9
Chapter Two	Pg # 38
Chapter Three	Pg # 61
Chapter Four	Pg # 88
Chapter Five	Pg # 113
Chapter Six	Pg # 129
Chapter Seven	Pg # 143
Chapter Eight	Pg # 159
Chapter Nine	Pg # 180
Chapter Ten	Pg # 202
Chapter Eleven	Pg # 217
Chapter Twelve	Pg # 250
Epilogue	Pg # 260

ACKNOWLEDGMENTS

To Cherry and Dawn, my earliest pre-readers – many thanks for your advice, suggestions, and friendship. I treasure both of you more than you know.

To Robin – I threw you into the mix at the last minute and appreciate it immensely. I look forward to many more moments of laughter and friendship.

To my sister – I will forever be grateful for the many glasses of wine and conversations on your closet floor. We may not get to spend tons of time together, but I cherish those times we do.

To my Aunt Kaye – there are never enough ways to thank you for being such a great sounding board for me. I treasure our relationship and am thankful every day that family can extend beyond what God gives us.

To my mother – I am blessed beyond belief to have a mother who is also my friend. Words cannot express how much your support means to me. Your feedback is always honest and exactly what I need. I love you more than words can say.

To my father – I cherish every one of our conversations more than you know. You are a rock of support and love.

To my daughter and my husband – you are both my life. Thank you for allowing me to follow my dreams and for walking with me every step of the way.

And, finally, to my friends at Gem's – for us, the journey will never end! I am so thankful for the laughter and support from the most amazing group of friends I have never met!!!

PROLOGUE

Cold. Dark. Empty.

For the first time in months, the weather actually complemented Rebekah's mood. Usually, if she was sad, the sun was shining; if she was ecstatic, it rained. But, today was different. Today, it was as if God was empathizing with her, completing the atmosphere with rain drops that mimicked the tears rolling down her cheeks. Her life would never be the same, and deep inside, she knew that.

"Bekah?" A soft, quiet voice called out from behind her. "Are you ready to go?"

"No," she whispered back, not even having the energy to turn and face her friend.

"I know, honey, but the cars are here and everyone is waiting on us. We have to leave."

"I don't think I can do it," Rebekah broke down, silent tears streaming down her face. She felt, more than heard, her friend cross the room, and before she knew it, Kate was standing behind her, wrapping her arms around her, and offering Rebekah the support she needed at the moment. Silently, they stood there together for several minutes, watching the sky open up and cry with the both of them. "We need to go," Rebekah murmured.

"I'm ready when you are," Kate replied, releasing her embrace and squeezing her friend's hand. "And, I'll be right there with you the whole time."

Rebekah turned to face her friend of so many years. The dark circles under her eyes were intensified by the dark hair that surrounded Kate's face, and she knew that this had hit Kate as hard as it had hit her. "I don't know what I would do without you," she said, as Kate pulled her in for another hug. "Thank you for being here."

"I wouldn't be anywhere else, and you know it."

Silently, the two young women left the room together and headed towards the living room where the rest of the family was waiting. The sea of black that greeted them was almost overwhelming to Rebekah, and she felt Kate's grip on her tighten. It shouldn't have amazed her that Kate could read her mind and would automatically empathize with her emotions; it had always been that way with the two of them. From the moment they first met in the seventh grade, they had a connection that blossomed into an immediate friendship. That friendship had grown over the years and it was that friendship, along with the love staring at her from almost every face in the room, that Rebekah was relying on to survive this day.

"Are you ready to go?" She heard her father ask from his position at the fireplace. Rebekah glanced at him and couldn't help but return to earlier days in her mind. She closed her eyes to banish the memories, but it was too late; images raced through her mind in no particular order. How many nights had they all spent together in this very room, she, Steve, Kate, John, and her parents? How many memories did these walls hold? How many secrets? In her recollections, she saw her father as a younger man: always smiling, always strong, always stoic. There was only one other time in her life when she had seen him almost crumble. As she forced her eyes open and looked through the tears brimming there, she saw him now, a graying version of his younger self. And now, it seemed like it would be the second time in her life he almost fell. She knew he was trying to keep it together for her, to be strong for her, but Steve was like a son to him, and he had already lost one child. Grabbing her coat from the closet, she slipped it on gently, and replied, "I'm as ready as I'll ever be."

Her father only nodded in reply. He reached his hand down to help her mother up from the ottoman that she was sitting on in front of him, and together, they crossed the room to join Rebekah and Kate. The man representing the funeral home entered the front door and addressed the family and friends gathered there. "We have three cars waiting and that should be enough room for everyone gathered here. Mrs. Thomas," he continued, turning to speak directly to Rebekah, "you will be in the first car. That car will lead the procession to the church. Once the service is over, your car will follow immediately behind the one carrying your husband."

Numbly, Rebekah nodded. This was too real for her, and it shouldn't be happening. Steve was too young; she was too young. They should be together right now, laughing, planning for their future, going through the steps to try and have a baby. She should not be planning and going through his funeral. But, there was no amount of wishing on Rebekah's part that would change anything; Steve was gone and she was the one left behind.

Rebekah felt her father's hand touch the small of her back as he ushered her from the house and into the waiting car. Her mother stood on the other side of her father, and Rebekah could practically hear the tears falling from her mother's eyes. There was nothing about this day that was easy for anyone. Steve may have been her husband, but he was the son that her parents never had. In some ways, Rebekah wondered if this was harder for them than it was for her.

In silence, they drove to the church; the sound of an occasional sniffle or sigh was the only thing that broke the monotony. That silence was slowly killing Rebekah because it was in that she felt completely alone. Raindrops danced across the windows as she watched the outside world fly by. She and Steve had both been so adamant about settling down in their hometown; it was where both of their parents were, and it was where they knew they wanted to raise their kids. Now, it was so painful to see all of the places that once represented so many happy moments and cherished memories.

In a daze, Rebekah felt the car stop and felt the strong hands of her father reach down to support her as she stepped out of the car. How many times had those hands supported her before? She gazed up at the man she had loved for so long and thought about the last time he helped her out of the car in this exact same place in front of the church. At that moment, there was no way she could have felt more alive. On that day, the sun had shone, and her father had watched her with such love and awe as he prepared to offer her hand in marriage to a man he had had grown to love. Today, he just watched her with sadness.

As he escorted her into the church and down the aisle, she could feel the congregations' eyes on her and knew the polite thing to do was to make eye contact and acknowledge their presence; however, she just couldn't seem to make her brain work. She could only focus on the coffin that was in front of her.

Once seated, the family pressed together, and although they had an entire row to themselves, the four of them crowded so close it was almost impossible to tell where one started and the other one stopped. Rebekah closed her eyes when she heard the minister say, "We are here to celebrate the life of Steven Andrew Thomas, brother, son, and husband." She knew she should be paying attention, but she was afraid that the longer she listened, the more she would lose it; so, she mentally forced herself to shut it all out. In her mind, she regressed to a happier time, a time she just wanted to get lost in.

They were sixteen when they first fell in love, although they had known each other for years. Growing up, it had always been she, John, and Steve. Her mother called them the three musketeers. They complemented each other because she reined them in some and they drew out her daring side. From the moment they entered kindergarten, they were inseparable. Once Kate came into the picture in junior high though, they actually drifted apart some. It always amazed Rebekah what hormones would do. Kate wasn't particularly fond of Steve, but she couldn't stand John. So, girls being girls, they stopped hanging out as much. She and Kate spent countless hours ooing and aahing over many young men in their school, and never once did either of them consider Steve or John an acceptable match for the other.

That changed one fateful day in high school. Kate and

Rebekah rode to school together every morning and afternoon in Kate's car as she was older and got her driver's license first. It was a beautiful spring day, and the girls had the windows rolled down and music turned up. The other car turned towards them so fast, Kate barely had any time to react. They were hit broadside, and Rebekah spent a week in the hospital. Kate was recuperating at home, and she rarely had the opportunity to come check on Rebekah. Although she had many friends who came by to see her, it was Steve who never left her side. By the beginning of the next school year, Steve and Rebekah were officially an item, and two years later, they were married.

Rebekah still laughed at how coincidental life had been. It turned out the other driver who had hit them was John. He felt such insurmountable guilt over what occurred that he never left Kate's side as she healed at home. She joked that he annoyed her, but Rebekah knew her well enough to know that she was lying. But even though both Rebekah and Steve knew that John and Kate were interested in each other, it wasn't until a year after their own wedding that the other two finally gave in and admitted it. They were married six months later, and the three musketeers officially became four.

Shortly after their wedding, John and Kate moved to New York, but the two couples stayed in touch, unlike many high school friends that grow up, move away, and drift apart. Both Rebekah and Kate began teaching, so that was another common connection for them. But, the biggest connection was their friendship; they had been with each other through the good and the bad, and always would be.

'Just like today,' Rebekah thought to herself, tearing herself away from the past and forcing herself back into the present. Once again, John and Kate were there supporting them. Kate sat with Rebekah to support her, and John stood with the pallbearers to physically support Steve for the last time. Rebekah watched as the group of men silently picked up the casket and carefully carried it out of the church. She knew she was supposed to follow, but couldn't seem to make her legs move. She felt Kate squeeze her hand in silent support and turned her tear-filled eyes up to meet her mother's gaze. Her mother reached out her own hand and Rebekah stood, drawing strength from those around her. Together, they made their way back down the aisle and to the car, waiting for the drive that would truly make everything final.

When they arrived at the cemetery, Rebekah and her family were seated in front of the coffin. The rain had finally stopped, and normally, the covering that stood above them protected the family from the intense heat of the Texas sun. Today, it simply formed a wind tunnel that allowed the frigid January air to whip through her despite the long coat she kept wrapped around her body.

She could barely listen to the words that the minister chose to use; it was simply just too difficult to focus. Yet, when she found her eyes wandering over the other headstones in the cemetery, she couldn't help but wonder how many other families had been torn apart. How many other young people were laid to rest too early in this place? She knew of at least one other, but that was just one of many. Death seemed so unfair at times. How was she supposed to go on with the rest of her life when her husband and best friend was no longer there with her?

Rebekah knew that she wouldn't be able to watch them lower the casket into the ground; that would just be too much. So, as soon as the minister was over, she rose from her chair, shaking the hands of many of the people who were there to pay their respects as she made her way back towards the car.

Kate watched her go, her arms clutching the coat around her small frame. Her heart broke for her friend and as she glanced at her own husband, she knew that she couldn't truly empathize with Rebekah; a part of her heart was lying in that casket, about to be placed in the ground. She and John had a future together, and while Rebekah still had her whole life in front of her, Kate knew her friend well enough to know that she would feel as if her life were over.

Slowly, Rebekah made her way back to the car, purposely avoiding turning her head and looking back. Looking back was too painful, looking back served no purpose. She knew many around her believed that she had her whole life in front of her, but her heart was being buried. Without her heart, Rebekah no longer saw any real reason to go on.

CHAPTER 1

Rebekah Thomas was tired. She loved her job, but it had been a long few years, though most would not know it by looking at her. The twenty-six year old woman may have carried the weight of the world on her shoulders for quite some time, but physically, she hid it well. A smile graced her face as her long, golden hair flowed past her shoulders with a healthy gleam. The only indication of the amount of emotional pain she was in resided in her eyes. Normally, her sapphire blue eyes sparkled with happiness and energy. Lately, they were a darker shade of blue, which only those she was close to understood as the mask of her pain.

Her exhaustion was why she had looked forward to this annual Government conference. As a middle school U.S. History teacher, she usually relished the chance to meet with other teachers from around the nation; however, this year it also gave her a break from her life, from her memories. Plus, she loved New York City; it was an amazing place. Living in South Texas was about as different from New York as you could get, and she needed something different. She loved coming here. Sometimes,

Rebekah could not get enough of New York. Everywhere she turned, people were bustling around her. Lights constantly flashed overhead and the smells were enough to drown one's senses. It was so hard to describe, a mixture of car exhaust, hot dogs, roasted nuts, and excitement all around her; and today, Rebekah could definitely smell the excitement.

Her weekend had been going well; the Civic Education Council went all out for this annual conference. They paid for her to have a substitute teacher while she was away, paid for her airfare, her hotel, at an amazingly wonderful location, and paid for her meals. There were 100 teachers at the meeting, two from each state. This was a chance for them to get together and share ideas on things that were working well in each other's classes and states. It was also a chance to talk about the new programs to promote civic education among young adults in America.

The best part of the conference though was after the meetings. They were finished around three o'clock in the afternoon each day, so there was always time for exploring the city, and this afternoon was no exception. She was with four other teachers, enjoying the atmosphere of Fifth Avenue. Standing on the sidewalk, Rebekah was doing more window-shopping than actual shopping because the more she walked the street, the more lost in her thoughts she became. Before she knew it, her mind betrayed her, and she regressed into thoughts of her past.

"Penny for your thoughts," she heard someone say behind her. Turning, she found Kate Sanders, her best friend.

"Hey, Kate," Rebekah whispered, trying to shake any negative thoughts from her mind.

"Bekah, we can go back if you want to."

"No. I need to be out and about for a while. I am just tired."

"That's understandable. You've had a rough couple of years."

"I have, but what's even more difficult now is trying to move on. Something inside tells me it might be time, but I'm so afraid."

"If anyone knows the importance of living your life to the fullest, it's you, Bekah," Kate replied. Part of her wished there was something she could do for her friend, but the intelligent part of her brain knew this was Rebekah's battle to fight. Rebekah had to come to terms with her past on her own time, in her own way.

"I know, Kate. I know I have to live my life. I know I have to let go of the past. I just don't know if I'm ready. Does that make sense?"

"Perfect. All I know is that when the time is right, you will know it. Until then, don't worry about moving on, and just take the time to enjoy your life."

Rebekah reached forward and drew her friend into a hug. It was times like this that made her so thankful she had Kate in her life when she lost everything. She was one of the few people Rebekah knew she could always count on. "I think I can do that. Now, how about we get the others from this store so we can continue?"

They tapped on the window and drew the attention of their friends. Each of the women was from different areas around the nation, yet they always enjoyed shopping Fifth

Avenue together every year. Grabbing their bags, the group began to make their way out onto the bustling sidewalk.

That is when they saw him.

Coming out of the store ahead of them was Jason Taylor. The man was undeniably gorgeous, and just about every woman in America wanted him. Standing almost six feet tall, his dark blonde cropped hair ended neatly at the base of his head, showing off the strong lines of the neck that curved into his broad shoulders. His body signified a regular workout, and it was evident through his narrow waist and his lean legs. His face was thin with chiseled features and he had a smile that had a way of melting almost anyone's heart. More amazing than his smile though were his crystal blue eyes, which most women in America had spent hours gazing into while he was on-screen. He had been acting in Soap Operas since he was five years old, and just recently, at the age of thirty, he had broken into his first blockbuster movie role.

For a second, it was as if time froze, as all the women around him stopped in their tracks, and an exciting buzz surrounded them. Rebekah heard a few screams, and they made her cringe; she hated it when people did that. But, in typical star fashion, Jason turned to face the women, flashed a smile and waved his hand. In almost an instant, people were swarming around him, asking for an autograph. The teachers with Rebekah turned towards her. "Go ahead," she said laughing. "I'm staying right here."

She watched as the mob engulfed the man. It seemed almost as if he had no room to breathe. Women were encircling him from all sides so no matter which direction he turned someone was there. Without missing a beat, he reached from one woman to the next, signing their receipts or any other paper they could find, and taking pictures with them. Never once did he lose focus of the women around him until he glanced down the street. His breath caught in his throat as his eyes devoured the form of the beautiful woman he saw. Laughter danced across her face, as she seemed to enjoy watching the spectacle he had created; yet she never made a move closer towards him. However, before he could lose himself in his thoughts surrounding her, a woman much closer to him blocked his view and forced him back to the task at hand. If he ever wanted to get away this afternoon, he knew he would have to finish with all these fans.

Ten minutes later, Jason prepared to leave. Most of the women had dispersed, and he was beginning to have a moment of fresh air. He glanced up, noticing for the second time that afternoon, the gorgeous blonde standing in front of the other store. Her long, straight, golden hair hung past her shoulders, gracing her back with soft curls at the edges. Although she was wrapped in a coat to block the frigid February air, he could still detect her small, feminine form. But, what grabbed his attention the most was her addictive smile; it seemed to light up the world around her. He could not tear his eyes away. She was simple, yet elegant, but he was not sure what to think of her. She was beautiful, but she never once approached him. Then he noticed the diamond ring glistening on her left finger. 'Oh well,' he thought to himself as he turned to walk away.

He had not even realized he had dropped one of his packages, until he felt a hand on his shoulder a moment later. Turning, he inhaled sharply as the blonde beauty was standing right in front of him. He was right, her smile was addictive, but even more so when he was able to gaze into her blue eyes. The look in her eyes drew her to him and piqued his curiosity.

"I'm sorry," she said in a voice that sounded like heaven to him. "You dropped this," she continued, handing him the package. "Someone would probably be very upset if you came home without it."

"Uh, thanks," he replied, finally finding his voice, getting embarrassed when he realized it was the Victoria's Secret bag.

She smiled as he took the package and extended her hand. "I'm Rebekah," she said simply.

He reached to shake her hand, surprised when he felt a jolt go through his arm as his hand touched hers and he relished in the feel of her soft skin against his. Jason was enjoying this. It was not often that he had a beautiful woman in front of him who was not screaming or asking for an autograph. "Jason," he replied, giving her hand a gentle squeeze.

"I'm sorry to have bothered you; I just didn't think you had noticed you dropped the package." She turned to leave, but stopped when she heard his voice.

"Look, there's a Starbucks right down the street. Let me buy you a cup of coffee to say thanks."

She turned again to face him, looking into his eyes. She could not believe she was standing in New York City, actually contemplating going somewhere with this stranger. The only thing she knew about him was what was reported in magazines and the TV so basically, she knew nothing real. But, even with all that, she somehow felt drawn to go with him. She glanced behind her to the group that was waiting for her. "Okay, just let me tell them to go on without me."

Jason watched her as she turned and walked away and he was surprised with himself as to how strong of a pull he was feeling towards her. He was not half as surprised as Rebekah was though, or the women she was with.

"He asked me to have coffee with him," Rebekah explained when she returned to her friends.

"Well, don't you have all the luck?" One of them replied sarcastically, with a smile plastered on her face.

"Go. Have a good time," another encouraged.

But, as it always was with them, it was Kate that Rebekah turned to for advice. "I feel like I'm betraying him," she almost whispered.

"Bekah," her friend practically scolded her. "You are not betraying him; you're getting a cup of coffee." Kate drew her friend into a quick hug, and then playfully pushed her away. "Go," she ordered. "It's not every day that a famous movie star asks you out."

"I'll see you back at the hotel later," Rebekah replied as she smiled the first genuine smile Kate had seen in a couple of years as she turned and headed back to where she had left him.

A second later, she returned to his side. She still could not believe she was doing this; it was so unlike her and even the teachers with her were surprised, because some of them had known her for years.

"Ready?" he asked.

"I think so," she replied, not really prepared for where

this one cup of coffee would lead her.

Jason and Rebekah exchanged small talk as they stood in line ordering their drinks. He showed her to a table, pulled out the chair for her, and took a seat next to her once she was comfortable.

"Thank you again for giving this back to me," Jason stated once they were both seated, indicating the bag now resting on the floor.

"Like I said," she replied, "I didn't think you realized you dropped it. Besides, someone would be disappointed if you didn't bring that Victoria's Secret bag home with you." She flashed a smile at him, and he could sense immediately that she was teasing him.

He shrugged his shoulders, trying to fight off the embarrassment. "My sister is getting married in a month. I figured she could use something nice."

"Well, you are a sweet brother."

"You have no clue. Do you have any idea how difficult it is for a guy to walk into Victoria's Secret and buy something?" She shook her head with a small smile, and he continued. "Well, it's even more difficult when it's his baby sister. I wanted it to be flannel, long sleeved, and ankle length."

She laughed again, and it took his breath away. "So," she asked. "If you don't mind me asking, what did you get?"

He glanced down at the table briefly before raising his eyes to meet hers. "Lotion and perfume," he replied, laughing.

"Chicken," she said, joining him in his laughter, thinking about how good it felt to laugh like this for a change. She did know how difficult it was for a guy to do that. Early in their marriage Steve had done that for her. He had wanted to surprise her, so he went all by himself and picked something out. By the time she came home that night, he had it wrapped and waiting for her. She could tell how embarrassed he had been.

"Rebekah?" Jason said her name, breaking her out of her reverie. "Are you okay?"

"Yeah. Sorry. I was just thinking about something." She decided to change the subject before he asked any more questions. "So, why were you left to do the shopping? Isn't that something your wife normally helps you with?"

Jason took a breath and rubbed his hand over his face. He had to get used to saying this. "I'm not married anymore. Carrie, my ex-wife, left a year ago. We were able to keep it out of the press until just the last few days, when the divorce actually became final."

"I'm sorry. I didn't know."

"No, that's okay." It was his turn to change the subject. "So, what brings you to New York?"

"I come here twice a year, once in February and once in June. I'm a teacher, and every year we have a Civic Education Conference in February."

"Okay, I'm sorry to interrupt," he broke into her sentence. "But, I have to ask. What exactly is Civic Education?"

With a laugh, Rebekah answered. "That's okay; most people don't know what it is either until it's put in a different way. Civic education is teaching the foundations of our government. It's combining U.S. History, historical documents, and government all into one."

"Okay," he drew out slowly, slightly unsure how exciting that could really be.

Sensing his hesitation and light skepticism, she continued. "What can I say?" she asked with a shrug. "It's a passion of mine." He watched as her eyes lit up as she talked, recognizing it truly was something she enjoyed greatly. "Anyway," she continued. "The conference is a good deal for the teachers. They pay everything for us to come up here for four days. So, that's what I've been doing. We meet all day, but then have the afternoons and evenings off." As she took a sip of her coffee, her ring glistened in the light.

"So what were you doing this afternoon?" He could not figure out why he was so intrigued by this woman in front of him, but that ring on her finger bothered him. He had to find a way to ask her about it.

She saw him staring at the ring, but she was afraid to open that wound so soon. She was drawn to him, but what was the point? He was some famous guy who probably did this with all the women he met, and she was going home in two days. "We were just walking around, taking everything in. I love coming here. It's so different from my home."

"Where's that?"

"Texas."

"Wow. I'd definitely agree on the different part."

"What about you? Where's home for you?"

"New York. Actually I live in small town about an hour from here called Newburgh. I was in the City to take care of some shopping."

They sat in silence for a few minutes; each lost in their own thoughts; enjoying each other's company.

"Okay, I have to ask," Jason stated, breaking through the silence. "How is it that you were one of the only people not running up and asking for an autograph earlier?"

"Ah, I'm sorry," she said with a laugh. "Did I bruise your ego?"

"No," Jason replied quietly, "It intrigued me. You intrigued me," he answered honestly.

Rebekah blushed and looked down. "I told you I teach, but I actually teach in a suburb. Every time I go somewhere, I always run into one of my students, or one of my students' parents. It's extremely hard to feel like you have your own life when you feel like you are constantly being watched. I know it's not the same scale as what you face, but because of that, I can sort of relate."

He could not believe this woman sitting in front of him. His own wife, ex-wife, had never understood the pressures of being in the spotlight. She always wanted to do what she wanted, when she wanted, never caring about the consequences, and she had been around the fame for years. Yet, here was this beautiful creature that lived in Texas, and she understood part of the difficulty he faced every day in his life.

When he did not say anything, Rebekah decided to continue. "Anyway, like I said, it was always difficult for me. I've always felt like I had to maintain a certain image for my kids. I teach eighth graders and they are very impressionable. As a teacher, I've always thought it was important to take on the responsibility of being a role model. I've always believed that what I do outside of school teaches them as much as what I do inside of school." She looked at him and was amused at the look of shock that still covered his face. "It's okay; you can say that I'm crazy. My husband always did."

Immediately, she regretted the words. She couldn't believe she just said that. It was something she did not want to get into. She looked at him and was surprised to see a look of defeat in his eyes. Instinctively, she began twisting the ring on her finger. Jason watched her, feeling surprisingly dejected. 'She is married,' he thought to himself. 'So why do I feel as if I've just been punched?'

Jason noticed she was still playing with her wedding ring. The silence between them was now uncomfortable, and he could sense she did not want to talk about this. He decided to ignore the statement for the time being. She had said her husband 'did' say that, and he could deal with past tense for the moment. Looking around, he decided to change the direction of their conversation. "We've been here for an hour already. Why don't you let me walk you back to your hotel? Where are you staying?"

Relief flooded Rebekah's face as she realized he wasn't

going to push for an explanation. How was it that this man seemed to know exactly what she needed? She smiled at him, "I think I will take you up on that offer. I'm staying at the Marquis Marriott in Times Square."

"Wow," he replied standing and offering her his hand. "They really are putting you guys up well aren't they?"

Taking his hand, she stood and again flashed him a smile that made his stomach flutter. "Yeah, they take pretty good care of us," she answered, staring into his eyes, almost getting lost in them. He gazed back at her, both of them forgetting the fact that her hand was still in his.

"Excuse me," a nearby woman said, tearing both of them out of the moment. "Aren't you Jason Taylor?"

Rebekah grinned at him, and they broke their contact, hesitantly. He turned from her and faced the woman. "Yes, I am."

Rebekah watched as he made some small talk with the woman standing there. 'What am I doing?' she thought to herself. 'I can't be falling for this guy. I'm going home in two days. I'll just let him walk me back and call this my lucky afternoon. That will be all.'

"Are you ready to go?" Jason asked, turning back to face her.

"As soon as you can tear yourself away from your fans there," she teased.

"Very funny. Come on." After putting his jacket on, he opened the door for her and placed his hand on the small of her back as he ushered her out of the coffeehouse. He did not leave his hand there long, but he still could not believe the feeling he got from this simple touch. For some reason, he felt he could not just drop her off at the hotel and walk away, but how did he propose anything else?

"Welcome to my life," he said as they started walking towards her hotel. "And before you ask, yes, it is always like this. But then again, you got a taste of that earlier."

"I told you I understood. The only difference is that the people who come up to me aren't complete strangers."

"Sometimes I think that would be easier."

"I don't know, a stranger may judge you, but you don't have to worry about running into them at school or church the next day."

"That makes sense. Plus, I can walk away from a stranger much easier than you can from a student or a parent."

Again, Rebekah glanced at him. She could not believe that this man she had met less than two hours ago understood something her husband never did. 'This doesn't make sense,' she thought to herself, struggling with her emotions. 'He can't understand me; he's just saying what he thinks I want to hear.' The only problem with those thoughts was no matter how hard she tried to convince herself that they were right, she could not. He just seemed too honest to be making this up. For some strange reason, she felt herself trusting him, and that terrified her.

Their conversation remained light and general as they walked towards the hotel together. They stopped at different stores along the way, enjoying each other's company, more than either of them thought possible. They shared some more about themselves, both of them walking at a slow pace, neither wanting the walk to end. All too quickly though, they reached the hotel. Rebekah turned to face him. Shyly, she tucked a piece of hair behind her ear. "Thank you for walking me back," she started, not sure if she should continue.

"Sure," he replied. "And thanks for giving this back," he continued, holding the bag up towards her, "Kacee will be very appreciative."

Again his breath was taken away as she smiled at him, a teasing glint in her eyes. "Sure she will. She won't know what to do without that lotion on her honeymoon."

"You think you're very funny don't you?" he teased back, joining in her laughter, which ended all too soon. "And," he continued after taking a deep breath, "thank you for spending the afternoon with me. I had a great day, better than I've had in a long time." He finished that last part quietly, so quietly she almost did not hear him.

She reached her hand out to him and shook his lightly as he took hers, losing himself in the feel of her small hand in his large, strong one. "I had a nice time too," she whispered back, too scared to say anything else. Her mind was telling her to run into that hotel, but her heart would not let her legs move. They stood there together for a moment, neither one wanting to break contact, but both too unsure of anything to admit it. Finally, she broke the silence. "It was nice to meet you, Jason." After another glance into his eyes, she dropped his hand and turned to walk into the hotel.

Jason sighed as he watched her walk away. He was not sure it was the right time to start anything, but he just had this feeling that he could not let her walk away. In the short amount of time he had spent with her, he already felt this amazing connection. He had to trust his heart on this.

"Rebekah!" he called out.

She turned back around, smiling nervously as she did. Within a matter of seconds, he closed the distance between them.

"Have dinner with me tonight," he asked.

"What?"

"Have dinner with me tonight."

Rebekah sighed. She wanted nothing more than to say yes to this man, but she did not know if her heart could take the pain again. "Jason, I had a wonderful time today."

"So did I," he cut in.

"But, honestly, what do you expect to come out of this? I'm going home in two days. Let's just call this an incredible afternoon and leave it at that. What else could you possibly want from me?"

Feeling slightly defeated; Jason quickly realized he was not ready to give up yet. "Hey, I'm not asking for a relationship here," he started as Rebekah dropped her head with a sigh. "And," he continued as he used his thumb and forefinger to gently lift her face towards his, "I'm not looking for a one-night stand." Her eyes twinkled at that last statement, so he decided to continue. "I like you. I had a good time today, and I would like to take you to dinner tonight. All I want from you is a chance to get to know you better. You're in town for two more days, and so am I. Why don't we take that time and spend it together? I would like to think that a wonderful friendship is starting here." He stopped at that, never intending to go on as long as he did.

Rebekah stood there for a minute, thinking about his words. "Okay," she whispered.

"Okay, what?" he questioned back, knowing full well what she was talking about, but wanting to hear her say it.

She smiled back at him. "Okay, I'll go to dinner tonight, on one condition."

"What?" he asked, ready to agree to just about anything just to get her to go.

"We don't go anywhere too dressy. I didn't exactly pack for a fancy dinner."

Chuckling slightly, Jason nodded, acquiescing to her request. "I think we can arrange that. Besides, I want tonight to be about us getting to know each other. If we go somewhere too fancy, someone there will cause a scene, asking for an autograph or something. I don't want us to deal with that tonight. Is seven okay?"

"Seven it is then," she answered with another smile. "I'll meet you in the lobby." Turning, she headed back into the hotel, glancing over her shoulder at him one last time.

Jason smiled more than he had in several months. "Now," he said to himself, "I have a couple of hours to find something to change into, and to find a hotel room. I think I will be staying here for the next two days."

Once Rebekah got upstairs to the meeting room, just about every teacher from the conference was waiting for her. All had heard of her meeting him this afternoon and they each wanted to know what Jason Taylor was really like. She graciously answered their questions, trying to get out of there as quickly as she could, wanting as few people as possible to know about tonight. Finally, she was able to leave. Taking Kate with her, she left for her room. "I'm having dinner with him tonight," she whispered as soon as they were out of earshot of everyone else.

"You're what?" Kate squealed. Although Rebekah and Kate were best friends, Kate lived here in New York. Between everything that had happened with her husband and the physical distance separating them it had been a long time since they had the opportunity to share secrets like school girls.

"He asked me to dinner tonight, and I'm going," Rebekah repeated.

"Good for you."

Rebekah's head whipped around and her eyes widened in shock. "What? No lecture?"

"No, Rebekah. I told you earlier. It's time you moved on with your life. It's been over a year," Kate finished quietly.

"I know, Kate. It's just, I don't know if I can do this again. And besides, what's the point? I leave in two days."

"So? Go, have fun tonight. Enjoy his company, and stop worrying so much!"

"Fine, then help me pick out something to wear that

doesn't scream 'teacher.'"

Two hours and many outfit changes later, Rebekah was ready to go. She had borrowed a blue, off-the-shoulder top from Kate, and had it on with her black pants. Her hair hung down past her shoulders, slightly curled, and she had a minimal amount of makeup on. "How do I look?" she asked Kate, giving a slight twirl.

"Amazing. Something tells me he will be speechless, and it is time for you to go down to the lobby."

"Thank you Kate, for your help, and for your words earlier."

"Have fun tonight. I'll see you at breakfast tomorrow."

They walked to the elevator together and Kate gave Rebekah a hug. She knew this was hard for Rebekah, but she also knew it was time. She had grieved long enough.

As soon as Rebekah stepped off the elevator in the lobby, she saw him. 'Good gosh, that man is sexy,' she thought, immediately trying to shake that thought from her head. "Just friends," she told herself, but she was having a hard time convincing herself of that as she watched him standing there in dark slacks and a gray, button up shirt. She could see his muscles outlined through the material of the shirt. When he turned around, he froze. She looked beautiful, and she was going to dinner with him.

"Hi," she said quietly as she got closer. When he did not respond, she gave a small laugh, thinking of Kate's words, 'he will probably be speechless.' Her heart gave a small flutter when she realized he was. "Earth to Jason," she called out, trying to get his attention.

He shook his head slightly; trying to convince himself this wasn't a dream. "Hi," he replied, grinning sheepishly. "You look absolutely stunning."

"Thank you. You don't look so bad yourself."

"Are you ready?" he asked, offering her his hand. She took it gratefully, and again, her heart fluttered at the simple touch.

"Yes," she replied, not removing her hand from his.

As they walked out of the hotel, Kate's words from earlier ringing in her ears, her small hand in his, she felt she truly was ready, for the first time in a long time.

They grabbed a taxi and headed towards Little Italy. "Is Italian okay?" he asked.

"One of my favorites." She was impressed by the fact that they took a taxi. She half expected him to try to impress her with a limousine and a fancy restaurant. But, in the short amount of time she had known him, she had learned Jason was a simple man, not one to show off that he had tons of money, and she liked that.

"So, where are we eating?" she asked.

"A little restaurant called Tony's. It's a small place, out of the way. They have some of the best food and music there. It's owned by some old friends of mine, so they'll be good about making sure no one tries to bother us."

Rebekah nodded her head, and they finished the rest of the ride in silence, enjoying one another's company. Once they arrived at Tony's, Jason helped her out of the car, paid the driver and escorted her into the restaurant. Immediately, two rather intimidating men greeted them.

"Tony, Paulie, how are you?" Jason asked, shaking their hands.

"Good, Mr. Taylor. Do you want your usual table?"

"Please." Again placing his hand on the small of her back, he guided her to follow Tony. He led them to a secluded table in the corner of the restaurant. Because of its location, it was blocked from the view of most of the other tables there. Just as earlier today, Jason pulled out her chair for her, and took a seat only once she was settled in.

Looking around her, Rebekah couldn't help but fall in love with the quaint little restaurant. Red and white checked tablecloths hung elegantly over each table and flames danced atop the wax-covered candles sitting on each table as well. Soft music was playing in the background, and tile mosaics graced the walls, each depicting country life in Italy. All this added to the atmosphere of being in some Italian villa.

Nodding towards the two men they had met at the door, she glanced at him with a teasing glint in her eyes. "So, what?" she asked. "Do you have connections with the mob or something?"

"Funny. You know, not every Italian male in New York belongs to the mob." He laughed and she joined him, again surprised at how comfortable she felt with him. "I've known Tony and Paulie for a long time. They know I like to come here when I need some peace and quiet, so this is where they always seat me. Most people don't even know when I come in here and I like that, especially when I just need to get away from it all. I've been here a lot in the past six months."

"Carrie," she stated quietly. He nodded his head indicating she was correct. Nothing more was said as the waiter arrived and they placed their orders.

A few minutes later they both sat quietly, sipping glasses of wine when Jason broke the silence. "I met Carrie in Newburgh years ago. She was an aspiring artist, and I was attracted to her. I had been injured on the set of the show, and she took care of me. I stayed with her for a while. It was better than going back to my family's house. They are a bit insane, but that's a different story."

She gave a small laugh as he paused to allow the returning waiter to place their food on the table. They began to eat. "Believe me, that, I definitely understand." She stopped to let him continue.

"Anyway, the longer I stayed with her, the more attracted to her I became. She wasn't perfect, and had some annoying habits, but I figured, who doesn't. I went back to work not long after I moved in with her. We fought about that a lot. Carrie got very jealous of any actress I worked with. She hated it when I did any sort of love scene. I tried to explain to her that it was a soap, and that's what I did, but she still couldn't stand it. I had a feeling we weren't going to last, but I stayed anyway. Over time, she resigned herself to the fact that I wasn't going to quit, and she stopped arguing with me about it. Eventually, I realized I could love her, and I asked her to marry me. I know now that was my mistake. I loved her, but I was never in love with her. Does that make any sense?"

Rebekah nodded her head, her eyes full of compassion. He could not believe he was saying some of this to her. No one knew about his early years with Carrie, not even his closest friends, or his sister; yet, here he was spilling his guts to a stranger, who was beginning to feel less and less like one with each passing minute.

"I think she felt the same way. One night, a year ago, after a huge fight, she moved out. She went back to waitressing at a little diner in town called The Cafe, which is what she used to do before we got together. She moved into her studio where she painted. I started working on the movie, so I wasn't around much. I always hated the idea of divorcing, so while I was gone, I thought about giving it another try. When I got back six months later, I realized part of our problem in the first place. She had been seeing some guy named Tim for the past year. When she found out I was home, she came to my old Penthouse that I had moved back into, not knowing I had found out about Tim. I asked her to leave that night and ordered the security guards in the lobby to never let her back in. I filed for a divorce the next day. It was finalized two days ago."

Rebekah reached her hand across the table and placed it on top of his. He turned his gaze up to meet hers, and could again see the compassion in her eyes. "I'm sorry," she whispered.

"Don't be," he replied simply. "I strongly believe that what's in the past is in the past. I've had six months to come to terms with this, and I have. I don't have any regrets about what happened, because that's what led me to where I am today." He paused and took a breath before he continued, looking into her eyes, "and believe me, I like where I am today." Gently he squeezed her fingers and she smiled at him. "You know what?" he continued. "Enough of that. Now you know all there is to know about my ex-wife. Let's think about something else." He stood up, his hand still holding onto hers. "Would you like to dance?"

"I would love to," she replied as he gently pulled her to her feet. Never letting go of her hand, he led her to a small area near their table. It was big enough for one or maybe two couples to dance on it, but the nice part about the space was that it, like the table, was secluded. Pulling her toward him, he wrapped his right arm around her waist, and continued to hold her hand in his left as she encircled her other hand around his neck. Neither said anything as they began to sweetly dance to the music; both too caught up in the nearness of each other. He smiled as he realized how perfectly she fit in his arms, and was hoping she noticed it as well. Unbeknownst to him, she was thinking the same thing. Closing her eyes, she took a tentative step towards him, and as he felt her slight movement he tightened his arm around her waist, pulling her closer. Closing his eyes, he leaned his head forward, resting his cheek against the side of her head, allowing himself to investigate her intoxicating scent.

Unsure of anything around them, the couple was lost in the dance and lost in each other. For a man who prided himself on control, he knew he was quickly losing it. The woman in front of him was absolutely amazing, and she was stirring feelings in him that he long ago gave up. His heart was beating rapidly in his chest and she was so close he could tell hers was beating the same way.

Before they realized it though, the music ended. Reluctantly, she pulled back slightly but remained in his embrace. Slowly, she pulled her left hand from around his neck, trailing her fingers down his arm until her hand was joined with his. For a moment they were both too afraid to speak; both had felt way too much in that embrace and neither quite knew what to do about it. Rebekah's eyes twinkled as she finally spoke. "You are an excellent dancer, Mr. Taylor," she whispered, not wanting to break the mood.

"Thank you," he replied just as quietly, his thumbs caressing her fingers. "Perks of the job." Their faces were inches apart, foreheads almost touching, hearts beating rapidly. Hesitantly, he leaned closer towards her as her eyes began to close.

"Excuse me, Mr. Taylor!" the waiter, exclaimed as he walked around the corner to where they were, causing both of them to jump apart. "I'm so sorry, Mr. Taylor."

"No, that's okay," Jason replied, glancing at Rebekah with a look of disappointment in his eyes. "What did you need?"

"I just came in here to bring you dessert."

"Thank you, you can set it down." Knowing the moment was lost he turned back to Rebekah. "Will chocolate do?" he asked with a smile.

"How did you know that was my favorite?" she answered, smiling back, walking towards the table. As he pulled out the chair for her to have a seat, he let his hand linger on her back for a second longer than he should have, and shooting chills down her spine.

He sat back down across from her, and they resumed their small talk from earlier. Neither mentioned what almost happened after their dance but the interest was still evident in each of their eyes. She intrigued Jason. He wanted to know more, and he still wanted to know about that ring on her finger. Something told him she could not be some 'easy woman' who would cheat on her husband; there had to be something else there. However, something also told him not to push and that she would tell him when she was ready.

Thirty minutes later, they were finished with dessert and ready to leave. Jason was not ready to take her back to the hotel yet, but he did not want to push; he had already talked her into going to dinner with him. Luckily, as he was getting ready to hail a taxi, Rebekah stopped him. "Do you want to take a walk before we go back?" she asked, almost shyly.

"Sure," he answered, trying not to appear too enthusiastic. He quickly forgot the taxi as they turned to walk down the street, stopping occasionally to look at the different shops.

"I was married for four years," Rebekah stated, so quietly, Jason almost could not hear her. She glanced up to see if he was listening. He met her gaze and nodded his head, silently telling her to go on with her story. She closed her eyes for a brief moment and took a breath before continuing. "I know that's a long time for someone as young as me. We were high school sweethearts, and I got married young. As soon as we were married, Steve and I began trying to have a baby. We never succeeded, and we continued trying for a couple of years. Nothing worked, so we finally went to see a specialist. I had countless numbers of tests run, and still the doctors were not able to find anything. They decided to do a simple blood test on both of us to check the Rh factors of our blood; apparently there can be some problem. We waited a week for those results, expecting the doctors to say, once again, they could not find anything. Finally, they called." Rebekah paused and Jason could tell how difficult it was for her to continue, but he watched her take a deep breath to steady herself, and then continue on with her story. "This time, it was with news we weren't expecting. Steve was diagnosed with cancer. We fought it, but within a year, he was gone." She stopped walking. "That was a year ago."

Nothing was said for a few minutes until Jason finally spoke. "Rebekah, I am so sorry," he said, truly wanting to take all her pain away. She looked up at him and could see the sincerity of his comment. He did not need to say anything else.

"Thank you," she whispered. They continued walking in silence for a moment, each lost in their own thoughts. She could not believe she had made it through telling that without crying. It was the first time in a year she had done that. "So, now you know I'm not some cheap woman trying to pick up some famous guy," she said jokingly, trying to lighten the mood a little.

"Cause of course, that was the impression you gave me from the beginning," he laughingly played along, knowing what she was trying to do. After a moment, he continued. "Seriously though, if you'd rather go back, I can get a tax…" but she cut him off.

"No!" It was her turn to try and not appear too enthusiastic. "This is probably one of the best nights I've had in a long time, and I am not quite ready for it to end yet. Unless you are," she finished, looking at him.

"Neither am I," he responded. Smiling at him, she closed her eyes as his fingers brushed a piece of hair behind her ear. It was a simple gesture, one that was meant to put her at ease. However, all it did was quicken both of their heartbeats, leaving each of them secretly longing for more. Pulling apart, they continued on their shopping journey, investigating just about every shop on the street before turning onto a new one, both walking slow in an effort to make the night last longer. They discovered more about each other as they walked, laughing from time to time, enjoying the silence in other moments. Somewhere along the way, Rebekah timidly reached her hand out and entwined her fingers with Jason's. He didn't say anything, just gave her hand a soft squeeze, indicating he was comfortable with this too; although for a reason he couldn't understand, he had this crazy desire to hold more than her hand.

Before long, they realized how late it was. Regretfully, he called a taxi to take her back to the hotel. He knew she had an early day of meetings the next morning, and he didn't want her to be too tired. Once they arrived at the hotel, he helped her out of the cab and walked her into the lobby. He followed her to her room, and they stood outside her door. Again, she took his hand and held onto it, neither of them sure of what to say.

Finally, Rebekah broke the silence. "Now it's my turn to say thank you."

"For what?" he asked, playing with her fingers.

"I had a wonderful time tonight, and I owe it all to you."

He smiled. "I had a great time too." Jason paused for a moment, almost too nervous to continue. "Do you…I mean…would you like to have dinner again tomorrow? We could go for another walk. It's Sunday, so things are a little slower in the city."

"I would like that, Jason. A lot." Taking a step towards him, she placed her lips on his cheek and gave him a soft kiss. "Good night, Jason," she whispered, backing away and opening her door. She turned and looked at him one last time before she shut the door, leaning on it from the inside.

He brought his hand to his cheek, and then to his lips. Sighing, he then touched the door, feeling her presence there. "Good night, Rebekah," he whispered back, turning to walk to his own room, anticipating what tomorrow would hold.

CHAPTER 2

The next morning, Rebekah woke, feeling more rested than she had in a long time. As her sleepiness began to leave, she wondered if the whole previous day had been a dream. 'No,' she thought to herself. 'It may have felt like a dream, but it was definitely real.' Almost as if to confirm her suspicions, she heard a knock on the door. Opening it, she found the bellman holding a vase of beautiful red roses. A huge smile spread across her face as she reached for them. She set them on the table and grabbed the note.

Rebekah,

Thank you for a wonderful evening last night. I enjoyed getting to know you and am looking forward to continuing that this evening. I'm in room 2111. Give me a call when you are finished with your meetings for the day.

Jason

"Wow!" Kate exclaimed, walking into the room. In her excitement over the roses, Rebekah had not realized she had left the door open slightly. "I take it dinner went well?" she asked.

"You have no idea," Rebekah answered. "It was not just dinner, it was the whole evening. We went to dinner, we danced, we talked, and we walked. I did not want the night to end, but Jason insisted we come back because I had such an early meeting this morning. He was concerned that I would be too tired. Kate, he is so thoughtful and caring, and…"

"And you're falling for him," Kate stated, breaking into Rebekah's gush.

"What? No." Rebekah replied, trying to keep her smile from becoming too big. "Maybe," she sighed. "I don't know."

"It's okay, Rebekah. You loved Steve; I know that. But, you are twenty six years old. You have your entire life ahead of you. He would have wanted you to be happy."

Rebekah absentmindedly twisted the ring on her finger. "I know Kate. Believe me, I do. And, if anything, this weekend has taught me that it is okay to do that. But, am I being realistic with myself? I like this guy, and I could tell that those feelings are not just one-sided. Last night, I could feel that there was definitely something there. I want to see him again and I am going to tonight. I just don't know what to expect out of this. He lives in New York and I live in Texas. Could we really make this work? Do I even want to try? Is he even interested in 'this'?"

"Those are a lot of questions for someone who didn't want to admit she liked the guy a few minutes ago!" Kate teased. Rebekah blushed and joined her friend on the bed as Kate continued. "I agree those are all good questions, but I also think you are putting too much thought into this. There is really only one question you need to be concerned with; what is your heart telling you?" Rebekah did not have to answer; the look on her face said everything. Kate finished by saying, "we go home tomorrow. Ask him tonight what he wants."

Rebekah shook her head in agreement, lost in her own thoughts. After a moment, they realized what time it was. "We have to get ready. Our meeting starts in about an hour." Kate nodded and left to go back to her room, both agreeing to meet before they went to the meeting.

As the group's meetings got started for the day, Jason lay in his bed thinking about the wonderful woman he had met the day before. In less than twenty four hours, she had stolen his heart, and if he was honest with himself, he did not necessarily think that was a bad thing. He smiled as he looked at his watch. By now, she should have received the roses he ordered last night. He hoped she liked them. Not every woman was a fan of roses, but they had a classic elegance about them, just like she did.

Realizing what time it was, he knew he needed to call his best friends. He was supposed to have gone home yesterday. He dialed the number, praying Nikki would not answer, and was relieved to get the answering machine. Once he finished leaving a message, he hung up, sighing. He loved Nikki, but he knew she would want to play twenty questions about why he was staying. Being honest with himself, he knew he did not want to share Rebekah just yet. Once he told Danny and Nikki, she would never leave him alone about it.

After showering and getting dressed for the day, he left the hotel to make arrangements for tonight. Sometimes he hated the extreme things people would do to please him just because he was famous, but today he was going to play it up. She was going home tomorrow and he wanted this to be a night she could not forget.

Rebekah had a difficult time concentrating on her meetings all morning. Every time she tried to think about Civic Education, or classroom strategies, or anything at all related to education, she could only think of the last twenty four hours with Jason. She never had any intention of letting him get to her the way he did, but now, she was not so sure she wanted it any other way.

Kate had spent the morning laughing at Rebekah. Finally, around lunchtime, she was able to tell her why. "Have you even looked at your handouts from this morning?" Kate asked.

Rebekah shrugged her shoulders. "Yeah, I looked at them earlier. What's the big deal?"

"The 'big deal,' as you put it, is that in addition to all of your other doodles on the pages, you have written his name all over them!"

Blushing, Rebekah hastily glanced at the papers in her hand. "Oh my gosh! You're right. I'm as bad as my eighth graders!" Quickly, she shoved the papers into her folder.

"I guess you have been thinking about him a lot, huh?"

"I've just been replaying everything in my head and I keep thinking about everything you and I talked about this morning. I'll be honest, Kate. I don't want to go home tomorrow."

"You don't exactly have a choice in the matter, Rebekah."

"I know," she sighed. "I don't really mean that. I guess I am just afraid that I will go home and find out that this weekend did not mean anything to anyone except me. After everything that happened with Steve, I don't know if I could handle that."

"Somehow I think that's highly doubtful."

"Why, because you have some 'feeling' about it?"

"No, because for the past ten minutes, he's been standing in the hallway, trying to catch a glimpse of you!"

"What?" Rebekah asked, her head whipping around. When her eyes met his, a huge smile broke out across her face. He gave a subtle wave and tried to control his own smile from invading his entire face.

"Go on," Kate softly nudged. "We still have half an hour left of lunch. You won't hurt my feelings if you leave."

"Thanks," Rebekah replied, heading towards the door. She tried to ignore the inquisitive stares she was receiving as she headed out of the room to meet him. She knew there were many who were beside themselves over the fact that Jason Taylor was right outside the conference room, but they were doing a great job holding back their desire to jump up and ask for an autograph.

As she walked towards Jason, her beauty once again took him aback.

"Hi," she practically whispered as she walked up to

him.

"Hi," he responded, just as quietly. "I'm not disturbing you am I?"

"No, not at all. We've been eating lunch and we still have a few minutes left. Do you want to sit down?" she asked, pointing to the tables and chairs that lined the halls around the meeting rooms.

They chose a table away from the crowded meeting room and both took a seat facing each other. Rebekah continued in her soft voice. "I have to tell you. I woke up this morning and was afraid yesterday was a dream."

"Me too," he broke in softly.

She glanced up at him and shyly bit her bottom lip before she continued. "Then, I opened my door to find someone holding a vase of the most beautiful roses." She flashed a smile at him. "Thank you for those by the way."

He shrugged his shoulders, trying to play it off as no big deal. "You're welcome. I just wanted to let you know I was looking forward to this evening."

"So am I. I'm actually glad you came by. All morning long, I've been trying to think of what to say when I called you later. Now, I don't have to." For a moment, they got lost in each other's gaze. "Wait a minute," she said, breaking them out of their reverie. "What are you doing here? Not that I'm complaining," she quickly added.

Jason grinned sheepishly, not wanting to admit that he came by because it had been too long since he had seen her. He still couldn't believe he was feeling this connected to her, and he didn't know what he would do when she went home. 'Oh well,' he thought. 'We'll cross that bridge tomorrow.' Finally, he answered her. "I had something planned for this evening, but now I need to change it and I wanted your opinion. It seems Mother Nature has different plans for us.

"What do you mean?"

"Haven't you been outside this morning? Or even looked out a window?"

"No. That's the life of a teacher," she replied, laughing. "We rarely see the light of day until at least three. What's going on?"

"It's snowing."

"Really?" she practically squealed, jumping up from the table, looking around. "Are there no windows in this place?" she asked, turning around to see Jason laughing at her. "What?" she asked, laughing back. "What are you laughing at?"

"You," he replied. "I've never seen someone get this excited about snow before."

"You do remember I said I live in Texas, right? We don't exactly get a lot of snow around Houston. It's been years since I've seen snow. So," she said, reaching out her hand, "you are going to help me find a window."

Laughing again, he took her hand and led her down the hall he had come from. She was right. Most of these meeting rooms and halls had no windows around to make it easier to see presentations. However, back on the main hall, there were windows everywhere, so that's where he would lead her. He glanced back at her and felt a tug on his heart at the twinkling of her eyes. He wasn't used to a woman getting so excited about something as insignificant as snow. At the end of the first hall they came to, they reached a window, and again he felt that tug as he watched her face light up.

She inhaled deeply. "This is beautiful!"

"Yes, it is," he said, referring more to the woman in front of him than the snow they were looking at. She glanced behind her and caught his eyes, blushing as she realized his hidden meaning. Softly, she squeezed the hand she was still holding.

They stood there in silence for several minutes, each reveling in the closeness of the other, enjoying the beautiful scene in front of them. Since it was at the end of the hall, there weren't many people around. Somehow, while they were standing there, he dropped her hand and wrapped his arm around her waist, drawing her back into his chest.

"I don't think I've ever seen this much snow before in my entire life," she said after a few moments.

"This is nothing. "It's not even a foot. We can still easily get around in this."

"You don't understand. When it snows at home, we have to make snowmen on the trunks of our cars or in the beds of our trucks just to make them as tall as us, because we never have enough snow to make a real one." She could feel him laugh against her back and she loved the way it felt. "So, what are our plans now?"

"Well I figured a picnic wouldn't be all that good in the snow, so I was thinking dinner and a Broadway show.

That's what I wanted to ask you about though. I know you were concerned with not having anything fancy to wear and I didn't want you to feel uncomfortable."

She was touched by his thoughtfulness, but it really didn't surprise her. He had shown multiple times in the past several hours what a caring man he was. "No, don't worry about that. Dinner and a play sound great. Which one do you want to see?"

"You pick."

"Are you sure? It might be some girly one," she warned.

"Whatever you pick is fine with me."

"I've always wanted to see Phantom of the Opera, but I already know it's sold out. A friend of mine and I tried to get tickets before we came up here. Other than that, I'm not really picky. You pick. Surprise me."

"Okay," he whispered, resting his chin on the top of her head.

They stayed there for a few more minutes before she broke away from the embrace. "I hate to do this, but I have to get back. I only have a few hours left of my meetings, and then we are finished until next year."

"You're finished around three, right?"

"Mm hmm," she answered, nodding her head.

"Why don't I meet you in the lobby around 4:30 and we'll go from there."

"Okay." She turned to go, but as she walked past him, she felt his hand on her wrist, turning her back towards him. Sapphire orbs crashed into crystal blue ones, and time stood still as their gazes connected. Bringing a hand to his face, she whispered, "I'll see you at 4:30."

All coherent thought left his body at the feel of her skin against his. He couldn't respond, so he just nodded his head and let go of her hand. As he watched her walk away, he thought, 'there is no way I can let her get on that plane tomorrow without telling her how I feel. I just hope I can make tonight special for her.'

The afternoon passed quickly for Rebekah. Her brief time with Jason during lunch enabled her to relax some. She was convinced her feelings were not one-sided and she had decided to no longer worry about what would happen tomorrow; she was going to enjoy tonight.

Three hours after lunch, her meetings were finally over. Knowing she probably wouldn't see most of the teachers the next day because of flight schedules; she said good-bye to them that afternoon. As the only teacher from the Houston area, she was flying home by herself. Grabbing Kate's hand, she dragged her from the room. Laughing, Kate asked, "I guess you want me to help you get ready again, right?"

"Actually," Rebekah responded, "I know what I'm wearing. I just wanted your company while I got ready."

"I'd love to. So, what are you going to wear?"

"I brought one simple, black dress just in case you and I were able to get tickets to a show. I told him I didn't want to go somewhere dressy last night, because this dress wouldn't have actually worked. However, I think it will be perfect for this evening."

They took the elevator upstairs and headed to Rebekah's room. The whole time she was getting ready, they visited and caught up on everything that had happened in the past year. Kate was going to drive home in the morning before Rebekah left for the airport. They promised to try and meet before Kate left. Just a few minutes before Rebekah needed to be in the lobby, Kate hugged her and headed back to her own room. Taking one last glance in the mirror, Rebekah turned to leave the room as well, but her eyes caught a glimpse of her hand. Slowly, she reached her right hand to take hold of her wedding ring. She twisted it and pulled it off her finger, bringing it to her lips. Kissing it softly, she whispered, "You will always be a part of my heart. I love you." She pulled the ring away from her hand and placed it in her suitcase. Kate was right; it was time to get on with her life. She would always love Steve and the life they had together, but it was time to move on. If nothing else came from this weekend, she had at least learned that. Turning the light off, she closed the door on the past, ready to embrace the future.

A few minutes later, she was in the lobby and within seconds, her eyes sought him out. Her breath caught in her throat as she checked out the dangerously handsome man in front of her. As his eyes caught her gaze, she knew he was doing the same thing and a smile tugged at her lips. Her dress was simple, yet showed off her figure well. It was knee length with a scoop neck in the front. It hugged her body in all the right places, and the skirt had enough of a flare that it would occasionally give any onlooker a glimpse of what was hidden beneath. He lost his breath as he stared at the stunning woman in front of him and once again felt like he was the luckiest man in the world.

"Wow," he whispered as she stepped closer to him. "You look amazing," he continued, his eyes telling more of what he wasn't saying with words.

"Thank you. You look pretty good yourself," she replied as a smile crept across his face.

"It's stopped snowing," he said quietly, purposely breaking the connection that was quickly being made before he lost all control. "I thought we would walk to the theatre if that's okay with you. It's not far."

"Sure," she answered, beginning to put on her coat.

He glanced at her coat, skeptical of the amount of warmth it would provide, but he reasoned that it was better than nothing at all. "Let me help you," he offered, reaching for her coat. Holding it open for her, she slipped her arms in. As she began to button it, she felt his hands gently pulling her soft tresses from inside the neck of her coat. Immediately, his small, intimate gesture sent chills racing through her body. "Ready?" he asked, offering her his arm.

She nodded, accepting his arm as they stepped out of the hotel. Because of the snow, the temperature had dropped several degrees from the night before. The extreme cold outside surprised her and he felt her shiver. He removed his arm from holding hers and he wrapped it around her, drawing her closer to him.

She smiled as she snuggled against his warm body. "I didn't think you would be prepared for this cold," he worriedly said.

"It's okay. Really, I'm fine. It's just not usually this cold, ever, at home. But, you said we weren't going far. I'll be fine." He nodded and responded by pulling her closer to him. They walked towards the theatre, enjoying the silence and nearness of each other. After a short walk, they reached the theatre. Rebekah looked at him with a surprised look on her face as she realized the name of the play plastered on the billboards. "What? How? I thought this was sold out."

He shrugged his shoulders, trying to indicate it was no big deal. "It is, but you said Phantom of the Opera was what you wanted to see."

Without thinking, she wrapped her arms around his neck and pulled him closer for a tight embrace. "Thank you," she whispered, not wanting to let go.

He responded by strengthening the hug. It amazed him how such little things seemed to bring her such pleasure. "Let's get you inside," he said, rubbing his hands up and down her arms in an effort to warm her.

She laughed as they walked into the lobby. "I'm afraid I'm not used to this weather. This is my winter coat, and I don't think it seems to be helping much!" He joined in her laughter as they made their way into the theatre and found their seats. Not only had he been able to secure tickets for them, but also he was able to arrange fabulous seats.

After removing their coats, they settled into their seats. She sat on his right; and tried to hold back the few remaining shivers as her body thawed out from the short walk. He looked at her with concern when he saw her shiver. "Are you alright?" he asked.

"I'm fine, I promise," she answered, placing her hand on his forearm, shooting an amazing sensation through her body.

"Good," he replied, covering her hand with his. He, too, had felt the jolt as she touched his arm, and he didn't want to lose that feeling. Gently he squeezed her hand and as the show started, she quietly laced their fingers together. For the next few hours, they enjoyed the show and enjoyed the feeling of holding on to one another.

Jason stole glances of Rebekah's face periodically throughout the course of the play. She was mesmerized and it was clear she was thoroughly enjoying their evening. He, on the other hand, was enjoying watching her much more.

Before either of them knew it though, the show ended. They stood and Jason smiled as Rebekah wiped away a few tears "What?" she asked, trying to figure out why he was looking at her like that.

He reached a hand up to her face and used his thumb to wipe away one remaining tear. Letting his hand linger on her face, he answered, whispering, "You are so beautiful."

She blushed as she brought her hand to cover his, getting lost in his crystal blue eyes. "Thank you," she whispered back, letting her eyes say it more than words ever could.

Jason used ever fiber in his being to break away from this gentle embrace. He wanted to kiss her so badly he could practically feel the silk of her lips against his. But, neither the time nor the place was right. There were still people all around them, trying to leave the theatre, and he didn't want to share that moment with anyone else but her. Trying to find his voice, he huskily asked, "Are you ready for dinner?" He was surprised to see a look of disappointment flash through her eyes. He knew she wanted the same thing he did and it only strengthened his resolve to wait. With the emotions her touch elicited, he knew their first kiss would be magical and he wanted to savor that moment. She nodded in response to his question and turned to leave the theatre. He grabbed both of their coats and his hand immediately went to the small of her back to guide her towards the lobby. Once there, he put his own coat on before helping her with hers. His arms never left her shoulders once her coat was on.

"Where are we eating?" she asked once they were ready to go.

"We're heading back to the hotel. They have one of the best restaurants there called The View. It rotates and you can see all of The City from there. It's beautiful at night. Will you be okay walking back, or would you rather we take a cab?"

"No, I'll be fine," she answered, snuggling towards him. He smiled and pulled her closer as they started the walk back to the hotel. "I still don't know how you managed to get tickets to that show. We must have tried everything before we came here, and everywhere we called, we were informed of its sold out status."

"I just made a few calls to some people I know. It's really not a big deal."

"Well, it is to me. I'm sure you had to do a lot to get those tickets. I've wanted to see that play since I was a little girl. You just made one of my dreams come true," she replied smiling.

'Hopefully, that won't be the last one I get to make one come true,' he thought to himself, but he answered her with, "well, it was worth it." And for him to see her smile because of something he did, he felt it really was worth it.

They reached the hotel in record time, both walking fast because of the cold weather. Stepping into the warmth of the lobby, he immediately ushered her to the elevator and pressed the button labeled "The View". She raised an eyebrow at him, but he just responded with a mischievous smile. Moments later, the doors opened and Rebekah gasped as they stepped into the restaurant. The place was amazing. It was elegant and beautiful and surrounded with banks of windows. Jason stood to the side watching her face light up. He loved that he helped put that smile on her face. It was now Rebekah's turn to be speechless and it wasn't until Jason helped her out of her coat that she finally found her voice. "You weren't kidding. This place is amazing."

"I thought you would like it," he replied as a man approached them.

"Mr. Taylor," he started, reaching out to shake Jason's hand. "I was glad that you called me to make your arrangements for tonight. I have your table ready, and I promise you there will be no distractions." He indicated that they should follow him and continued talking as they did. "I'm placing you in one of the private areas of the restaurant. You will have all the same outside views as the rest of the guests, but will be completely secluded."

Rebekah marveled as they continued to follow the man she could only assume was the manager. He led them to a private room that she wouldn't have even noticed if she was there if she were a regular guest. The room was gorgeous; the lights were dimmed; yet it was easy to see with all the white lights that were draped around the plants in the room. There was a table for two set in the center of the room with a smaller table near it. They took their seats as the manager continued talking. "I took the liberty of using your suggestions Mr. Taylor, and your dinner is already ready. There is wine over there," he indicated a table to the side, "and your dinner is on your table. You dessert is also on the table by the wine. If you need anything else, just press this button and one of the waiters will be in here immediately."

Jason nodded his head, and the manager left, leaving the two of them alone. Rebekah shook her head in disbelief. "I guess he wasn't kidding when he said we wouldn't be disturbed."

Suddenly, Jason was worried about her being uncomfortable. "I hope this wasn't too presumptuous," he began, but Rebekah cut him off.

"No," she whispered, placing her hand in his. "It's perfect."

His face relaxed into a smile at her touch and he stood to pour both of them a glass of wine. They began enjoying their dinner, keeping the conversation light. They shared many of their interests and were not surprised when they realized many of theirs were the same. Neither of them discussed tomorrow, but no matter how much they tried to ignore the topic, it seemed to hang over their heads. They were both still nursing their first glasses of wine by the time they were ready to eat dessert, and soon they had finished even that. Rebekah took another sip of her wine and stood up, walking towards the window. She stood there looking out for a moment and smiled when she felt

Jason's eyes on her. Turning, she motioned for him to join her. Seconds later, he was behind her wrapping his arms around her waist as she pressed her back against his chest. She laced her fingers with his as he dropped his head to inhale her intoxicating scent, trying to commit her to memory, before resting his head against hers. The restaurant rotated so slowly, you almost wouldn't notice it and they stood there silently taking in the scene around them.

"This is peaceful," she stated quietly, letting out a long breath and relaxing into his arms.

"It is," he whispered back, not wanting to break the spell they were creating. He knew a discussion was coming, but he wanted to hold onto this moment for as long as he could. His thumb lightly caressed her fingers and he realized for the first time this evening that she was no longer wearing her wedding ring. He smiled as he unconsciously ran his thumb across her ring finger causing her to stir in his arms and he knew what was coming.

"Jason, what happens tomorrow?"

The question was out, and now they would have to deal with it. The moment of truth was here, and it was time to see where things stood.

"You could always stay here," he responded, gently nuzzling her neck.

"Very funny," she said, turning herself in his arms so she was facing him. "Not a possibility." No matter what either of them wanted, the reality was, she had to go home and so did he.

"I know," he replied, trying not to get lost in the depths

of her eyes. He took a deep breath. "What do you want to happen?"

"I don't know," she answered honestly. "I know what I feel, but how realistic is it to think we could do anything about it? Plus," she looked at him shyly, "I don't even know if you want to do anything about it," she lied. She could already read his eyes as if they were doorways to his soul. She knew how he felt, but she needed to hear him say it.

"I do," he whispered, drawing one hand from around her waist to push a piece of her hair behind her ear. She sensed he had more to say, so she remained quiet, allowing him to continue. "I wasn't expecting this. Who would've thought that while shopping for my sister's wedding, I would meet this amazingly beautiful woman I feel like I've known my entire life? I don't know what will happen in the future, but I do know I have no intention of letting you get on that plane tomorrow without the guarantee that I will see you again. I've spent forty-eight hours with you happier than I've been in a long time. I would be a fool to throw that away."

A smile crept across her face as he confirmed what her heart had been telling her since she first met him. "I feel the same way, but as much as I want to stay here, I have a hundred and fifty students expecting me to be in class the day after tomorrow. You have work to get to as well. So how do we guarantee we will see each other again?"

"Simple, you agree to come with me to my sister's wedding."

"Jason, I don't know," she broke in, pulling away from his embrace and turning to face the window.

"Look, there's no pressure here. All I said is if you agree to go, that is my guarantee. The wedding is in a month. I say we take the next month getting to know each other. We'll e-mail, we'll talk on the phone and if in a month, you're no longer sure, you just won't come."

She stood silent for a moment, watching the craziness of New York City disappear in the serenity of the moment. That's how she felt when she was with him, serene and complete. "Is it really that simple for you?" she asked.

"I know nothing about this is simple, but I also know I'm willing to take a chance." He reached out and took hold of her arm, gently turning her to face him. "All I know is in the short time we've been together, you have given me a glimpse of who you are, and you've left me longing for more. I won't walk away from that." Still holding onto her arm, he stepped closer, drawing her towards him at the same time; their eyes locked onto each other's.

"Okay," she whispered, letting out a soft breath, "I'll go to your sister's wedding." Hearing her words, he finally decided to give into the longing he had been fighting all day. Tentatively, he stepped towards her, closing the remaining distance between them. His eyes sought hers to make sure she wanted this too. Sensing her desire, he gently cupped her face in his hands, drawing her lips to his. They felt like the silk he had imagined, and immediately, he felt her reach her arms around his neck fully giving into the passion surrounding them. He intended the kiss to be short, but all rational thought quickly left his mind and he let his heart take over. His hands left her face and swept through her hair settling around her waist as he sweetly and gently explored her. She stepped closer if that was even possible as he discovered her mouth with sweet caresses she never imagined possible. They were lost in the moment, lost in each other, but eventually the magic ended, as the need for oxygen became more desperate than their need to be held by one another. Breaking away, they rested their foreheads together.

"I've wanted to do that all day," he stated quietly.

"So have I," she replied honestly, relishing in the feeling of being in his arms as his fingers ran sweetly up and down her back. She sighed as she turned back around in his arms, again letting her back rest against his chest, and she smiled as she felt him draw her close and place a sweet kiss on her neck. As they stood there together, neither one could ever remember feeling so complete; they just fit together.

She didn't know how long they stood there, but eventually they knew it was time to go. Reluctantly, they broke apart, both acknowledging that fact. Hand in hand, they left their private dining room and were surprised to see the restaurant was not only empty, but also closed. "What time is it, Jason?" she asked.

He glanced at his watch and grinned sheepishly. "Two in the morning."

"Oh my gosh! That manager was serious when he said we wouldn't be disturbed," she exclaimed as they got on the elevator. "You know they only didn't come in because of you. Do you get this special treatment everywhere you go?" she asked, her eyes hiding a teasing glint.

"Only when I ask for it," he replied, simply.

"And do you ask for it often?" she asked, biting her bottom lip as she looked up at him.

Wrapping his arms around her waist and pulling her closer, he answered, "No," as he leaned forward to capture her lips in another sweet kiss. Just as he thought the kiss might deepen, he heard the elevator ding, indicating they were on her floor.

They walked down the hall silently, each processing what had happened this evening. "Will I see you again?" she asked once they reached her door. He glanced at the floor and she could tell he wanted to ask her something. "What?" she prompted.

"I was hoping I could take you to the airport in the morning. I'm not taping tomorrow, so I have the day off."

"I would love that. I have to leave here around ten in the morning. Will that work for you?"

He laughed inwardly at her sweet soul. He had offered to take her to the airport, and she was worried if her already set schedule would blend okay with his non-existent schedule. "I'll meet you in the lobby at 9:45."

"That sounds great." Neither of them said anything else, nor could they seem to move. "Goodnight," she whispered, trying to force her legs to turn. Finally, she seemed to gain control again of her body and she began to turn towards the door when she felt his hand on her arm. Turning around, she immediately lost all sense of control as she felt his lips come crashing down on hers. Gone was the sweetness from before; the kiss was still gentle, but this time, it was driven by passion. Again, they hungrily opened their mouths to each other. Now though, she did most of the exploring and was surprised when she heard a moan escape from her own mouth. This time, it was Jason who broke the kiss, staring into her eyes and gently caressing her face.

"Goodnight," he whispered, placing a searing kiss on her forehead. "I'll see you in the morning." And with that, he turned to walk down the hall.

'Yes, you will,' she thought as she entered her own room, already thinking of what surprises the new day would bring.

CHAPTER 3

The next morning, Rebekah lay in bed reveling in her memories from the night before. She was so wound up when she came in that she completely packed. Now, she had several hours until she was supposed to meet Jason in the lobby.

Jason. Just thinking his name brought a smile to her face. She still couldn't believe she was dating Jason Taylor. Somewhere in the back of her mind, she kept expecting someone to wake her up from this dream. But, she was positive this was no dream; it was too real to be a dream. Rubbing her thumb across her lips, she closed her eyes and imagined him kissing her. She knew last night that he wanted to take things farther, and while she got lost in that last kiss, it would have been so easy to get completely consumed in him. But, she didn't want to rush things, and she loved the fact that he had the strength to walk away. It made her care about him and to want him even more. And, she was so glad he offered to take her to the airport. She wanted to see him one more time before she had to get on that plane.

Stretching, she got out of bed and headed to the shower. She wanted to get dressed so she could visit with Kate before she left for home. Stepping into the shower, her thoughts drifted back to Jason, wondering what he was doing at that moment.

Jason rolled over in bed; stretching and bringing his mind back to reality from…from what, from a dream? But it wasn't a dream; she wasn't a dream. She was real and he was so thankful she was. Never could he have imagined a woman so magnificent, but there she was holding his hand, smiling at him, smiling because of him, kissing him. His eyes closed as he imagined her touching him, running her fingers through his hair, kissing him. He groaned just thinking about it. If she only knew what she did to him with her simple touches. It had taken all of his strength to walk away from her last night, but he didn't want to rush things. Everything had been amazing so far, and he didn't want to do anything that would give her one moment of regret. Besides, although People magazine had labeled him a ladies' man several times, he wasn't exactly the kind of guy who just jumped into bed with a woman.

Standing, he headed to the shower. He glanced at his cell-phone and knew he had to call Danny and Nikki again. Nikki was going to throw a fit over the fact that he just left a message and then never called back. Rubbing a hand over his tired face, he decided to call them after his shower. He stepped inside and his thoughts drifted to Rebekah, wondering what she was doing at the moment.

Just as Rebekah was finishing getting dressed, she heard a knock on the door. She opened it to find Kate there. As Kate walked into the room, the first thing she noticed was Rebekah's missing wedding ring, but she chose not to say anything about it. Instead, she decided to focus on the huge smile that was plastered all over her friend's face. Kate couldn't stand it any longer. "Okay, spill it!" she ordered.

"What?" Rebekah asked nonchalantly.

"Don't 'what' me Rebekah Thomas! You know darn good and well what I am talking about! I want to know how last night went, and I want to know why you look as if you could explode from happiness at any moment."

"Kate, you have no idea what an amazingly romantic man Jason Taylor is," Rebekah swooned, falling onto the bed.

"Okay, so fill me in."

"Well, he started by taking me to see Phantom of the Opera, which by the way, he secured tickets for in less than four hours. Then we went to dinner. Did you know there is a restaurant here?"

"I know there's a buffet place several floors up, but no offense, that doesn't sound real romantic!"

Rebekah laughed and threw a pillow at Kate, which she skillfully ducked. "No! There's a restaurant at the top that rotates giving you an amazing view of New York."

"The View?" Kate asked. Rebekah nodded as Kate continued. "I've heard about that place before. In fact, that's the restaurant Meg Ryan's fiancé takes her to in Sleepless in Seattle. Is that where he took you?"

"Yeah, but he had arranged all of this ahead of time, so when we got there, we were given this private dining room, hidden from the view of any other guest. We had dinner, talked, stood together looking out the window, and kissed."

"You KISSED him?"

"Mm hmm."

"And?"

"And what? Was it a mind-blowing, earth-shattering, body-numbing kiss?"

"Well?" Kate asked, getting frustrated she was having to pull all these details from her.

"Okay. I've made you suffer enough. Yes, it was all of that, but Kate, it was so much more. I felt complete with him, in a way I've never felt before. I loved my husband, you know that, but what scares me is that I'm falling for Jason harder and faster than I ever fell for Steve."

"Rebekah, I know that you loved Steve, and I know that if he had survived the cancer, you would have spent the rest of your life happy with him." She watched Rebekah sit up on the bed and gently touch her ring finger and she continued. "But, you were in high school when you fell in love with him. It was honest and true, I don't doubt that, but it was young. You've grown since then. You have faced something most women never have to face, and you survived, coming out a stronger person. I told you this the other day. Steve would have wanted you to be happy, and I haven't heard this much happiness in your voice in over a year. If Jason puts that happiness there, I say, hold onto him."

Rebekah's face broke into a huge smile at this last part. "I plan to," she whispered.

"So," Kate asked. "I guess you two decided to continue seeing each other then?"

Rebekah nodded. "I agreed to come back in a month for his sister's wedding. Until then, we are going to keep taking the time to get to know each other." She paused and took a breath before continuing. "I'm just not ready to give him up yet, and he feels the same way about me."

"Oh, Bekah!" Kate exclaimed, pulling her in for a hug. "That's great. I am so happy you two met, and that you decided not to throw this away because you are scared."

"Well, I'm still scared, but I'm willing to take the chance." Rebekah broke from the embrace, wiping a tear from her eye. "You'd better get going Kate. You have a long drive, and I have to finish getting ready to go home." She paused before continuing. "Thank you, Kate. You've always been a good friend to me and supported me. I don't know what I would do without you."

"I'll miss you Bekah. Call me and keep me updated on everything."

"You know I will," Rebekah replied, hugging her friend one more time. Once Kate had left, Rebekah leaned against the door, anxiously wishing time would pass quickly so she could see Jason again, and yet hesitant for it to pass because that would mean she would have to leave him. She sighed and bustled about; taking care of a few last minute items, all the while, her mind and heart was trained on Jason.

Jason glanced at his cell phone again. He had taken a shower and gotten dressed. No longer having an excuse not to call, he picked up the phone to call Danny and Nikki. It wasn't that he didn't want to talk to them, he just knew Nikki well enough to know she would want to know every detail of this girl who had captured his heart. This time, he was ready to share Rebekah; he just knew it would be an exhausting phone call. Dialing the number, he smiled at her familiar voice, and he knew immediately she had recognized his number on caller I.D.

"JASON TAYLOR! I know that's you!" he heard Nikki yell through the phone.

"Nikki, stop yelling!" he admonished through the phone and laughed when he realized Danny had said the same thing in the background. "I was just calling to let you two know I would be coming home later today. I'm not sure when though."

"Jason, what is going on?" Nikki asked, this time a little more calmly. "You were supposed to be home two days ago. This isn't like you. Please tell me everything is okay with you and the divorce. Carrie didn't try anything there, did she?"

"No," he smiled. It was just like Nikki to worry about him. "Carrie didn't try anything, and I am officially divorced from that crazy woman. I just stayed because I met someone."

"Well, Jase. I'm glad she didn't try anything there, but you're not going to be happy… Wait a minute; did you say you met someone?"

Again, Jason smiled. He loved it when this woman, who was like a sister to him, got so caught up in what she was saying that she paid no attention to him. "Yes, Nikki. I met an amazing woman while I was here. She is why I stayed. Once I see her off today, I'll come home. Now, what am I not going to be happy about?"

"Oh no you don't, Jason Taylor! You can't just dump that on me and try to change the subject! Who is this girl? How did you meet her? What is going on there? This isn't like you to just do something like this for some girl."

"She's not 'some girl' as you quaintly put it, Nikki. She is the most amazing woman I've ever met, and you will get a chance to meet her in a month. She's coming to Kacee's wedding." He heard her take in a large breath of air, preparing her body for the next round of questions, so he decided to cut her off. "Nikki, you can play twenty questions when I get home. For now, know that I'm fine, and will be home some time tonight. I'm not taping today, so I'm in no hurry to leave here."

"Fine, Jason," she replied, letting out that long breath, but mentally preparing herself for the onslaught of questions she would have for him later. "Danny and I are both taping today, so we might not be home when you get here. And, we still need to talk about what Carrie has done."

"Okay, Nikki, but not now. I don't want anything to ruin this happiness I am feeling. I'll be home later." With that, he hung up the phone, knowing word for word the conversation that was taking place this time moment between Nikki and Danny. But, he wasn't concerned about that. All he wanted to do was go see Rebekah.

Ten minutes before Rebekah had to meet Jason in the lobby, she heard a knock on her door. Opening it, she was surprised to see Jason standing there. "Good morning," she said as a huge smile broke out across her face. Taking his hand, she led him into the room. "What are you doing here? I thought I was supposed to meet you in the lobby," she said.

Jason smiled as he watched her ramble. She was so beautiful and he couldn't believe it would be a month before they would be able to see each other again. He didn't want to lose her. Realizing he hadn't answered her yet, he quickly spoke. "I just thought I'd see if you need help with your luggage."

Once again, Rebekah was struck by his thoughtfulness, but she also detected a hint of sadness in his voice. She didn't want to lose him, but she was still partially afraid to believe in this too much, lest reality set in and break her heart again. Not wanting to voice her concerns, she again let a smile grace her face. "Thank you. I'm ready to go if you want to go ahead and leave."

"Your chariot awaits, my lady," he responded with a deep bow, laughing when her eyes twinkled and he noticed the smile on her face become genuine. He too detected the bittersweet atmosphere that surrounded them and he wanted to try and lighten the mood. He grabbed her bags as she took her coat and purse, and together, they left the hotel.

Fifteen minutes later, they were sitting in silence in a cab. Jason reached his arm around her and drew her closer, trying to memorize the feel of having her in his arms. He didn't want to wait a month to hold her like this again, but he could see no other options. Before either of them was ready, they reached the airport and he helped her out of the cab, grabbing her luggage. Together, they walked to the security checkpoint, that being as far as he could go without a ticket. Pulling her into a tight embrace, he could sense how she was feeling. Placing a sweet kiss against the top of her head, he whispered, "are you okay?"

She nodded her head in response, because she didn't

trust her voice to speak.

"No you're not," he whispered. Taking her face in his hands, he gently tilted it until their eyes met. "What's wrong?"

Tears threatened to fall from her blue eyes. She tried to break away from his gaze, but knew it was a useless battle. "I don't want to leave you, and that terrifies me."

Gently, he used the backs of his fingers to stroke her face. "I don't want to leave you either, but we don't really have another option. What terrifies you about this?"

She sighed and succeeded in pulling away from his gaze and his embrace. "Jason, I didn't even fall for my husband this fast, and that scares me. In the past two days, I feel like I've met someone who, for the first time, sees me, someone who sees the real me. I know I agreed to come back for your sister's wedding, but part of me is afraid that between now and then, you will change your mind and my heart will be broken again." By the time she finished speaking, her face was pointed towards the floor, and she was wringing her hands nervously. She couldn't believe she had just said that.

Jason took her hands in his, to not only steady her nervousness, but his own as well. "Rebekah, look at me." Slowly, she brought her eyes up to his, and almost immediately got lost in his gaze. Patiently, she waited for him to begin, but she wasn't prepared for the sweetness of his words. "I never expected to meet anyone like you. Even when I decided to marry Carrie, I thought that was what a true relationship was supposed to feel like. In forty-eight hours, you have proven that theory wrong. I know you are scared and I know neither of us is sure of what will happen in the future. But, I can promise you this, I will not break your heart, because if I did, it would be like breaking a part of my own."

This time, the tears fell freely down her face. "I don't know how to respond to that."

"Like this," he whispered, as he leaned forward and captured her lips in his. Slowly, his hand left the side of her face and slid down her neck, caressing her shoulder, down her arm. He pulled her closer to him, if that was even possible, and willingly opened his mouth as she softly searched for the entrance. Their kiss deepened as they explored the warmth of each other's mouths. Each moment in that kiss sent them closer to the point of no return, and neither of them wanted to come back from that edge. To the passerby, they looked like a devastatingly handsome couple, so in love with each other that they couldn't bear to part. What those onlookers didn't know was that was exactly how they felt, even if they hadn't said those words to each other. A kiss that was meant to serve as an answer to the unknown soon turned into a promise: a promise of the future and a promise of love. But, eventually, they began to run out of oxygen and the kiss ended. Foreheads touching, they remained lost in each other's embrace.

"I have to go," Rebekah whispered.

"I know," he whispered back, gently caressing her arms and back. "Will you call me when you get home, so I know you landed and the flight went okay?"

She nodded, slowly beginning to work her way out of his embrace. Eventually, the only things that still touched were their hands. One last time, she glanced up and got lost in his gaze. "Jason…"

"Shhh," he whispered, bringing a finger to her lips. "I know."

Again, she nodded and dropped his hands. Placing her carry-on bag onto the x-ray machine belt, she went through the metal detector and wiped a few tears from her eyes. Glancing behind her, she looked at him one last time before she turned to head towards her airplane.

Thirty minutes and many tears later, she was sitting on her plane. She was looking forward to going home, but she couldn't wait to get back here again. Closing her eyes, she could still taste him on her lips. One month seemed so long.

"Ms. Thomas?" a voice spoke, calling Rebekah out of her reverie.

"Yes?"

"There seems to be a problem with your seat. Would you please grab your carry-on luggage and follow me?"

Rebekah sighed and began to gather her belongings. She wanted to be left alone with her thoughts of Jason, but no, she had to follow some flight attendant to…first class? She was standing in first class.

"Ms. Thomas, we apologize profusely for the mix-up with your seat. Here is your new boarding pass, and here is your seat."

"There must be some mistake," Rebekah broke in. "I don't have a first class ticket." But, the flight attendant wasn't listening. Once she handed Rebekah the paperwork, she showed her to her seat. Rebekah shook her head and took a seat. The flight attendant turned to leave but not before she handed Rebekah a note.

Rebekah,

I wanted to join you on the plane this morning, but I was afraid it would make it even harder to say good-bye. I hope you don't mind being moved to first class. If I can't be here with you at least you can have a restful trip home. I can't wait to see you again.

Love,
Jason

She smiled as she read the note and thought of him. She knew that as reality set in over the next few weeks, she would be able to hold onto these thoughts of the past few days and look forward to the thought of seeing him in a month. She didn't know what the future might bring, but she couldn't wait to find out.

Several hours later, Rebekah's flight landed and she was headed home. The airport was an hour away from her house. She had left her car at home and since her parents lived close to her, they dropped her off. Now, she was so glad her father came to pick her up. He had always been one she could easily talk to, and he immediately noticed the happiness in her eyes, but knew her well enough to know that she would talk about it when she was ready. She had always been close to her parents. That's why she and Steve had decided to stay in their hometown after they got married.

Rebekah loved her parents dearly; they were a little crazy at times, but she didn't know how she would have survived Steve's death without them. But, she knew her parents well enough to know that her mother would be driving her crazy about now, trying to figure out why she appeared to be so happy. She wasn't sure how her parents would deal with her dating someone like Jason Taylor. In fact, she wasn't sure how her parents would deal with her dating someone at all. They had loved Steve like the son they never had, and they had been almost as devastated as she had been at his death. But, Rebekah knew she couldn't keep Jason a secret. Her mom knew her too well, and she would notice the change in her countenance. For the first time in over a year, she had a true smile on her face and a twinkle in her eye, and Jason was the one responsible for putting it there. She couldn't contain the smile from breaking out across her face as thoughts of him invaded her mind; however, her father soon broke into those thoughts.

"Did you have a good trip?" he asked, hoping she would explain to him why she looked so happy.

"You have no idea," she replied, still beaming. 'Was now the time to tell him?' she thought to herself.

"Well, you look good, very rested. Was your flight okay?"

Thinking of the restful flight she had just experienced, because of Jason, made her smile only become larger. Taking a deep breath, she decided to tell him. Her father was always the more rational member of the family. "Actually, my flight was great. I had the opportunity to fly home on first class."

"First class?" he asked, a little shocked. "Was there a mix-up with your flight?"

"Not a mix up, per se, but an upgrade." She turned to look at him, so she could watch his reaction to what she was going to say next. "I met someone over the weekend and he upgraded my seat without me knowing, so I could have a restful trip home." There, it was out.

She watched her father as he sat there for a moment. The shock of what she was saying registered on his face, and she was trying to figure out what he was thinking. Unexpectedly, a smile appeared on his face as he exclaimed, "honey, that's wonderful!"

Now, it was her turn to appear shocked. "You're not upset?"

"Why would I be? I love you and I want you to be happy. I know you're trying to hide it, but I haven't seen you this happy in over a year, and I've missed that twinkle in your eye."

"Thank you, Daddy," she whispered

"Don't thank me, just tell me about him."

'Uh, oh' she thought. 'How do I tell him I'm falling for a movie star? Deciding it would be best to start out small, she took a deep breath and began. "He's amazing, Dad. He's kind and thoughtful, and very romantic. You'd actually like him." Rebekah laughed to herself as she thought how much she felt like she was back in high school again, getting permission to date some guy. But, her family was her lifeline, she kept nothing from them, and it didn't matter to her that she was a twenty six year old widow; she still wanted to share her life with her parents.

"So," her dad asked. "Does 'he' have a name?"

"Jason." She replied, pausing before she added the last name. "Jason Taylor."

"You know, I think there is an actor with that name."

"There is," she answered, not offering any more information.

"He isn't the same Jason Taylor, is he?" he asked, glancing sideways at her.

Turning to catch his eye, she replied, "He is." Her father just nodded his head, and that concerned her. She didn't need his permission to see Jason, but she definitely wanted him to be happy for her. He still hadn't responded and now she was worried. Sighing, she asked, "what Dad? Go ahead, you can say it."

"There's nothing I need to say. I trust you. You've always had good instincts about people, and if you trust this man with your heart, I trust you."

"Thank you. That means a lot to me. I just hope Mom feels the same way. I know how much she loved Steve."

"We both did honey, but Steve is gone. He would want you to be happy and if you feel like you can be happy with this man, then I say go for it." He noticed a smile creep onto her face as he finished that. "What?" he asked.

"Nothing. It's just that a friend of mine said the same thing to me in New York right after I met him."

"Kate, right?" he asked. Rebekah nodded. "Well, Kate's always been one smart lady, and Jason seems like a wonderful man. I'm happy for you honey."

Again Rebekah nodded. She settled back against the seat, letting her mind drift to Jason. Needing to hear his voice, she couldn't wait to get home so she could call him. She closed her eyes and thought about the events of the weekend, wondering what he was doing now.

"Nikki, I'm back!" Jason yelled, walking into the Penthouse across from his. He considered Danny and Nikki family more than his own family.

"I'll be right there," she yelled from upstairs, so Jason took a seat on the couch. He had known Danny and Nikki for years now and although Nikki drove him crazy sometimes, he loved her like a second sister. He always laughed about when he first joined the show they all worked on together. Actually, he was re-joining the show; it was the soap he started on as a five-year old. Now, thirteen years later, he was back, and they were giving him a girlfriend, played by none other than Nikki Carlson. She was two years younger than him and flirted with him horribly. He couldn't stand her at first, but she was persistent. For the next two years, she chased after him and he continued to turn her down. Finally though, she turned 18, and he realized how good-looking she had become. Giving in, he asked her out, much to her excitement.

The date was a disaster. Nikki drove him ten times crazier on the date than she ever had on the set. There was no way he could continue to see her, but he didn't know how to end it. They were still in a relationship on-screen, and he didn't want to cause problems there. That was when he decided to never date someone on the show again; it was way too difficult. Fortunately, for him, it wasn't an issue very long. Danny Camarrelli joined the show, playing a cop. At first, their storylines were not joined, but once Nikki's character stole a car, all of their paths met. Danny was the cop, Nikki the criminal, and Jason, the boyfriend set to bail her out. A friendship began to form on-screen as well as off-screen. Within a few weeks, Nikki had Danny wrapped around her finger, even though he was four years older than she was. Five years later, they were married, and now the three of them were each other's family. The only time they ever had any difficulty was when he was married to Carrie; Nikki detested her, and now he knew why.

But, that didn't matter now. All that mattered was Rebekah. Smiling as her image filled his mind; he wondered if her flight had gone well and hoped she hadn't minded being bumped to first class. Needing to hear her voice, he hoped she would call soon.

"What are you so happy about?" he heard Nikki ask as she came down the stairs and stood by the couch. "Oh, that's right," she continued. "Your best friend didn't call and dump information on you and then never call back."

"Okay, okay Nikki. I'm sorry. But, I didn't want to talk to anyone but her this weekend. Hey at least I called in the first place. I could have made you worry."

"Alright, Jason." Nikki replied sarcastically, taking a seat next to him on the couch. "I'll let this go for now, but only because I want to hear about this girl who has apparently captured your heart. Who is she? How did you meet her? What is she like? Where...?"

"Slow down Nicole!" a voice ordered from the doorway.

"Daniel," she responded, getting up from the couch to hug him.

"I want to hear all of this too, but if you'll stop plowing the poor guy with questions, and let him talk, I'm sure you'll know everything you want to know. Right, Jason?"

"He's right, Nikki," Jason replied. "If you'll just sit down and be quiet, I'll tell you about her."

"Fine," she muttered, pretending to be angry. "But, I want the whole story."

"Well," Jason began. "I had been shopping for Kacee's wedding, when I walked out of a store and was mobbed by a group of women."

"Typical!" Nikki broke in.

"Nikki!" Danny warned. "Let him finish!"

Jason shook his head and smiled as he looked at his family surrounding him. It was like a comedy show around here, especially with Nikki around, but he loved every minute of it. He couldn't wait for Rebekah to meet them. "Anyway," he continued. "I noticed this amazingly beautiful woman a few shops back. She never approached me for an autograph and I started to walk away, but a gentle hand on my shoulder stopped me. Turning around, I saw her standing in front of me. I swear it was as if an angel stepped down from heaven to appear before me." Jason's eyes glazed over with happiness as he remembered the way she looked that day. Her long hair was down, framing her face and looking like silk strands that were begging to be touched. But, what got to him the most were her eyes. They were like sparkling sapphires, and the more he got to know her, the more they seemed to sparkle and come to life. He couldn't wait to get lost in that gaze again.

"And???" Nikki's voice broke through his thoughts.

She and Danny had noticed the look on his face and were both smiling at the thought of their friend in love. He may not have said it yet, but they both knew that this woman, whoever she was, had stolen Jason's heart.

"Sorry," he replied sheepishly. "She had stopped me because I dropped a package and she wanted to return it. I asked her to grab a cup of coffee, and we spent the rest of the weekend together. She's planning to come here in a month for the wedding."

Nikki was beside herself. "That's it?" she asked incredulously. "That's the end of your story?"

"No Nikki. That's not the end. Actually it's just the beginning." He smiled as he felt his phone vibrate in his pocket. Glancing at his watch to see the time, he knew it had to be her. His smile spread across his face as he answered it. "Hello?"

"Jason?" the voice on the other end of the line asked. "It's Rebekah."

"I hoped it would be you," he responded, standing to leave the Penthouse as he mouthed 'goodnight' to Danny and Nikki. He could hear Nikki protesting to Danny that he was leaving, and as he stepped into the hallway separating their Penthouses, he could picture the mess he had left Danny with. But he had something more important on his mind. Rebekah. "Did your flight go well?" he asked.

"Very well," she replied and he could almost hear the smile in her voice. "By the way," she continued, "thank you for my surprise. I've never flown first class before." She paused before continuing. "I just wish…" but she stopped herself.

"Wish what?" he asked quietly.

"It's nothing."

"Rebekah, you know you can tell me anything." He heard her sigh on the other end of the line, and immediately he wished he could wrap her in his arms and never let her go.

"I just wish I hadn't had to leave," she finished.

"I know, but you have to teach tomorrow, and I have to go back to work. Isn't that what you reminded me of last night?"

She smiled at the mention of that fabulous evening they had had the night before. It already seemed so long ago. "I know," she sighed. "I can't thank you enough for the wonderful weekend."

"It was my pleasure, but I didn't do it alone. You made it pretty special yourself."

"Okay," she replied laughing. "We were both involved in making it an amazingly wonderful, fantastic weekend. You know though. You've created quite a problem for yourself."

"Really," he responded, laughing as well. She could always draw him in with her laughter; it was like music to his ears and his heart. "And how, may I ask, have I created a problem?"

"Because, you've already spoiled me so much, you're not going to have anything left when I come up there in a month."

His heart caught in his throat. She really was planning to come back in a month. "Maybe I like spoiling you. Why, do you have a problem with that?"

"A problem with being spoiled by you? On the contrary, I think it's one of my new favorite past times. I'm just trying to keep from getting too used to it."

"Why? I don't plan on stopping anytime soon."

It was her turn for her heart to be caught in her throat. "Good," she whispered. "Jason. I hate to do this, but it is kind of late here. I have to teach tomorrow."

"Okay then. Good night Rebekah."

"Good night Jason," she whispered back, but after a second she realized neither of them had hung up the phone.

"Rebekah?"

"Shhh," she whispered. "I know." With that, she hung up the phone as he smiled. 'Twenty-nine days left,' he thought, 'and I haven't even begun to spoil her yet.'

The next morning, Rebekah awoke to the shrill ring of her phone. She knew immediately it would be her mother. Sighing, she rolled over and grabbed the phone. "Hello?" she answered, half asleep, working to will away the sleepiness in her voice.

"Hi, it's Mom."

"Good morning, what are you doing up so early?"

"I felt bad that I couldn't be there last night. Your Dad said you had a good time on your trip."

Wake fully spread through Rebekah's mind as she thought back to the weekend, for the hundredth time. "Yeah, you could say that I had a good time," she answered smiling.

"Good. You needed a break. Do you want to come by the house this afternoon after school?"

"Sure. I'd love to come by. But, I'll have to stay to catch up on few things. I'll see you this afternoon. Goodbye Mom."

"Have a good day, sweetie."

Flopping back on the pillows, Rebekah sighed. Getting up so early was the difficult thing about teaching middle school students in her district, and Rebekah was actually glad her mother had called to wake her up; however, she was a little worried about this afternoon. She knew her mother well enough to know she might not be thrilled her daughter was seeing someone. Immediately her mind swept to Jason. She couldn't help but wish it were he who had called her this morning. Although she hadn't experienced it yet, she couldn't imagine anything better than waking up in his arms and hearing his voice first thing in the morning. Closing her eyes, she projected herself back to the last time she felt his arms around her; it was at the airport, and she didn't think he wanted to let her go anymore than she wanted to walk away. She knew she would definitely use that memory to get her through the next few weeks.

An hour and a half later, Rebekah was in her classroom. She had missed her students, and unbelievably, they had missed her as well. They all wanted to know how her trip was, and of course they wanted the details. She gladly divulged them, every class period; but she kept Jason to herself. It was one thing to share the news with family, but she wasn't ready to share the fact that she was dating him with anyone else. Once the students settled down, she was able to teach her lesson. She was about halfway through it during third period when the door opened. One of the student aides walked in carrying a vase of roses. Her face radiated happiness, as she knew immediately whom they were from. Setting the roses down, she reached for the note.

Rebekah,

I know you had to leave your roses in New York when you left, and I know you were upset about that. So, now you have some more at home. There are twenty nine roses here; one for every day I will be missing you. I can't wait to see you again.
Jason

If it was possible, her face was lit up even more; her cheeks felt hot, and she knew she was blushing. He wasn't kidding when he said he wanted to continue spoiling her.

"Who are they from miss?" one of the students asked from the back of the room.

Rebekah looked up and her eyes softened before she answered. "Someone very special to me." And he was; more special than anyone else knew.

Several hours later, Rebekah left for home. She wanted to drop off the roses at her house before she headed to her parents. Those roses had caused quite a stir at school amongst not only the students, but the teachers as well.

Most had seen her receive flowers before, because Steve always sent them on her birthday. But, she hadn't received flowers in so long. Of course, everyone wanted to know whom the flowers were from. Fortunately, she was able to dodge the question well enough so as not to give out too much information.

Finally, she reached her parents' house. Taking a deep breath, she used her old key to open the front door. She loved the fact that her parents still lived in her childhood home. She remembered when her father wanted to sell the house; she had cried on Steve's chest all night. Just about the time she had made peace with the fact that her house would be sold, her parents had decided to stay. Walking in the house, she was surrounded with the familiar smell of vanilla mixed with her mother's perfume. "Mom?" she called as she walked into the living room.

"I'm in the laundry room," she heard her mother's voice call back. Hurrying through the kitchen, she found her mother taking the laundry out of the dryer. After giving her mother a quick hug, she grabbed one of her Dad's shirts and started helping her mother fold the laundry.

"How was your first day back?" her mother asked.

"Long," she replied. "But, it was good. I missed my kiddos."

"You usually do." They stood folding in silence for a few minutes before her mother broke that silence. "You look good though; very rested, and your eyes have a light to them I haven't seen in a while."

Rebekah knew her mother was fishing. It often amazed her how perceptive her mother could be at times. When she was growing up, she always tried to convince herself her mother didn't know anything. As she grew older and got married, she realized she was wrong. Her mother knew more than Rebekah ever wanted to admit, and this time was a perfect example of that. Hesitantly she answered the question, not wanting to give away too much information, but wanting not to lie to her mother as well. "It was a very restful flight, and I had a highly enjoyable time while I was there." There, that wasn't a lie; she would bring in the rest slowly.

"Was Kate there this year?"

Rebekah's eyes misted at the thought of her friend who had been such a good help to her. "Yes, she was. We had some good conversations."

"That's good. Anything exciting happen?"

Okay, she couldn't hesitate anymore. Setting down the shirt she had finished folding, she saw her mother glance over at her, noticing the smile she can never seem to control every time she thinks of Jason. Taking a deep breath, she responded, "Yeah, actually something exciting did happen. I met someone."

Her mother had resumed folding the laundry when Rebekah started talking, but at her last statement, her head jerked up. "You did?" she asked.

"Mm hmm," she replied, nodding her head.

"Well, tell me about him."

She smiled as she repeated to her mother the same thing she had told her father the night before: Jason was wonderful, caring, thoughtful and romantic. She even finished with the same statement she had given her father. "You would really like him, Mom."

Putting down her laundry, Rebekah's mother turned to face her. "Are you sure you're ready for this?"

"I'll be honest, Mom. I didn't think I was. I fought my attraction to him. I tried to stay away from him. But, there is something about him, about us, that just makes sense. You know I loved Steve; if he were alive, we wouldn't be standing here having this conversation. But he's not. I'm a twenty-six year old widow who is turning twenty-seven in two weeks. I have my whole life in front of me, and I should live it. It's taken me awhile to figure that out, but I've finally realized that Steve would want me to be happy." Rebekah paused, trying to give her mother a chance to take everything in, and trying to catch her own breath. Even she hadn't realized the full impact of what Jason made her feel. "I've found someone who makes me happy Mom. I trust him with my heart, and I'm asking you to trust me."

Silence filled the room as trepidation filled Rebekah's heart. Even the washing machine was silent. Rebekah knew she didn't need her mother's permission, but she wanted her to share her happiness. Tears filled both of their eyes as her mother drew her into a hug. "Of course I trust you Rebekah. I just worry about you. You were hurt so much by Steve's death; we all were. I just don't want to see you hurt again. If you trust this man, I know we will too."

They stood there in each other's embrace for a few minutes, mother comforting daughter, and daughter reassuring mother. As they broke apart, Rebekah whispered, "thank you. I was so worried you wouldn't be happy for me or that you wouldn't want me to see anyone again. But, Mom there's something else. You know this man, or at least, you know of him."

"How?"

Again taking a deep breath, Rebekah answered, "His name is Jason Taylor. He plays Brad on the soap opera you've been watching for twenty-five years."

"*That's* the man you're seeing?" she asked incredulously.

"Yes," Rebekah answered, cringing slightly as she prepared to be bombarded with criticism and concern from her mother. But, she was met with only silence. Catching her mother's gaze, Rebekah noticed a gleam in her eye. "What?" she asked.

"Nothing," her mother replied nonchalantly.

"Mom." Rebekah continued in a warning tone, and still she received no response. "Mother!" Rebekah practically yelled. "What is so amusing?"

Rebekah's mother broke into laughter as she prepared to answer her daughter. "It's just," she tried to get the words out through fits of laughter. "It's just that he's *hot!*"

Rebekah's eyes widened in shock as the realization of what her mother said hit her. Then she broke into laughter that matched her own. "Yeah, he is," Rebekah agreed.

CHAPTER 4

The next couple of weeks were amazing for both Jason and Rebekah. They talked so much, and so often; they were getting to know each other in ways they never thought possible. He told her about his childhood and growing up with his family, the Jensen's. He told her how crazy they were: always causing one problem or another, continuously lying, constantly fighting. When he pulled off a stunt on the show and injured himself, he moved in with Carrie, because he couldn't stand the idea of moving back in with his family. He loved his mother, his grandmother, and his sister, but everyone else, he could do without. Being an actor, he had his last name legally changed when he was twenty; going by Taylor instead of Jensen.

She told him of her childhood as well: the joys of having two loving parents and an older sister, the pain of losing that sister when she was twenty. The thought of her sister still pained her. Her sister was killed in a car accident three months after Rebekah's wedding. She also laughed as she remembered the last family vacation they took; it was her senior year, and her sister had just gotten engaged. Their parents wanted to take one last vacation with just the four of them. They went to Maui for a week that December, and she reminisced about falling in love with that place. She tried so hard to get her parents to let her go to the University of Hawaii, but of course, she didn't go. She admitted that it was times like this, what was happening in her life now, that she really missed her sister, but she was leaning more and more on Jason.

He told her about Danny, Nikki, and their whole background. He explained how they lived across the hall from one another, and they were basically each other's family. She told him about Kate, and how, since her sister's death, she had come to see Kate as more like her sister. Thinking back to when she and Jason first met, she told him about Kate and her wise words. Jason then told her he needed to thank Kate if he ever saw her again.

After a while, they even started sharing their hopes and dreams for the future.

A week and a half after Rebekah returned home, they were having a conversation, again, about family. After Jason had explained about his family, or lack thereof, Rebekah couldn't help but be concerned. "What do you do for holidays?" she asked.

"Usually, I spend them with Danny and Nikki. Occasionally, I get together with my sister and mother, but holidays are often the times when my family is the worst. I can't stand to be around them. At Christmas, I always make it a point to go by my Grandmother's house to see her, but I never stay long. Why do you ask?"

"I just hate the thought of you being by yourself on holidays. No one should be alone on holidays, especially you."

Jason smiled as her words lit up his heart. They hadn't been together that long; yet he could hear the genuine concern in her voice. "I'm never alone Rebekah. Family is what you make it; I have Nikki and Danny and they are my family. Nikki never lets me celebrate a holiday totally by myself."

"What about your birthday? How do you celebrate that?"

"Oh, since it is in the summer, what we do varies, but I promise, I'm never alone."

"Good," she replied. Ever since he told her about his real family, she couldn't help but worry about it. Worrying about him came as natural to her as caring about him. She wanted him to be happy.

"What about you?" he asked. "How do you spend your holidays?"

"With my family. It never mattered where we were, as long as we were together."

Again, her words warmed Jason's heart. He had always wanted a family like that. Sure, he loved Danny and Nikki, as well as a few members of his own family, but he had always wanted that solid foundation. Hoping he had found it in Carrie, he married her, but he knew now they never had that kind of connection. Rebekah on the other hand, was different. It was as if she had breathed new life into him; a life he hadn't known was missing. He craved the day when he could hold her in his arms again. There were only two and a half more weeks until Kacee's wedding, but that seemed like an eternity. "And your birthday?" he asked.

"Usually dinner, somewhere, anywhere; again it didn't matter as long as we celebrated as a family. Since my birthday is in early March, we never know what the weather will be like; sometimes warming up, sometimes still cold. So, we always felt dinner was a safe activity."

"Uh, Bekah? You do know it's early March now, right?" he asked surprised. He knew she probably wasn't planning on telling him when her birthday was, but apparently it was right around the corner, if he hadn't missed it already.

"Oh my gosh. I wasn't even thinking about that. Last year, I didn't exactly feel like celebrating, and the year before, Steve was too sick."

"So, when is it?" he asked, praying she would tell him.

"Saturday. My birthday is exactly two weeks before Kacee's wedding."

Jason almost felt his heart stop in his chest. He was so glad she had mentioned the wedding because he had wanted to ask her if she still wanted to come, but didn't want to push her. Now, the time seemed perfect. "Do you still want to come?"

She heard the hesitation in his voice, and was surprised to find it there. Didn't he know how much she needed to see him, to be with him? Couldn't he feel how much she just needed him? Her body ached to be in his arms, and although she cherished every moment of their conversations together, it wasn't the same as looking into those eyes as she spoke. She laughed inwardly as she thought back to every one of her afternoons the past week and a half; she had started to tape his show, just so she could see him. She missed him so much. "Yes, I do," she whispered, "if you still want me to come."

It was Jason's turn to be surprised. How could she even question whether he wanted her here with him? Didn't she realize how important she had become to him? He lived for these few stolen moments on the phone, but it wasn't enough. She was a craving the phone couldn't satisfy. "Of course I still want you to come. That hasn't changed. Just tell me when you want to fly in, and I'll take care of the ticket."

"Jason, you don't have to do that."

"No, I invited you; I'll take care of the plane ticket. I just can't wait to see you."

"I can't wait to see you either. The wedding is on Saturday, so how about I come in Friday night. I'll have to leave after school on Friday. That won't cause a problem for you, will it?"

"Not at all. Kacee's wedding rehearsal will be over by the time you are able to land. Don't worry about it!"

Their conversation became quiet for a few minutes, as they were lost in their own thoughts. Finally, Rebekah broke through. "I have a confession to make," she said, with a hint of laughter in her voice.

Picking up on that hint, he asked, "what confession?"

Barely containing her laughter, she admitted, "I've been taping your show everyday just to see you."

"I can't believe you're actually watching that garbage," he replied, joining in her laughter.

"Hey! It's the only way that I can see you. Plus, your storyline isn't that bad. The whole thing is actually quite amusing."

"It's not amusing, it's annoying. And that storyline isn't worth anything. It was fairly decent, now it's about to be ruined!" Jason hadn't meant to snap, but the moment she mentioned his show, it was like all the light of the conversation drained away. He didn't want to tell her why he hated the direction of his storyline, but he knew he couldn't keep anything from her. In just these few short weeks, she had become a confidant for him. Plus, he had to reassure her before she saw anything on screen.

Rebekah immediately detected the tension in his voice. Had she said something wrong? She figured he would be amused at her watching his show, or at least touched she was trying to see him. "Jason? Is everything okay?"

Silence was her only answer. Hearing his tense breathing on the other end of the phone, she knew he was still there. Deciding to give him time, she joined the silence and waited. After a minute, he began to speak. "I'm sorry for snapping. It means more to me than you realize that you care enough to watch that show just to catch a glimpse of me." Taking a deep breath, Jason paused before continuing. "I just received some news about my storyline yesterday, and I wasn't very thrilled about it. I got a warning from Nikki, but I didn't believe her." The truth was, he was too happy to pay attention to Nikki. Now, he wished he had, because maybe he could have stopped it.

"Do you want to talk about it?" she asked quietly, hoping he would. She wanted Jason to trust her with everything, just as she was beginning to trust him.

Jason sighed. "The morning we left New York, Nikki

started to tell me about something involving Carrie. I was too happy with the weekend we had just had to even care about anything my ex-wife did. Now I realize I should have paid attention. Carrie was hired a while ago to do some painting at the studios. She really is pretty talented, and they wanted some walls painted with artwork directly on them for the show. Of course, she agreed. Well, apparently, while I was on my three-day vacation, she managed to get some face time with one of the writers. He was impressed with her and convinced the idiots in charge that she needed to be hired. They actually broke down and hired her; that's what Nikki was trying to warn me about."

"Did I miss something?" Rebekah asked in a state of disbelief. "I know I'm not in the acting industry, but do they normally put artists on the show as actors?"

"Not normally, but unfortunately for all of us, she actually used to act. She's done mostly plays, nothing major, but she can act. She's fairly decent; she just never appeared interested, until now." That was the part that made no sense to Jason. Why, all of the sudden, did Carrie want to act, and why his show?

"Are they putting her in your storyline?" Rebekah asked.

This was the part he was dreading. They had such a good thing going here and he didn't want to risk losing her; he couldn't lose her. "Rebekah, not only are they putting her in my storyline, they are making her my new love interest."

He cringed at the immediate stillness of their conversation. Maybe he was crazy for trying to bring Rebekah into all of this. She had already been deeply hurt when Steve died. The last thing he wanted to do was hurt her, but he was afraid he just did. "Rebekah?" he whispered.

"I'm here," she replied quietly. "I was just thinking. How do you feel about all of this?"

Jason was beside himself. Here he was, worried about hurting her and wondering if he was asking too much by having her with him, yet she was worried about him. "I won't lie, Rebekah. I'm not happy about it. I didn't say anything last night, because I was hoping to change their minds today, but no such luck. They are set to go ahead with this. But, that's not my main concern."

"So, what is?"

"You."

"Me, why?"

"Rebekah, I don't want to hurt you. You've already faced so much pain, and it would kill me to think that I caused you anymore."

"Jason," she broke in, "how would you cause me any more pain?"

"I don't think you understand what this will mean. She'll be a love interest at first, but eventually they might put us together. If that happens, we will have to do love scenes together, and make them look real. I don't want you to have to deal with that."

Rebekah was quiet for a moment and when she finally responded, her voice was thick with emotion. "Let me ask you something."

"Okay."

"Do you still love Carrie?"

"Of course not. You of all people should know that."

"Okay then," she continued, her voice still soft. "Do you have any intention of dropping what we have started to go back with her?"

"Rebekah, why would you even ask that?"

"To prove a point to you." She paused; wanting to make sure she had his full attention. "Jason, I know what you do; you act. That means whether you are kissing Carrie or anyone else, you don't mean it. And I don't care how real you make it look, it will never be as amazing as that first kiss we shared, or any kiss from that point on. I know you have a hold on my heart, and I know you wouldn't do anything to break it. I trust you Jason, completely."

Jason was speechless; he had to collect his thoughts, because he didn't know if he trusted himself to answer her immediately. Finally, after what must have seemed an eternity to Rebekah, he answered her. "Thank you, Bekah," he practically whispered. "No one has ever understood me the way you do. I know this is crazy, Rebekah; we only met a few weeks ago, but so help me girl, you have a hold on my heart too. So many people would look at us and say we are rushing things, that in the end, this won't last. I couldn't disagree more. I don't give my heart away easily; in fact, I don't believe I've ever fully given it, until now. You have nothing to worry about with Carrie or anyone else. I would never risk losing you."

"Jason, if you want to keep fighting to keep from working with Carrie, that's fine. I want you to be happy.

But, I want you to do it for you, not me."

"Okay," he whispered, exhausted from the lateness of the night and the emotion of their conversation. He wanted nothing more than to push those silky blonde strands from her face, wrap his arms around her, and kiss her good night. "Rebekah, we need to go."

"I know," she replied, fighting off a yawn of her own. "I just hate this part of our conversations."

"I do too. But, I'll see you in a few weeks. Until then, just know that I…,"

"Shhh, Jason," she whispered. "I know."

Suddenly, two and a half weeks seemed too long for Jason.

Jason was miserable. For four days he had fought the upper echelon against him and Carrie working together, and still they wouldn't change their minds. It might have made sense to him if no one there knew of their past together, but many of them did. In fact, one of the writers even took him to dinner several times after he and Carrie separated. Now, he was one of the main writers pushing for Carrie in Jason's storyline.

He hated this. Moreover, he hated what it was doing to him. Ever since this new development came about, he had barely spoken to Rebekah. Sure, they spoke every night, but their conversations were limited and always short. This is what he hated the most. He missed her, but he couldn't bring himself to relax about Carrie; something was going on there, he just couldn't put his finger on it.

Shaking the thought from his head for the hundredth time that day, Jason once again allowed his thoughts to drift to Rebekah. Her birthday was tomorrow. More than anything, he wanted to get on a plane and fly out to Houston, but he had to work on Sunday. That was the other thing he hated about this. Because the writers wanted him and Carrie together so quickly, they had to actually tape some scenes on the weekend.

"Dammit!" he yelled, slamming his hand onto the table in front of him. No matter what he did, he couldn't keep the thoughts of Carrie and work from streaming into his mind. He couldn't take it any longer. He knew Rebekah was at school, but he had to hear her voice. Quickly dialing her number, he counted the number of rings until her voicemail picked up. Instead, he heard her angelic voice.

"Hello?"

Jason was so caught up in this unexpected surprise he forgot to answer.

"Jason?" she asked quietly, recognizing his number on her caller-id screen. "Is that you?"

"It's me," he responded almost as quietly.

Rebekah's heart tore at the tiredness in his voice. She knew his problems at work were weighing heavily on his mind, and she didn't know how to help. "What's going on?" she asked hesitantly. "Are you at work?"

"I'm on a short break," he answered, pausing before continuing, "and I just needed to hear your voice. I called to leave a message on your voicemail. What are you doing answering? I figured you would still be in class."

"No," Rebekah smiled, realizing he was relaxing by the tone in his voice. "We're on a half day schedule today, so the kids are already gone. I'm just taking care of some work in my room. Any particular reason you needed to hear my voice?" 'Not that there needs to be,' she thought. She loved the fact that anytime he got stressed, he seemed to call her.

"I'm sure you can guess. I can't stand the thought of working with Carrie, but no one seems to care. We start taping our first real scenes together in about an hour, and there is nothing more I want to do right now than leave this studio," 'and fly to Houston,' he added in his own mind. "You know, I've never had a problem pretending to love any woman on the show, but I don't want to do it with her."

"What are you going to do?" The last thing Rebekah wanted to do was push Jason. He needed to make his decisions based on his needs, not what he thought she needed.

"Suck it up and deal with it, for the moment. There's nothing I can do."

"I'm sorry," she whispered. "I know there's no reason for me to be, but I hate that you're unhappy."

Jason's heart rate increased at the sweetness of her words. He loved that she cared about his happiness so much. It amazed him how a three-minute phone conversation could have him so relaxed. If only he could have her next to him. But, that was impossible, at least for now. "Thank you Rebekah."

"For what?"

"For just being you." There was so much more he wanted to say, but now wasn't the time. "So, onto happier topics. What are you planning to do tomorrow for your birthday?"

"Nothing but the usual: dinner at five o'clock with my parents. I'll probably talk to Kate also. She always calls on my birthday."

"Dinner, huh? Where at?"

"The Steakhouse. It's probably one of the oldest restaurants in my hometown. I've known the owners since I was a little girl."

Jason's mind was flashing images of Rebekah in a small restaurant, surrounded by family and friends. He just wished he could be one of those people. "Sounds like you have a wonderful evening planned. I know you will enjoy it."

"I will," 'but all I really want is to see you,' she thought to herself.

"By the way, I'm mailing your flight information tomorrow. It's an e-ticket, so all you will need is the papers I am sending you. I can't wait to see you again."

"I can't wait to see you either."

Sighing, Jason continued, "I've got to go. I only have about five minutes before we begin taping the next scene."

"Alright. I'm glad we at least got a few minutes to talk."

"Me too." Taking a deep breath, Jason contemplated

telling her exactly what was on his mind. "Rebekah, I…"

"Shhh. I know." She replied as she hung up the phone. And, for the first time, she really was beginning to know. In just a few minutes, Jason's whole demeanor had relaxed, and she smiled as she realized at least part of that was because of her.

Placing his cell phone in his pocket, Jason leaned his head against the wall, a smile tugging at his lips. He was falling in love with this woman. Everything about her radiated through his body. He needed to be with her, to feel her in his arms, her lips against his.

Work that afternoon was easier for him because he finally figured out how to get through his scenes with Carrie: Rebekah. Every time he had to respond in a loving or desirous manner towards Carrie, he just kept picturing Rebekah, her lips, her body, her voice, anything he could think of. She was the one responsible for getting him through the day. By the time he drifted off to sleep that night, he could no longer even think about work; she invaded every one of his thoughts, and that was the only way he wanted it.

The next morning, Rebekah awoke with a start before sighing and plopping back onto her pillows. She didn't want to get out of bed. Birthdays and holidays were still a little difficult for her. Steve used to work so hard to make these days special; he would bring her breakfast in bed, bring her flowers, do anything he could to make her feel as if she was the queen of the world. Now, in this house and in this bed, she just felt alone. But, that wasn't entirely true either. She wasn't alone, not any longer. Jason was beginning to permeate each and every one of her thoughts. She felt like he was with her everywhere, but it wasn't enough. She needed to see him, to feel his arms around her, and she knew these thoughts and desires were increasing her feelings of being alone. Pushing those feelings away for the moment, she focused on the day at hand. It may have been her birthday, but she still had a lot to accomplish. Forming a list in her mind, she showered quickly, got dressed, and headed out to start her day.

Hours later, an exhausted Rebekah walked through her kitchen door and sank onto her couch. Accomplishing everything on her list was the only thing keeping her up at the moment. She was a little disappointed by the fact that she hadn't heard from Jason all day. Part of her was expecting to be woken up by a phone call from him this morning. But, she couldn't complain; she knew he was busy.

After a quick nap and a change of clothes, she felt re-energized and was ready to go. Applying her last bit of lip-gloss, Rebekah headed out to meet her parents. She didn't know what she would do without them. At least she wasn't fully alone; she would always have them to rely on. Walking into the restaurant, her eyes sought them out right where she knew they would be. Her parents were anything if predictable; they had occupied the same table for years. Her father was notorious for keeping his family waiting, just so he could sit at "his" table. They even had the same seats: her father facing the door, while her back was pointed towards it.

"Hey, sweetheart," her father said, standing and pulling her into a hug.

"Happy Birthday," her mother chimed in, pulling her into a hug of her own. "Did you have a good day?" she asked as they were sitting down.

"Busy," was her response, and it was true. There was only one thing that would make this day good, and she wasn't holding out any hope for that. Rebekah couldn't help but notice the worried look that her parents exchanged, so she quickly continued. "But, it was fine. I was able to get a lot done. I missed Kate's phone call though. I'll call her back later."

"And Jason?" her mother asked. "Have you spoken to him lately?

"Yesterday." Rebekah knew her mother was still worried about her and Jason. To be honest, she was still some too. If only she could see him again. She knew seeing him would end her questioning. Every time she looked into his eyes, she felt as if she could read his soul. She only wished she could read it now. 'Two weeks,' she thought to herself as her father's voice broke into her thoughts.

"How about we eat?" He said. "Stan and Janet already placed our order, knowing what we would want. It looks as if the food is finally here." Rebekah laughed to herself again. Stan and Janet were not only the owners, but close friends as well. It was just like them to take care of her family and just place the order of what they knew would be wanted. Rebekah and her parents continued visiting throughout their meal. When it was over and the plates had been cleared away, her father asked, "how about you open your presents?"

"Presents? You know you guys didn't have to get me anything," she replied, but the sparkle in her eyes gave her true feelings away. Quickly, she ripped the paper out of the first bag. Just as she suspected, it was a book. Without fail, every year, her father picked out a book for them to read together. She would read it first, and then pass it on to him. The cycle would end as they discussed it over a father-daughter lunch. It was one tradition Rebekah never wanted to end. "Thanks, Dad. I'll start it tonight."

Hesitantly, she reached for the other gift. She had an idea as to what was in it, and she wasn't sure if she wanted to open it. Fingers shaking, she pulled at the ribbon and tore the tape, ripping the paper. Opening the box, a soft cry escaped her mouth.

"It's a new hybrid," her mother said quietly. "It's been so long since you worked on your roses, I thought maybe you would like to start again."

Rebekah nodded, not yet ready to respond. Gingerly, she ran her fingers over the small plant. Of course, there were no blooms on it; that was the way she liked to start all of her roses. Thinking of the neglected rose garden in her backyard, she realized how right her mother was. It had been too long since she tended to it. She was in the rose garden when they got the call from the doctor, and she hadn't stepped foot inside it since. At one point in time, that garden was her refuge, her place of healing; then it became her place of pain. But, her roses were hardy; they had survived despite her efforts at neglect, just like her heart. After numerous attempts at neglect, Jason slowly entered her heart. Her heart had healed, and even started to thrive again, maybe it was time for her roses to do the same. "Thank you, Mom. I love it."

"So," her Dad broke in, trying to lighten the mood, "can you deal with only two presents this year?"

"Oh, I suppose so. I guess I can't be too greedy."

From behind her she heard, "would you like one

more?"

Immediately, she recognized that voice; how could she not after nights of endless conversations. Spinning in her seat, her eyes connected with those ocean blue ones she had longed to see. Before she knew what was happening, she was out of her seat and in his arms. "Jason," she whispered, not wanting to let go.

"Happy birthday," he whispered back, tightening his embrace of her. He still couldn't believe he was here, but when he had woken up that morning, he decided he had to see her. And, in that moment, he knew it was worth it. Feeling her in his arms was the only thing he needed. "I think we have an audience."

"I think you're right," she replied, reluctantly pulling away from his strong embrace. "Come here. There are a couple of people you need to meet." Taking his hand, she led him to her parents. "Mom, Dad, this is Jason. Jason, my parents, Jim and Susan Williams"

Reaching out his right hand, Jason shook her father's hand before pulling her mother into a quick hug. "It's a pleasure to meet you both," he said, barely able to tear his eyes away from Rebekah.

"It's a pleasure to meet you too," her father replied. "Unfortunately, we can't stay much longer." He turned to give his wife a look that told her not to say anything. He knew what his daughter needed more than anything was some time alone, and he planned on giving it to her.

"Dad, you don't have to go," she replied, her eyes giving her true feelings away.

"I know," he answered, kissing the top of her head.

"Happy Birthday, Rebekah."

But, Rebekah didn't hear her father's response. She was concentrating on the dangerously handsome man in front of her. "How did you manage this?"

"I got up this morning, called the airlines, and booked a flight out here." Giving into his longing, he reached a hand out to take hers, needing to feel her skin against his.

"Funny. Seriously, I know you have to tape tomorrow. How did you manage to rearrange that?"

"I didn't," his fingers continued to caress her own. "I'm only here for a couple of hours. I just needed to see you."

"I'm glad you came." Rebekah couldn't believe he would endure a two and a half hour flight, just to see her for a few hours. "Do you need to eat?"

"No. I ate on the plane."

"Good. Let's get out of here." They had both noticed the stares that were surrounding them. Not many stars ended up in her small town, and she didn't want to deal with anyone but him right now.

He didn't even have to answer. Standing, he held out his hand for hers and quickly escorted her out of the building. Once in the parking lot, she directed him to her truck. "You don't exactly seem like a truck person," he said, laughing.

"I'm not. This is my Dad's. My car is having some work done to it. That's why you're going to drive." She quickly tossed him the keys to the truck.

Cocking his head to one side, he playfully replied, "I can't say I've ever driven a truck before."

"Yeah, well I would venture to say you've never flown two and a half hours to visit a teacher before either," she played back.

Hanging his head in shameless defeat, he opened her door for her and walked around to the other side. Once in, he prepared to start the truck, when he felt her soft touch on his arm. That was all it took. Turning towards her, he took her face in his hands and gently lowered his lips to hers. Softly and tenderly he caressed her lips as she returned the motion, her tears sweetening the kiss. Pulling back before it turned into something neither of them could control, he whispered, "I've missed you so much," his thumbs wiping the tears from her eyes. "Why are you crying?"

"I'm so glad you came."

"Me too." He punctuated that thankfulness by drawing her into another embrace, never wanting to let her go. Kissing her gently, but quickly this time, he asked, "where to?"

Rebekah slid over next to him and directed him to a close friend's rice field. The stock pond there was the closest thing to a lake, and there were a few trees around it. There hadn't been much rain yet, so the mosquitoes weren't bad; this was a perfect evening. Once he turned off the ignition, they climbed out of the truck and he followed her to the bed of the truck. Releasing the tailgate, she hopped up and motioned for him to join her. He leaned his back against the wall of the bed and drew her to his chest, enclosing her in his arms. The sun was hanging dangerously low in the sky, its setting rays painting the horizon. Birds chirped in the distance and crickets danced in the grass while frogs croaked their loneliness around the pond. "I definitely agree about the different part," he whispered against her neck, letting his lips linger there for a moment.

"Hmm?" she asked, fighting the loss of control that was building in her body at that movement of his lips against her neck.

"When we first met, you told me New York was so different from your home. Being here, I would have to agree. It's so peaceful here. Is this your land?"

"No. It belongs to a friend. It's just such a good night for sitting outside; I wanted to take you here."

"Well, it's definitely beautiful." They sat there for a few minutes before she felt him shifting, trying to draw something from his pocket. "Happy birthday," he whispered again, handing her a small box.

"Jason, you didn't have to get me anything. You being here is enough of a present for me."

"I know, but I wanted to. Now open it."

Giddy with anticipation, Rebekah quickly opened the box to reveal a beautiful heart-shaped locket. The light engraving on the front drew her attention, and she gently rubbed the letters R.T. "Jason, it's beautiful."

"Open it."

Gingerly unlocking the clasp, her eyes welled with tears as she read the words engraved inside on the left. 'You have a hold on my heart.' Turning to give him a hug, she whispered, "thank you. I love it." Withdrawing from his embrace, she took the necklace from the box and handed it to him. "Put it on me."

His fingers moved the hair from her neck, loving the feel of her bare skin against his fingers. He placed the necklace around her neck and after several tries, was able to successfully clasp it. He smiled as her hands went to the heart and her fingers twirled it. Leaning back against him, she whispered, "You have a hold on my heart too."

His arms tightened around her as his lips again found her neck. Turning in his arms, she drew his lips from her neck to her own hungry ones. Excitement and need soon took over as he nibbled on her bottom lip, causing her lips to part. That was all the space he needed. Passion seemed to control both of them as a sense of completeness and hunger overtook their bodies. Her back pressed against his right knee, which was propped up in the tailgate as his left hand softly ran down her neck and her arm, his fingers lightly touching her skin, stirring emotions within her that she was afraid she wouldn't be able to control if they continued much longer.

Hesitantly, she pulled away, breathlessly whispering, "Jason, we can't do this."

"I know," he replied, dropping his face into the warm crevice of her left shoulder. This wasn't the time or the place for this to happen. "But, I won't deny that I want you."

"I do too, but I can't. Not yet." Pulling completely from his embrace, she pushed herself off the bed of the truck and walked towards the stock pond, leaving a very confused Jason behind. After a moment, she felt his presence behind her. Knowing he wouldn't push her, she started talking. "You need to know something about me Jason. I'm not some 'easy' woman."

"I never thought you were Rebekah." Placing his hands on her shoulders, he turned her to face him. "You have to know that."

"I do. I just need you to understand something." Bringing a hand to his face, she whispered, "You have no idea what you do to me. Just being near you awakens senses I thought were dead; you even ignite feelings I never knew existed. But, I've never," she paused, "how do I say this?"

"You've never been with anyone other than Steve," he completed the sentence for her. She nodded her head, dipping it towards her chest, dropping her hand from his face. Softly, he kissed the top of her head, and then used his thumb and forefinger to tilt her face towards his. "I want you Rebekah. But, I want you when it is right for both of us, not a moment before. We've only known each other a few weeks. I'm not going anywhere. We have a lifetime ahead of us."

Once again, she felt herself getting lost in him, in his eyes. They truly were windows to his soul, and she could tell he meant every word he said. He truly understood her. "Jason, I…"

"I know," he replied, drawing her lips towards his. Reigning in his own desire, Jason held back from deepening the kiss too much. He seemed to lose all control around her, and he couldn't afford to do that. But, he didn't have to worry about that very long, because, as usual, their need for air surfaced before their desire to break apart, but they had no choice.

Resting her head against his chest, she asked, "When do you have to leave?"

"Now." The silence that surrounded them was deafening. "It took me almost an hour to get here from the airport."

"Do you need me to drive you back?"

"No, I don't want you coming back, alone, that late at night. I've arranged for a cab. I just need to call and tell him where to pick me up." He pulled out his phone and proceeded to give the driver the address Rebekah had given him. "He'll be here in ten minutes," he said quietly, pulling her back against his chest, wanting to hold onto her for as long as possible.

She nodded, afraid to speak. This man simply amazed her. Not only would he give up his only day off this week to come see her, he understood her reluctance to move forward too fast. She didn't want him to leave, but she knew he couldn't stay. They stood there in silence for several minutes before she turned in his arms.

"What are you thinking?" he asked, brushing a piece of hair behind her ear.

"I don't want to let you go," she answered honestly, staring into his eyes, reading emotions she knew mirrored her own.

"I don't want to go. But, I'll see you in two weeks."

"That seems so long."

"I know," his fingers traced the sides of her face as she

leaned into his touch. Needing to feel her closer, he lifted her lips to meet his. Again, he tasted her tears and his own threatened to fall as he realized this time they weren't tears of happiness. He deepened the kiss; trying to tell her in that one touch everything he was too afraid to tell her with words.

Rebekah felt herself falling over the edge with that kiss. After this moment, she knew she could not live the rest of her life without this man. She had tried to keep herself from wanting him, needing him, loving him; but, in the end, her heart won out over her mind. She knew in that instant, she was in love with Jason Taylor.

The sound of tires broke them apart. His heart broke at the look in her eyes. Taking her hand, he pulled her to the cab with him, trying to maintain contact for as long as possible. Withdrawing some papers from his pocket, he handed her the flight schedule for Kacee's wedding. "Two weeks," he whispered, opening the door and climbing in.

"Call me tonight when you land so I won't worry."

He nodded, holding her gaze in his as he shut the door and told the driver to leave, his body already aching with the loss of her in his arms. He wrenched his head in the cab to catch one last glimpse of her.

Rebekah saw him turn his head, so she offered a feeble smile and small wave. She stood there until the taillights were the only things she could see. "I love you," she whispered.

CHAPTER 5

Butterflies graced Rebekah's stomach as she boarded the plane, smiling because Jason placed her in first class again. Her nervousness extended beyond seeing Jason again to the more nefarious task of meeting his family, both blood and extended. Jason's infamous stories of his crazy family both intrigued and terrified her. She had jokingly referred to her family as insane when they first met, but after hearing his stories of lies and betrayal, she knew she had no idea what insane meant. It seemed his father was a constant schemer who often pulled other family members into the fray, either willingly or unwillingly. 'Oh well,' she thought. 'There's no use in getting worked up now. I'll meet them soon enough.' Dropping her head to one side, she drifted off to sleep, anxiously awaiting her arrival in New York, her mind filled with dreams of the past month and anticipation for the future.

Two and a half hours later, she was awakened by the pilot's voice announcing their arrival before a jolt ran through her body as the plane touched the ground. She began collecting her things, and after a brief taxi, the plane finally came to a standstill. Almost immediately, she was able to un-board the plane, again, she reasoned, another perk to being in first class. Sometimes she hated the new airline security procedures, because she wanted nothing more than to see Jason immediately, but she would have to wait until she reached baggage claim for that. Upon entering baggage claim, she looked around, eagerly awaiting being in his arms. To her dismay, she couldn't find him anywhere.

Suddenly, a voice whispered behind her. "Rebekah." Turning, she found herself immediately being swept into his strong embrace. "I'm so glad you are here," he continued, whispering into her hair.

"Me too, more than you know," she responded just as quietly.

Breaking the embrace, he placed her bag on his shoulder and picked up the handle to her small rolling suitcase. "Do you have anything else coming off the plane?"

When she shook her head no, he looked at her with an amused expression. "What?" she asked.

"Nothing. It's just that most of the women in my life have always prided themselves in the fact that they pack more than they need. It's always been like a competition with some of them: who has the most bags. And here you are, with one small suitcase and shoulder bag."

"Well, I'm not like most women," she smiled lightly, biting her bottom lip and turning her head slightly to look up at him.

Bringing a hand to her face, his voice remained quiet,

but now she picked up a tone laced with desire. "No you aren't." They stood there for a moment, his thumb lightly caressing her cheek. "Let's get out of here," he continued his voice still husky.

"Okay," she whispered back. Lacing her fingers with the hand of his that wasn't carrying her luggage; she let him lead her to the awaiting car.

Although the ride to Newburgh was really an hour, to the couple inside, lost in their own conversation, it was seemingly short. Rebekah was regaling Jason with tales of her day and her students, while Jason was explaining his father's latest debacle at the rehearsal. All too soon, he slowed the car as he turned into the parking garage of the building where he lived. Stepping out of the vehicle and walking to the other side, Jason opened the door to help Rebekah out. Finally, he grabbed her luggage and ushered her inside the elevator, slipping in a key and pressing the penthouse button. As soon as they stepped off the elevator and he opened the door to his home, Rebekah couldn't help but laugh.

"What?" he asked caught off guard by her laughter.

"How long have you lived here Jason?"

"Off and on for several years, but steadily the last six months. Why?"

"It's empty!" Rebekah's eyes slowly took in the main living area in front of her. It consisted of a couch and two recliners by the fireplace, a desk by the wall and a pool table where a dining table probably should have been. "Seriously, Jason, there is nothing here!" she stated, turning to face him, her eyes twinkling with laughter.

He shrugged his shoulders. "I don't need much: a place to sit, a place to work, and a place to relax. Besides, there's also a TV here," he pointed to a small cabinet beside the fireplace, "where I work on some stuff for the show. And, there's a table in the kitchen, so you don't have to think I'm a heathen or anything when I eat at home!" The truth was this place didn't feel like a home to him anyway; it was a place for him to stay at night. His home was somewhere else. Where? Well, he hadn't quite figured that out yet. "If you're through making fun of my place, I can show you to your room."

"Ah. Did I offend the great Jason Taylor?" she raised one eyebrow as she slowly walked towards him. Inches apart, she placed one hand on his chest. "I'm sorry. What can I do to apologize?"

Picking up on her game, he wrapped his arms around her waist and pulled her as close as he could get her. "I'm sure you can think of something," but he was barely able to finish his sentence as her lips pressed against his. All coherent thought left his mind as unrelenting passion swept through his body. He had missed her so much, and he was only beginning to realize how much. Having her in his arms again was indescribable. If he wasn't careful, he was going to lose himself in her, and right now, that wasn't a luxury he could afford. Breathless, he pulled away, keeping her drawn to him. "Let me show you to your room."

Rebekah could only nod her head; her own senses still reeling from that kiss. In a daze, she followed him up the stairs to the first door on the right. Setting her stuff on the bed, Jason turned to find Rebekah stifling a yawn. It was late; her flight hadn't even gotten in until eleven, and they had a long day ahead of them. Quickly closing the distance between them, he drew her into a warm embrace. "It's late.

Why don't you get settled for the night?" She nodded, further snuggling into his embrace, willing away the sleep that was slowly overtaking her body. Tightening his embrace, he continued, "Danny and Nikki want us to come for breakfast in the morning. Is that okay with you?" Again, she nodded, now too tired and too calm for words. Slowly, he lifted her face to his and gently pressed his lips against hers. The kiss was short and sweet, but it spoke volumes. Foreheads resting against each other, he whispered, "Get some sleep."

He was almost out the door when her voice stopped him in his tracks. Her heart was screaming for him to stay. She needed to tell him, but she wasn't convinced the time was right. "Jason," she began. "I…"

"I'm glad you're here, Bekah," he broke in quietly. His eyes told her he knew what her heart was saying. "Good night," he whispered, backing out of the doorway and keeping a hold of her gaze until the closing door broke the view.

Rebekah sighed as she changed clothes and crawled into bed. She was exhausted, yet she felt oddly comforted by the fact that he was only a door away. Before she could even question the motives of him not staying with her, she was asleep.

The next morning, Jason woke with such a feeling of completeness. She was here, in his house. He felt as if he was the luckiest man in the world. However, he couldn't fight off this cloud overshadowing them, they couldn't continue like this. Somewhere in the past month, he had fallen in love with Rebekah Thomas. He had yet to tell her, but he was sure she felt the same. The question became what happened next? She lived hundreds of miles away and was as settled in her life as he was in his. Where did they go from here? Shaking those questions from his head, he decided to let Nikki know they were coming for breakfast.

Quietly, he slipped out of bed, not wanting to wake the sleeping angel in the next room. As he walked by her room and felt her presence, it was all he could do to keep himself from opening the door just to see her. He had wanted nothing more the previous night than to crawl into that bed and hold her as they slept. However, he didn't want to rush her; he wanted it to be her invitation.

Sighing, he continued moving past her room, down the stairs, out the door, and over to Danny and Nikki's. Knocking to announce his presence, he opened the door, calling out. "Nikki? Danny? You guys here?"

Jason raised an eyebrow as Nikki came out of the kitchen. "Please tell me you are not cooking breakfast, because if that's the case, I think I'll take Rebekah to The Café." His eyes twinkled with laughter as Nikki prepared to defend herself.

"Very funny, Jason. And don't even think about taking her there. Danny's been getting ready for this breakfast all week. You know he's dying to meet her."

"Oh, Danny is, huh? Well, if Danny's the only one who wants to meet her, tell him to come over later." He finished that last part by heading towards the door, pretending to leave.

"Again, you're the comedian," was Nikki's response, causing him to turn back around laughing. "You know very well I want to meet her too. Someone has to make sure she's good enough for you."

Jason's eyes turned serious as he rubbed a hand over his face and sighed. "Look, Nikki, I want you to be nice."

"Of course I'll be nice. I'm always nice."

"Yeah, just ask Carrie how nice you can be."

"Okay, Taylor! Do not throw that in my face. Was I not right about her?"

"Yes, my ex-wife was a sadistic, crazy woman. Can we not talk about her please?"

"You're the one who brought her up," she shrugged.

"Fine, and I'm the one un-bringing her up."

"So," Nikki broke in. "When do I get to meet Ms. Wonderful?"

"At breakfast. She's still asleep and I didn't have the heart to wake her up yet. It's only six in the morning her time. I just came over here to tell you we would definitely be coming for breakfast."

"Okay then, we'll see you around 8:45."

Jason turned and headed towards the door to leave, but turned around before going through it. "Nikki," he called out.

"Don't worry Jase. I'll be on my best behavior. Besides you're so totally different about her than you ever were with Carrie. I already know I will love her too."

"Thank you, Nikki," he replied leaving their Penthouse and heading over to his own. As he closed the door behind him, he could hear water running upstairs. Immediately, his thoughts turned to her, naked, in his shower. Eyes closed, he leaned his body against the door, resting his head there. He could imagine the water running down her goddess-like body. Her golden tresses would be darkened and heavy with the water, as her hair would only slightly cover other areas he shouldn't be thinking of. As his mind began trailing lower down her glistening body, he heard the water shut off, and he prayed she had been in that shower long enough to drain his hot water. If ever there was a time he needed a cold shower, this was it.

Keeping his eyes closed, he let his mind linger in those thoughts longer than he should have, his body obviously aroused by the desires coursing through his veins. Before he knew it, he heard her padding softly down the stairs. By the time he had his eyes open, she was headed straight for him. Immediately, she noticed his eyes had turned a darker shade of blue, noting his current state of mind. As her eyes took in the rest of his form, his eyes devoured her figure, detailing the robe clinging to her still damp body as leftover water droplets fell from her hair, only aiding his fantasy. "Good morning," he tried to speak, but his body betrayed his mind as he enveloped her in a passionate embrace. Lips against lips, he almost lost it as she sensed his desire and forced her tongue into his mouth. Hungrily, they tasted one another before he broke the kiss and made his way down her jaw line towards her neck, his tongue sensuously lapping the water from her skin. "Jason," she moaned softly, her voice dripping in ecstasy.

At the sound of her voice, the rational portion of his brain regained control of his body, and he used all his strength to pull away from her, leaving his arms to rest lightly around her waist. "Beck," he whispered softly, wanting, no needing her to understand his actions. If only he could understand them.

Dropping her forehead to his chest, she lazily murmured, "Mmm, good morning to you too. You know, I could get used to starting my days off this way."

"Yeah?" he gently ran his fingers through her now slowly drying hair. "You have no idea how much I agree with that."

Suggestively, she pressed her hips against his still aroused form. "I think I have an idea." She glanced up at him with a smile on her face.

"Rebekah," he began, but her index finger against his lips quickly quieted him.

She replaced her finger with her lips as she placed a sweet and gentle kiss there. "I know, more than you understand." She wanted nothing more than to tell him exactly how she felt, but they had to be at breakfast soon and she didn't want to rush that moment. "Why don't you go take a shower and I'll finish getting ready."

Jason could only nod his head yes as his eyes followed her retreating body up the stairs. He wanted her, more than he had ever wanted any other woman. No one had ever had the ability to make him lose control the way she did. Pressing his fingertips against his temple he shook his head and thought of the cold shower that awaited him.

An hour later a much more in control Jason treaded down his stairs to find Rebekah curled up on the couch reading through his newest script. Laughing, he placed a kiss against the top of her head and asked, "What are you doing?"

"I just wanted to see if Brad saves his sister from the cave."

"So, does he?"

"What do you mean, 'does he'? Haven't you even read through that yet?"

"Nope."

"Nope?"

"I memorize my stuff the night before. If I'm correct, that doesn't happen until Friday. That's a whole week away!"

Exasperated, Rebekah rolled the script and playfully hit him across the chest. 'So, when do we meet this family of yours?"

"Now, if you're ready. Look, I don't want you to be uncomfortable. If you don't…" but he was quickly cut off with her lips against his. After they broke away, he grinned and said, "I need to be shut up like that more often."

"Keep mouthing off and you will be."

She brushed past him, but stopped as his hand reached out and spun her around to face him, pressing her body against his. Again, she noticed the color change in his eyes. "Promise?" he asked.

"Don't start something you can't finish Taylor," she commanded, her voiced laced with desire. She knew she was playing with fire, but at this point, a part of her didn't really care. They had been apart so long.

Jason dropped his head into the warm crevice where her shoulder and neck met. He smiled as he realized how perfectly his head nestled there, and he knew the rest of their bodies would fit together perfectly as well. "Let's go to breakfast," he whispered into her neck, placing sweet kisses there.

"Okay," she was the one to break the embrace, knowing if they didn't leave then, they might not leave at all. Taking her hand, he led her across the hall to Danny and Nikki's"

"Are ya'll the only ones on the floor?"

"Ya'll?"

"Yes, it's Texan for you all. Don't make fun of me and answer my question."

Laughing, he replied, "Yes, it's just us. There were originally four penthouses here, but we bought the ones next to ours so we could have the whole floor." Knocking to announce his arrival for the second time that morning, he opened the door. "Nikki, Danny, we're here."

Both of them came from the kitchen, smiles on their faces. Danny reached them first and immediately stuck his hand out to shake Rebekah's. "You must be Rebekah," he stated. "I'm Danny, we've heard a lot about you."

"Likewise," she replied, shaking his hand and returning the warm smile. Darting her eyes towards Nikki, she could sense the other woman sizing her up. Usually, a girl's concern about meeting the family was in regards to the mother, but in this case, Rebekah had to win over Nikki. "Something smells good," she smiled again as she said that.

Jason had come up behind her, snaking an arm around her waist. "That's because Nikki didn't cook it."

Reaching behind her to slap him on the chest, she responded, "No, it's because *you* didn't cook it."

"Hey!" Jason exclaimed, feigning hurt.

"I like this girl," Nikki finally chimed in. "Who wants to eat?"

Placing a sweet kiss on Rebekah's cheek, Jason ushered her into the dining room. Once he had Nikki's attention, he quickly mouthed, "I told you."

As soon as Rebekah wasn't looking, she mouthed back, "You were right."

The conversation was light and comical during breakfast. Rebekah took everything in, enjoying Jason's family. Their time together this morning reminded her of the Saturday morning breakfasts with her own family. Several times, she was able to catch Jason's eye, and she knew he loved every minute of this. For a brief moment, she let her mind wander to what it would be like to be here every morning, but she quickly put that thought out of her mind. Jason wasn't ready for that, was he?

For the first time, Jason felt like his family was complete. He and Carrie had breakfast over here numerous times, but never had he enjoyed it as much as this morning. He knew that was because of Rebekah. She brought a light into his life. He wondered what it would be like to have her here every morning, but he couldn't ask that of her. Again, the questions from that morning raced through his mind. He refused to let her out of his life, yet he didn't know how to keep her there.

After a couple of hours at the table, both couples realized how long they had been there. Standing, Nikki began clearing the dishes from the table. "Here, let me help," Rebekah said, standing and gathering the plates near her.

"That's not necessary," Nikki responded.

"I know, but I won't take no for an answer." Nikki nodded her head and both ladies headed into the kitchen.

"I like her Jase," Danny smiled at his best friend.

His voice suddenly quiet, Jason replied, "So do I."

"So then, what's wrong?"

Jason laughed. "You know me too well." Standing, Jason followed Danny's lead into the living room, taking a seat on the couch. "I'm falling in love with her, Danny. I can't stop it, and I don't think I want to."

"But…" Danny prompted.

"But, she lives hundreds of miles away. She has a life there. I have a life here. How can this work?"

"That's something you two have to work out yourselves. Have you talked to her yet?"

"No."

"Jase, there's part of your problem. Talk to her."

"I will. I just need to straighten my own thoughts out first."

"I can understand that." Both men quieted, each lost in their own thoughts. After a moment, Danny continued. "It's awful quiet in there. Do you think we should check on them?"

Laughing, Nikki responded to Rebekah's joke with, "they're probably out there trying to decide if they need to come rescue you."

"Probably. You're not that bad though."

"Thank you. I'm glad someone in this family appreciates me."

Rebekah couldn't help but smile at the way Nikki said 'this family', as if she was included in that grouping. "It was just Carrie you couldn't stand, right?"

Setting the dishtowel down on the counter, her eyes narrowed, and Rebekah could see the dislike starting to form in Nikki's eyes. "Can you blame me? Look, I don't know how much Jason has told you about Carrie, but I just don't like her. She treated him like crap, and now she has wormed her way onto our show. I know she is working some angle, I just don't know what it is yet."

Rebekah just stood there, taking everything in. She really didn't feel it was fair for her to comment on Jason's ex-wife.

Nikki, noticing her obvious discomfort, continued, "I'm sorry. We shouldn't be talking about her. Not when there are happier subjects to talk about, like you and Jase."

"DAMMIT!"

Both women heard the yell from the living room and rushed in there. Rebekah knew immediately it was Jason. She would recognize that voice anywhere. She just didn't know what happened to get him so upset. When they reached the living room, Jason was standing, cell phone to his ear, fury in his eyes.

Rebekah glanced towards Danny just in time to see him mouth, "Kacee" to Nikki. Turning her attention back to Jason, she tried to catch his gaze to let him know she was there. Within a second, he turned to face her. His face immediately softened, but she noticed his eyes were also filled with a different emotion: worry, but worry for whom?

"Kace, I'm sorry for yelling. No. No. It won't be a problem. I'm just glad you called to let me know. Thanks. Now, you stop worrying. Today is about you. I love you, and I'll see you later." As he hung up the phone, he addressed the whole room, but it was clear he was talking to Rebekah. "Carrie is coming tonight." He was amazed when there was no change in her eyes, just the same concern and maybe love that was there moments ago.

Behind her, Rebekah heard Nikki asking, "how, why?" but she wasn't concerned about it. She was more concerned for the man in front of her. Silently, he asked her if she was okay and almost imperceptibly, she nodded her head indicating she was.

After her answer, Jason turned his attention to answer Nikki. "Jake, my brother," he added for Rebekah's benefit, "invited her. She convinced him that Kacee would want her there."

"Does she?" Danny asked.

Jason shrugged his shoulders. "They were friends once. I just don't want to deal with her. I don't want anything to ruin tonight."

Even though they had an audience, Rebekah knew she needed to offer Jason the comfort only she could give. Closing the distance between them, she wrapped her arms around his neck and gently but quickly kissed him. "Nothing is going to ruin tonight."

Returning the embrace, he whispered in her ear, "What would I do without you?"

"You'll never have to find out."

CHAPTER 6

Hours later, a much calmer Jason was dressed for the wedding and waiting on Rebekah. Because of his line of work, he owned his own tuxedo, but it wasn't very often that he wore it for something other than award shows and dinner. Leaning against the back of the couch, he smiled as he thought of her earlier. No one had the ability to calm him like she did. As soon as he saw her face, it was as if his whole body relaxed. They ended up spending the rest of the morning and the afternoon with Danny and Nikki. So many times, he got caught up in just watching her with them. It was like his family was complete, the way it was meant to be, and she was the one who completed it. He couldn't wait for Rebekah to meet the rest of his family; he just hoped they wouldn't embarrass him too much. He knew they would love her immediately, just as he had. He paced back and forth at the bottom of the stairs, realizing he was more nervous about how Rebekah would feel about his family than how his family would feel about her.

"Breathe, Jason," he heard from the top of the stairs. 'It's going to be fine." As he turned to face her, he felt as if his world was moving in slow motion. His breath caught in his throat as his eyes swept over her form. A sapphire blue, floor-length dress graced her body perfectly, scooping off her shoulders, sleeves resting at soft points against her wrists. Her golden hair was twisted up in the back, allowing her slender neck to be seen. She illuminated his stairwell, but it was more than her simple beauty; it was as if a light radiated from her, guiding his heart towards hers.

Almost clumsily, he stepped towards the bottom stair. "You know, this really isn't very nice of you." He reached his hand out towards her as she gracefully walked down the stairs.

"What?" she curiously asked, taking his hand and stopping in front of him.

Drawing her into his embrace, he quietly responded, "It's just probably not fair for you to look more beautiful than the bride."

Kissing him softly, she whispered, "Thank you." Slowly, she started to head towards the door, but stopped when she felt his hand on her wrist. Turning to face him, she was surprised at the intensity of emotions in his eyes.

"I'm serious," he whispered. "You have no idea how beautiful you really are."

Blushing slightly, she reached a hand up to his face, knowing her eyes were mirroring his own. "Jason, I…" but she was cut off as the door suddenly opened.

"Are you two ready to go?" Rebekah heard Nikki ask. As Nikki took in the sight before her, she began to immediately apologize. "I am so sorry. I'm not used to knocking." Her eyes pleading, she tensed as Rebekah turned around.

"It's okay, Nikki. Really, don't worry about it. You're right, we need to get going." Grabbing her purse from the table by the couch, she headed for the door.

Jason, on the other hand, remained frozen in place. He wasn't really upset with Nikki, he was just positive of what Rebekah was going to say. Again, he noticed Nikki's apologetic eyes. "It's okay, Nik. Just knock next time."

"I promise," she solemnly swore. "Come on Jason. Let's go see your baby sister get married.

Twenty minutes later, they reached the church. As Danny and Nikki entered the church ahead of them, Jason felt Rebekah hesitate slightly and he turned to face her, concern in his eyes. "You okay?"

Answering him, she nodded still trying to convince herself. This church looked so much like her hometown church where she and Steve married. Both were small town Methodist churches and this was the first wedding she had been to since he had passed away. Forcing a wry smile, she continued trying to convince Jason. "I'm fine. Let's go in."

He simply nodded and ushered her into the building. Somehow, he knew she wasn't fine, and he had a good idea as to what was wrong. But, he also knew this was not the time to bring anything up. By the time they passed through the Narthex and headed into the Sanctuary, she had a full and genuine smile on her face as if the ghost haunting her memories had suddenly disappeared. He had already decided he wanted the introductions to take place at the reception; he wanted nothing to interfere with

Kacee's wedding.

Rebekah gazed in awe at the small church. Roses and lilies graced the choir rail as candles stood on almost anything still. Together, the flames created a soft, romantic atmosphere throughout the church. Stained glass windows stood magnificently all along the side walls and a simple, yet beautiful cross hung on the front wall of the church. Joining with Danny and Nikki, the four began to make their way down the aisle towards the family pew. Kacee had wanted a small wedding, so there were only two bridesmaids and two groomsmen. Jason was so glad that her fiancé had two brothers because that allowed him the opportunity for him to sit with Rebekah instead of having to leave her alone.

Rebekah immediately noticed the glances of the multitude of people in the room; she was even sure she kept hearing Jason's name in hushed whispers coming from many of their conversations. Jason more sensed than felt her body tense. "You okay?" he asked, for the second time that night.

She smiled numbly, allowing all of this to sink in. "How do you do this all the time?"

"Do what?"

"Everyone is staring at you and I know they are talking about you."

"Not exactly."

It was her turn to question him. "What do you mean, 'not exactly'?"

Turning his head sideways to slightly face her, he

offered her a grin that mixed his apologies and sheepishness. "Actually, they are looking at you, and the reason you keep hearing my name is because they are wondering who the beautiful woman on my arm is." By the time he finished, a full smile appeared across his face as he noticed the blush that started to creep over Rebekah's. They had reached their pew and after taking their seats, he leaned over, giving her a soft kiss on her still blush-ridden cheeks. "And, you are beautiful," he whispered, delighting as her already red cheeks became even more red.

After sitting there for a few moments, Jason noticed someone out of place standing by the side door. Tapping Danny to get his attention, he nodded his head as if pointing to someone. "What's he doing here?"

"I don't know," Danny replied, "but it can't be good." The two men exchanged glances and sighed. "Let's go, Jase."

He nodded his head in agreement and turned to face Rebekah. "I'm sorry. There's something I have to take care of. I'll be back in a few minutes."

With that, he and Danny were out of their seats. By the time they made it over to the gentleman, another man had joined them, this one much older. She heard Nikki sigh next to her. "What's going on?" Rebekah asked.

"See the older fellow there? That's Quinton Jensen, Jason's father," Nikki answered.

"Okay, but why do they look so tense over there?"

"I don't know how much Jason has told you about his family, but they have a tendency to pull crazy stunts to make things go their way. The other man with them is Bradley Wells. He's a multi-millionaire, Kacee's ex-boyfriend, and the man her father wanted her to marry. My guess is Quinton brought him here to stir things up before the wedding. If Jason and Danny hadn't seen him, he probably would have proceeded through that door, found James, the only love of her life, and started something."

While Nikki was explaining everything, Rebekah was watching the group of men. Jason's father certainly didn't look happy, but Jason had a determined look in his eyes. After what looked like several more forceful words on Jason's part, Bradley turned and left the Sanctuary and Mr. Jensen went to join the others in the back of the church waiting on the procession. "Good heavens. Jason said his family did insane things, but I never expected something like this!"

"This is nothing. Believe me, they've done much worse. It amazes me what they do to their own family members in the name of love. I am so glad Jason doesn't have much to do with them. He has his own family now, and we are who he relies on. Besides, now he has you as well." She gave Rebekah's hand a small squeeze as they watched Danny and Jason walk back towards them.

'Yes, he does have me,' Rebekah thought to herself as Jason resumed his seat next to her. He slipped his arm around her back as she whispered, "everything okay?"

"It is for now." Before he could continue, the organist began playing and the grandparents were seated. Rebekah closed her eyes as she fought the flashes that ran through her mind: images of her grandmother walking slowly down the aisle; her sister, a huge smile on her face; her mother, kissing the tears off her cheek; her father, offering her his arm to escort her down the aisle; Steve. The images had no rhyme or reason, and although she tried, she couldn't control them. Just before Rebekah lost herself in the memories, the wedding march started, and they were all on their feet to watch the bride walk down the aisle. She was radiant. Rebekah smiled to herself as she watched Jason become mesmerized by watching his baby sister walk down the aisle, almost wondering what his face would look like if it was she walking down it, towards him.

They took their seats and as the minister asked, "who gives this woman to be married?" Images again raced through her mind. However, this time, the images were different. She was still the bride, but her father wasn't giving her away, Steve was. He was no longer the groom, Jason was. Reaching her small hand over, she wrapped it in Jason's and gave his a small squeeze. He glanced down at her and realized the smile on her face and twinkle in her eyes was real, and full of love. Somehow, he knew that whatever memory was haunting her from earlier had disappeared. Their fingers remained intertwined throughout the rest of the ceremony. As was customary with most Methodist weddings, the ceremony was quickly over, and the happy couple glided past them. The minister dismissed the congregation and they headed towards the reception.

Once there, Rebekah felt her head begin to swim. She had been introduced to so many people, she could barely see straight. One after another they seemed to come, all curious about the woman on Jason Taylor's arm. In addition to that, there was a photographer around every corner. Not only was the wedding photographer there, but media people as well. Everyone wanted a picture of the happy couple, or at least the bride's famous brother. After an hour of this, Jason noticed her predicament. "Meet too many people?" he laughingly asked

"You have no idea. I don't think I'll ever be able to keep them straight, except your family of course. And, other than that episode with your father at the church, your family has been perfect."

"Kinda scary, I know. But, they do seem to be on their best behavior tonight. Do you want something to drink?"

"Sure." Placing a quick kiss on her cheek, Jason left the table in search of drinks. Rebekah took in the sight around her. She had watched Jason's sister all night, and she truly looked happy. As Rebekah continued to scan the room, she noticed a small brunette she hadn't met yet. An emerald gown stylishly draped her slender form, and her hair was coiled high on her head, adding the illusion of height to her petite frame. The woman glanced across the room in Rebekah's direction, and Rebekah was almost positive that a sign of jealousy flicked through her cold, brown eyes. She was attractive and seemed to have a swarm of people around her, and there was something vaguely familiar about this woman, but it wasn't until Rebekah heard someone call, "Ms. Taylor," that she put two and two together; this was the infamous Carrie, and she was headed in Rebekah's direction. Having no desire to have a run in with her, Rebekah left the table in search of Jason, to no avail. She was sidetracked: first by his mother, then, his grandmother, and finally, his sister.

After almost twenty minutes of searching, she finally noticed him by the bar, a glass of wine in each hand, and clearly sidetracked himself, by Carrie. As she made her way closer behind Jason, she could pick up the conversation.

"The wedding was beautiful Jase," Carrie said quietly. Rebekah noticed the muscles in the back of his neck tense at the sound of Carrie calling him Jase.

"Yes, it was Carrie."

"Did it remind you of something?"

Sighing, Jason searched for an exit from this conversation. He wanted to talk to Carrie as little as possible. "What should it remind me of?"

"Our wedding silly. Of course, Kacee wasn't as beautiful as I was, but their ceremony was so much like ours." She placed a hand on his cheek and unbeknownst to Jason, made eye contact with Rebekah. "How could you forget that?" she whispered saucily.

Just as Jason was shifting to remove Carrie's hand, another photographer flashed his camera, but before he could take another picture, Jason shot him an angry look. Finally, he was able to shake off Carrie's hand. "Easy Carrie. Kacee's wedding was nothing like ours, and her marriage will not be either. Now, if you'll excuse me, I need to find my date."

"Yeah, she's cute, Jase. Probably wouldn't want to leave her alone too long." A coy look appeared on her face as she watched the curiosity cross his.

"What is that supposed to mean, Carrie?" Jason set the glasses of wine on the table, preparing himself for one of Carrie's episodes.

"Nothing at all, my love. She just seems to enjoy all the attention she has received today. I mean, who wouldn't. It's always nice to be on your arm. Too bad she doesn't look as good on it as I do."

"Carrie," Jason warned, his voice taking on an angry

tone. "Leave Rebekah out of this. In fact, don't even try to compare yourself to her."

"Ahh, what's the matter Jase? Afraid Mary Poppins over there doesn't measure up? Are you missing what we had?" Her hand rested on his arm, almost as if she was claiming what was once hers. Her eyes darted around her ex-husband's form, glancing at Rebekah, giving her a silent message to back off.

However, Jason remained oblivious to all of this. His anger remained directed at the woman standing in front of him. It amazed him sometimes that he had even married her. Harshly grabbing her wrist, he jerked it off his arm. Lowering his voice, Carrie almost became frightened at the tone his voice took on. "I want you to listen to me, and make no mistake about what I say to you." He paused making sure Carrie was fully listening. "There is nothing between us, and there never really was. So understand this, do not go near Rebekah. She is the most important thing in my life, and I will not let you ruin this. Now, leave."

"Jason," she began protesting, but he refused to hear any of it.

"You twisted Jake's arm to get in here tonight, so go back to him. I don't want you around me or the woman who owns my heart."

Jealousy and anger flashed through Carrie's eyes. 'Who does he think he is?' she thought to herself as she turned to walk away from him. But, she felt secure that she had done the damage she worked for. Rebekah was standing close enough to hear everything, and Carrie didn't picture her to be the one to stay around when she obviously didn't belong.

Jason watched as his ex-wife made her way through the crowd. He felt nothing but contempt for the brunette who had once belonged in his life. Sighing and picking up the wine glasses, he longed to find Rebekah, so he was surprised when he turned, and almost ran directly into her. "I guess you heard that?"

"Mm, hmm," she replied, lifting one of the glasses from his hand and taking a small sip. "Are you okay?"

"Fine."

"Jason," she practically scolded him. She could see he wasn't 'fine'.

"Beck," he placed a soft kiss against her forehead. "I promise, I'm fine. I don't want to think about her or anything else but the beautiful woman I have in front of me. You know," he continued, lifting the half-empty glasses from their hands and placing them on a nearby table, "I don't think I've had the honor of dancing with you tonight."

"Well then, that's something we must definitely remedy," she played along, taking his hand and following him onto the dance floor. Almost immediately, he swept her into his arms and glided her across the dance floor. "Have I told you that you are an excellent dancer, Mr. Taylor?"

"I've heard that a time or two." Their bodies slowed as the music changed. In that one moment, Jason pulled her closer and rested his head against hers, pulling her hand into his chest. "I'm glad you were here with me tonight."

Pulling back slightly, Rebekah lost herself in his gaze. "There's no where I'd rather be," she answered honestly before allowing herself to settle back into his embrace.

They were both so lost in each other, in the moment, that they lost all track of reality, forgetting the scores of eyes that were plastered on them. Nikki, being ever observant, had watched the exchange between Jason and Carrie, along with the subsequent conversation of Jason and Rebekah. She laughed inwardly to herself as she watched Jason in the two situations. While talking with Carrie, Jason's body was tense, his eyes constantly shifting as if looking for the quickest way out. With Rebekah, he was completely different; he was lost in her. The moment she approached him, his whole body relaxed and his eyes never once left hers. As they glided across the dance floor, someone could have easily mistaken them for a couple that had been in love for years; they completed each other that well. Nikki had lost track of Carrie once Rebekah entered the picture. Quickly scanning the room, she found her on the other side of the dance floor, watching them dance, her eyes narrow and her lips pressed in a thin line. Grabbing her glass of champagne, Nikki headed over there. "They make an amazing couple, don't they?" she sweetly asked, once in earshot of Carrie.

"Who? Kacee and James?"

"Nice try, Carrie. I've been watching you. You can't take your eyes off them. And, I know what you are thinking."

"Really? Well, by all means, enlighten me," Carrie scoffed towards Nikki. They had never been the best of friends; actually to be honest, both women strongly disliked the other. Hearing Nikki's interpretation of her feelings ought to be highly amusing.

"You're wondering why he never looked at you that

way. It's eating you up inside, because from the moment they walked into the church, everyone has been commenting on how wonderful they look together. You haven't been the center of attention tonight. You threw that away, and it's killing you."

"Once again, you have no clue what you are talking about." Carrie's eyes flashed though, and Nikki knew she was right on the mark. "That woman has not even crossed my mind. She is a filler for Jason, someone he's using to get over me."

"Really? So, that would be the reason he walked away from you to get lost in her embrace." When Nikki received no response, she knew she had made her point. She decided to close with one last remark before walking away. "Just remember Carrie, you are the one who selfishly threw away his love. And now, he's moved on. Whatever plan you have in your mind, forget about it. It's too late." With that, Nikki turned and headed back towards her husband, silently congratulating herself. She pictured Carrie's face in her mind as she walked away, and she didn't have to turn around and see her to know how it looked at that exact moment. Anger would be boiling inside her; she hated it when Nikki was right, and right she was. Jason had moved on, and she couldn't be happier.

All too soon, the music ended and Jason and Rebekah were brought back to reality. It was time to see the bride and groom off. Amidst birdseed, bubbles, and rose petals, they did just that before joining with Danny and Nikki and heading home.

Once they said their goodnights, Jason and Rebekah entered his penthouse. "I'm going to go change," Rebekah said. Jason headed upstairs as well, quickly changing out of his tux into more comfortable clothing before returning downstairs.

It was apparent to him how tired they both were. He still wanted to talk to her about her reactions at the wedding and he wanted to make sure she was okay with everything that happened with Carrie. But, they were both exhausted. Maybe it would be better for them to talk about all of that later. He was brought out of his reverie as she came back down the stairs in a pair of black pajama bottoms and a pink shirt. He motioned for her to join him on the couch. Once she did, he immediately wrapped a blanket around them, enclosing her in his arms in the process.

"The fire is nice," he heard her whisper sleepily.

"Yeah, it is," he replied, placing a sweet kiss against her forehead. "But, it's even nicer because you are here with me."

The room quieted as each became lost in their own thoughts. Both knew there were many questions unanswered. Where did they go from here? What happened next? Other thoughts fled through each of their minds, but for the moment they were content to remain in each other's embrace. Tomorrow might be the moment of truth, but they were going to get lost in tonight.

CHAPTER 7

The next morning, Rebekah woke up more relaxed than she had in quite some time, and she couldn't quite figure out why. That is, until she stretched her body and realized she was still in Jason's embrace. For a month, she had dreamed about what it would feel like to wake up wrapped in his arms. Now, she was finally experiencing it. She never anticipated spending the night like that, and she was positive he hadn't either. They were just enjoying the evening, the fire, and each other's presence when they apparently fell asleep. Now, Rebekah found herself lying as still as possible, she wanted to savor this moment as long as she could.

Jason felt her stirring in his arms. He had been conscious for almost twenty minutes, relishing in the feel waking up and holding her. He closed his eyes and thought back to the night before. They had sat there, wrapped in the blanket, her head on his chest, enjoying the crackle of the fire and the atmosphere they created together. Eventually, she had shifted her body so she was lying on the couch, motioning him to join her. He never intended to fall asleep. They hadn't said much, but he intended on waiting until she was asleep before carrying her to her bed. Before he knew it though, he was waking up, his head buried in her soft tresses. Inhaling slightly, he allowed her soft scent to invade every one of his emotions. He had never felt this alive. Once he felt her stirring more, he bent his head forward, placing his lips against the silk of her cheeks. "Good morning."

A smile broke out upon her face as she allowed herself to remain lost in his embrace a little longer. "Good morning yourself."

"I'm sorry about last night. I intended to carry you upstairs, but…" he was cut off as she began shaking her head.

"No. Don't apologize. I slept better last night than I have in over a year. Don't be sorry." She pressed her back into his chest, wrapping his arms more tightly around her waist, a move he willingly obliged.

Placing a sweet kiss on her neck, he asked, "What do you want to do today?"

"I don't care. I don't have to leave until late this afternoon."

The thought of her leaving again ripped him apart. He didn't even know when he would be able to see her again. "Well, as much as I would like to, we can't stay like this all day. Why don't you get dressed, and I will take you to get some breakfast."

"Okay," she responded, still not moving. She wanted to stay in his arms forever.

After several minutes, he whispered, "Beck, you do

know you have to move for us to accomplish this, right?"

"Mmm hmm," she answered, still not moving. His hand snaked further around her waist, and just as she thought he was going to draw her closer, his fingers slipped to the sides of her waist, and he began tickling her mercilessly. "Jason!" she screamed while gasping for air. "Stop!"

"Are you going to get up?" He let his fingers soften, as his tickling became less, expecting her to say yes.

"No," she replied defiantly.

"Fine, we'll do this the hard way," and he began tickling her all over again. With the strength in his body, she was unable to gain control of the situation. Running out of oxygen from laughing so much, she started gasping for air, making a strange sound as her gasps mixed with her laughter. Without much grace, she fell from the couch and landed on the carpeted floor. He looked down at her, his eyes twinkling with merriment. "See, told you we could do it the hard way."

"Very funny," she replied with a serious voice; however, her eyes too hid her own laughter, and her true emotions soon came out.

Gently, he brought a hand to her face, thumb caressing her cheek. Their eyes locked onto one another's and quickly, they became lost in each other. "You'd better get ready," he whispered. Nodding, she numbly stood from her position and headed towards the stairs. He marveled at her beauty, even at such an early hour; there was no one to compare to her.

As Rebekah got dressed, she also silently began packing

her things. She didn't know what they were doing that afternoon, and she didn't want to be caught off guard. A tear slipped out of her eye. She didn't know what to do; she didn't know if she should tell him how she felt. Their worlds were totally different, and she had gotten a taste of that last night. Everywhere they turned there was some person begging for a moment of her time or some photographer with a camera stuck in her face. She didn't know if she could deal with that. But, then, on the flip side, she didn't know if she could walk away from him either. Sighing, she added her last item to the small suitcase and headed out the door. She would let her heart be her guide today.

Jason was already waiting when she reached the bottom of the stairs. He noticed the melancholy look in her eyes, and chose to wait to tell her how he felt. Ushering her out of the penthouse, he decided to enjoy the day with her.

When they stepped off the elevator in the lobby, they were instantly greeted with a bright reflection from outside. Heading towards the door, they immediately realized that as they were snuggling on the couch the night before, the outside was blanketed with pure white snow.

"Wow!" Rebekah exclaimed, eyes shining. "I have seen more snow in the last month than in my entire life. I still can't get over how beautiful it looks."

"Beautiful, yes, but not great to drive in. The Café is only two blocks away. Do you mind walking?"

"Not at all," she answered, buttoning her coat and pulling on her gloves. "But, may I ask why we can walk and not drive?"

"Sometimes, these light dustings are more dangerous.

People can't always judge how much snow is on the ground." Taking her hand, he led her out of the lobby.

During the walk there, Jason pointed out various places of importance: different shops, churches, and buildings. Rebekah, pressed close to him in an effort to block out the cold, was only half-listening. She was thinking about this evening; she only had several hours left. Even as they reached The Café, ordered breakfast and ate, those thoughts continued. She wasn't her usual animated and bubbly self, and she knew Jason was noticing it.

By the time they left breakfast, he had all but completely joined her in her silence. They clung to each other as they walked back and as they reached the small yard in front of his building, Jason decided he couldn't take it any longer. He wanted, no needed, to hear her laugh. So, before she could react, he had abruptly stopped, crouched down in the snow, formed a snowball and threw it at her.

"Hey!" Brushing snow from her coat, she shot him a semi-angry look.

"What are you going to do about it?" he challenged.

Flashing him another angry look, Rebekah bent forward, wiping snow off her coat and jeans. "You know, Jason. You shouldn't have done that."

"Why not?" He really hadn't anticipated her anger; he was just hoping she would smile again. Now, he was worried he had maybe gone too far. "Look, Beck, I'm sorry."

"You should be," she replied, a mischievous glint appearing in her eyes. This time it was he who was caught off guard as a snowball hit him square upside the head. She could barely form her words through her laughter. "At least I can hit straight!"

"Really?" Jason asked, picking up another handful of snow. He formed it into a ball as Rebekah eyed him cautiously.

"You wouldn't."

"I thought I couldn't hit straight."

"Jason!" she warned, but it was too late. Swiftly, he hit her with another snowball, this time with accurate aim. "Alright! That's it! You don't know what you just started." Rebekah threw another snowball at him.

Over the course of the next ten minutes, Jason and Rebekah lost count of the number of snowballs thrown, most with highly accurate aim. Before she knew what happened though, Rebekah lost control of the situation. Jason, grabbing her around her waist from behind, held a handful of slow dangerously close to the opening of her coat. She knew what he was thinking. "Jason," she practically begged, trying to push off what she feared was the inevitable. "Don't even think about it."

"What?" He whispered into her ear, his hot breath causing a tingling sensation on her frozen neck.

Rebekah closed her eyes, allowing the sensations he was causing to stream through her body. Trying to regain some control, she quickly reopened them. "Don't even think about throwing that snow down my coat."

Still pressed against her body he flattened his other gloved palm against her stomach, pulling her closer. "What snow?" he asked, opening his left hand and letting the snow fall to the ground.

Her body relaxed as she realized he dropped the threatening snow. "Thank you."

"You're welcome," he answered, drawing his lips close to her neck.

All of the sudden, Rebekah's eyes shot open wider than before, her heart racing as she began to scream. "Jase!" She tried to pull his freezing glove from her neck. Trusting him when he emptied the snow from his hand, she wasn't expecting him to place that same snow-encrusted hand against her neck. Fighting to get out of his embrace, she angrily asked, "Why did you do that?"

The tone of his voice immediately caused her to stop her fight of breaking free from his arms. "Maybe because it would give me the perfect excuse to do this." His sensual lips made their way to her neck, scorching the previously frozen sensitive skin. He watched her close her eyes again and melt into his embrace, arching her neck away from him, allowing him easier access to the slender column of her throat. Moving higher, he let his teeth graze against the sensitive spot behind her ear. He smiled against her silky skin as he heard a quiet moan escape her lips. Reaching her ear, he gently nibbled on the lobe, feeling her tremble under his assault on her senses. Around them, the snow began to lightly fall, adding more to the moment than either of them thought possible. Jason stopped his tender ministrations and leaned closer, whispering quietly, inaudible to anyone other than her, "I'm falling in love with you, Rebekah Thomas."

Eyes still closed, her heart caught in her throat. She wondered if he really said that or if she imagined it.

Almost as if he had read her mind, he turned her in his arms, their foreheads resting against each other, "Open your eyes," he softly requested, needing to make sure she heard him. The moment he looked into her eyes, he knew they mirrored his own; they both swirled with love. Bringing a hand up to her chilled cheek, he let his thumb trail her cheekbone. Never letting her eyes fall from his, he continued. "Actually, what I said isn't true." Her eyes darkened slightly as confusion replaced the love there. He waited a moment longer before explaining. "I'm not 'falling' in love with you, I've already fallen. I love you Rebekah. You are unlike any other woman I have ever met."

Tears glistened in her eyes as the sweetness of his words hit her heart, causing it to soar. She felt as if she was flying and her knees buckled slightly, making her glad she was in his strong embrace. He loved her! She covered the hand on her cheek with her own, pressing her gloved fingers between his, intertwining them together. The snow swirled around the two of them, but she had never felt so warm. The electricity sparking between the two of them was more intense than anything she had ever felt before. Willing her heart to slow done, she began to respond. "Jason. You are unlike any man I have ever met. When we are apart, I long to be with you; when I finally am, I never want to leave. I never thought I'd love again; I didn't want to risk the pain of losing someone again. But you changed all of that for me. " Rebekah took a deep breath in an effort to calm her nerves. She never imagined saying these words again. "I..."

"JASON!" Nikki's voice sliced through the air as well as the moment,

Deeply frustrated and highly annoyed, Jason sighed.

"Just ignore her," he implored.

"JASON TAYLOR! I KNOW YOU CAN HEAR ME."

"Dammit Nikki! What do you want?" Jason's quietly uttered as his body tensed with anger. Never had he wanted to physically harm a woman, but he was damn close now. He couldn't have set that moment any more perfectly if he tried; now it was ruined. There was no way to recapture that. He glanced back over at Rebekah who was still in his embrace. "Maybe she'll go away."

"Jason," they heard again. "I'm serious, you need to see this."

"Fine!" He yelled back. "We'll be there in a minute. "Noticing Rebekah shivering, his concern turned to her. "You're cold."

"A little," she managed to respond, her teeth chattering.

"Let's get you inside." His hand on her back, they began heading to the door. "Why didn't you say anything about being cold?"

She shrugged her shoulders. "I was enjoying the moment."

Jason couldn't hold back his smile. "I was too."

She hesitated slightly and they stopped walking. "Jason, I," she turned towards him, getting lost in his gaze. "I had a good time today," she whispered, her eyes lowering.

Turning her back towards the door, he quietly replied,

"me too, Bekah."

His body was still tense as they stepped off the elevator. Noticing his door was open; he knew that's where Nikki was. He wanted to deal with this quickly. Rebekah only had a couple of hours until they would have to leave for the airport. He knew this was hard for her: she was so ready for love but so afraid at the same time. They were so close outside until Nikki ruined it. Rubbing a hand over his face, he sighed and entered the Penthouse, coming face to face with Nikki. "What in the hell is so important?" His eyes flashed with annoyance.

"Jason. Rebekah. I'm sorry, really, I am." Nikki knew she had interrupted something important by the look in his eyes. But, she had to tell them. "I really am sorry."

Rebekah smiled, shaking her head and indicating it was no problem. Jason, however, was a different story. He was still upset and both women knew it. "Fine," he replied gruffly. "You apologized. So, what's the big problem?"

"I went to the grocery store," Nikki began.

"*That's* your problem?" Jason was incredulous. He couldn't believe this was what she had called him here for.

"Just listen Taylor and stop interrupting me!" Jason shot her a cold look and took Rebekah's hand. Leading her to the couch, they sat down and looked expectedly at Nikki. She took that to indicate he wouldn't interrupt. "Anyway, I was in line, scanning the headlines. Most of the trash magazines update on Sundays and I always like to check out the new gossip. That's when I saw this." She handed him a tabloid newspaper.

Rebekah felt Jason's body tighten in a controlled rage as he read the paper in front of him. She glanced at it as well and heard a sharp intake of air coming from her throat as she took in the picture in front of her. There, on the front page, was Jason and Carrie. She had her hand on his cheek, and Rebekah knew immediately it was from last night. Carrie looked radiant; Jason, looked indifferent. However, what captured her attention the most was the left corner; there she was. Even worse was the caption. It read: *TAYLOR'S REUNITE WITH MISTRESS LOOKING ON!*

Mistress. She was being classified as the mistress, People at home were going to read this and there was nothing she could do about it. She couldn't collect her thoughts. Her palms began to sweat and she knew her eyes were growing wider by the second, but she couldn't process anything. She heard Nikki and Jason talking, but she couldn't comprehend what they were saying.

"Jason, I'm sorry," she heard Nikki say.

"You have nothing to apologize for. I'm glad you told me."

Nikki gave Rebekah a concerned glance. "She's not used to this garbage, Jason. I just thought it would be better for her to find out while you were around, before she went home." Jason nodded his head in agreement as Nikki excused herself.

'Home. Mistress. Reunited. Mistress.' Words ripped through Rebekah's mind, but despite her best efforts, refused to form a logical thought. Her breathing was shallow and her hands were trembling.

"Rebekah," she heard Jason call softly, yet she couldn't focus on him. "Beck," he pressed again, pushing a silky strand of hair behind her ear. She shivered, not only from his touch, but the snow covered coat she still wore. "You're freezing."

"I need to go change," she quietly rose from the couch, never really acknowledging his touch. As she climbed the stairs, thoughts finally began to form. She was in shock. Never had she thought of the personal effect of the tabloids, until this very moment. Being with Jason came with a price; that, she knew. She had even known there would be invasions of privacy, but never had she expected her character to be attacked. She didn't know what to do; she didn't know what to think. Without changing, without even taking off her coat, she sat on the edge of her bed, elbows on knees, and head in her hands.

Ten minutes later, Jason found her in that exact position. His heart broke as he watched her. He remembered the first time he ever faced the media; it was infuriating, but it was nothing compared to what she was facing. She hadn't bargained for any of this. She was just a girl who gave her heart to some famous guy, and essentially, had just been labeled an adulteress.

Heading towards the bed, he knelt in front of her and placed his hands against her shoulders, gently pushing her back, raising her from her slumped position. Slowly, he began to unbutton her coat, slipping it off her shoulders and down her arms. Once finished, he tugged at the gloves still on her hands, succeeding in removing them as well. She looked broken. He joined her on the bed, running his fingers up and down her arm.

Lovingly, he drew her to him, sighing with relief as he

felt her body relax into his. He silently debated within himself. Maybe he should let her go, walk away now and spare her any more moments like this. However, as soon as that thought entered his mind, he dismissed it. He couldn't let her go. She had become like breath to him; she was his oxygen.

Jason kissed her forehead, trying to draw some reaction from her. "Bekah," he whispered. "I'm sorry." It was all he could think to say. He just wished he could undo all of this for her.

"I know," she responded, not moving her face from his strong chest. Her body remained soft against his hard one. She knew it wasn't his fault, but she was angry; she didn't know who to lash out at. Placing her hand on his chest, she whispered, "Jason, I…"

"Shhh. I know." And he did, he just didn't want her to have to express any more emotions this afternoon. He wanted to protect her from everything. Unfortunately, for him, expressing her emotions was exactly what she intended on doing. A dam broke inside her and he was the only target in sight.

Pulling harshly away from his embrace, she angrily asked, "You know? What do you know?" By this time, she was off the bed, fire in her eyes. She had so many feelings running through her body, and although she knew better, he was going to bear the brunt of them. "Do you know what it is like to be called your mistress?"

"You know that's not true."

"Yeah, I do, but Jason; I have parents who will be at the store today. I have students who will be there as well. They don't know."

"They know you, Beck. That's enough."

"Do they, Jason? Do I?" Her body slumped against the chest of drawers in the bedroom, using it for support. "I don't even know if I know myself. I don't even know what I want."

Jason's head dropped, and immediately, his eyes filled with pain. Rebekah wished she could take those words back, but it was too late. She knew they weren't true, she just didn't know how to respond to any of this. She softened her voice, trying to convey the right emotions, but she didn't trust herself to approach him.

She couldn't blame him for this, but she didn't know if she could stay. With her back against the dresser, she crumbled to the floor. Almost inaudibly, she continued. "Do you know what it's like to lose someone you love, someone you thought you'd spend the rest of your life with? Do you know what it's like to wake up one morning and realize you are alone?" She raised her eyes to meet his, trying to focus through the tears starting to form.

Jason shook his head no, but he was terrified he was going to find out; in fact, he was afraid he had already lost her. "The pain is indescribable," she continued. "It's as if a part of you is gone. You shut yourself off and vow to never again open your heart to that kind of pain."

He slid off the bed and crawled to where she was sitting. When he reached her, he placed his hand on her shoulder, trying to pass some of his strength and love on to her. "You're not going to lose me." He tugged gently, trying to draw her to him, wanting, no, needing to hold her and soothe her trembling body. Willingly, she leaned into his embrace; afraid it might be the last time he held her that way.

Everything about their relationship had been a fairytale so far: romantic, loving, sweet, and, she worried, too good to be true. This one afternoon snapped her heart back to reality. Love was painful, not only losing that love, but being in love as well. People were going to get hurt and she didn't know if she could risk it again. Pushing back slightly, she gazed into his eyes; where she saw everyone her of own emotions mirrored. She could see the intense love, devotion, and concern there, and it scared her. "I can't do this."

He sighed and dropped his head. This is what he was afraid would happen. He didn't want to push her; he loved her, but he couldn't force her to stay. "Okay," he whispered, refusing to make eye contact with her. Instead, he ran his fingers over her hands, memorizing them. He wanted to remember everything about her when she walked out of his life. Taking a deep breath, he tried to wipe the agony from his face as he glanced up at her. "I'll be downstairs. We can leave for the airport whenever you are ready."

Standing, he offered her his hand to help her up, but she refused it, choosing to stay on the floor. Her voice was thick with emotion as she requested, "please, just call a cab instead." Jason simply nodded and turned towards the door.

Fifteen minutes later, he called her name, alerting her to the awaiting cab below. As she walked down his stairs, her heart tore at seeing him. She didn't know if she had the power to walk away from him, but she knew she couldn't stay. He stood by the doorway and she noticed he bristled with pain as she approached him. "I'm sorry, Jason, for everything."

One last time, he turned to face her, fighting to control his own voice. "Don't be, I don't regret anything that has happened between us. I never will." With that, he watched the woman he loved walk out of his door and out of his life. For the first time ever, he had to wonder, is love enough?

CHAPTER 8

An hour and a half later Rebekah sat at the airport, silently wiping tears from her eyes. She felt as broken as she had after Steve died. 'How had she fallen for Jason so quickly?' she wondered. In just a month he had become everything to her. When they were apart, she longed to be with him; when they were together, she felt whole, complete. What made this whole day worse was that she didn't know if she had done the right thing. She loved him, she had no doubt of that; but she walked away. 'Was she doing the right thing, or was she simply running from her fears?' Lost in her thoughts, Rebekah barely heard the airline workers call for the various flights to board. She only hoped she had the strength to board her flight when the time came.

Jason ran breathless into the airport. Minutes after Rebekah left his apartment, he realized he was wrong to let her walk away without putting up a fight. This wasn't what she wanted; he was positive of that. She was reacting to the situation and running from her fears. So, he decided to go after her, praying he would reach her before she boarded that plane and walked out of his life forever. Approaching the counter, he switched into "famous" mode and flashed a smile to the lady behind the counter.

"Oh my gosh," he heard her squeal. "You're Jason Taylor!"

"In the flesh."

"Wow! I can't believe this! I am such a fan of yours."

Jason glanced at his watch, anxious to be finished with this conversation. "I'm glad to hear that." Again he flashed a smile, mesmerizing her.

"What can I do for you?"

"Actually, I need a favor," he glanced at her nametag, "Betty."

A deep red blush quickly spread across her face at the mention of her name coming from Jason Taylor's lips. "Anything you need, Mr. Taylor."

"Jason," he insisted. "We're on a first name basis now, Betty."

"Okay, Jason."

"I need to see someone who is leaving on your Houston flight in forty-five minutes."

"Sure, I just need to see a credit card."

"You need a credit card for me to go back and see this person?" he asked incredulously.

"Yes sir. I need something to charge your ticket."

Jason groaned in frustration. "You don't understand. I don't want a ticket. I just need to get to one of your gates. This is not difficult!"

Now it was Betty's turn to be frustrated. "I understand Mr. Taylor, but in order for you to get to a gate, you have to go through there." She pointed a bony, heavily jeweled finger towards the security checkpoint as she continued. "In order for you to go through there, you need a ticket. No credit card, no ticket, no ticket, no getting through the security checkpoint, and no getting to the gate!"

"Fine!" Yanking out his wallet, he withdrew his credit card and slammed in on the counter. He was running out of time and he knew it. Usually, they started boarding the plane thirty minutes ahead of time. That only left him fifteen minutes.

"Would you like first class?"

"I don't care," he roared, wanting to pull out his hair. "Just hurry, please!"

After what seemed like an eternity, she handed him his ticket. "Gate E30."

"Thanks!" he yelled behind his shoulder, briskly walking towards security. By the time he reached security, he had his cell phone, wallet, and keys in his hand ready to place on the belt to run through the x-ray machine. The guard on the other side motioned for Jason to walk through and the moment he did, the monitors went off.

"Please take off your shoes and step to the right," the guard ordered him.

Jason knew it was useless to argue. Airline security had become so tight in the New York airports, and the more of a fight he put up, the more time he would lose; right now, his time was too precious. Standing with his feet spread apart slightly, he impatiently waited as another security guard waved a wand over his shoulders to his palms and back towards his chest, then sweeping over his legs. Once the guard was assured Jason was not a danger to national security, they allowed him to leave. Slipping his shoes back on, he glanced at his watch and took off for gate E30. 'Ten minutes left,' he thought, praying he wasn't too late.

Quicker than he thought possible he made his way to terminal E, searching for gate 30. As he reached gate 25, he heard, "now pre-boarding flight 3791 to Houston Intercontinental Airport. At this time all frequent flyers, passengers needing assistance, and first class passengers may board."

"Damn," he muttered under his breath. For the first time, he regretted putting her in first class. He slowed as he reached gate 30, scanning the waiting area for her. A glimpse of a blonde in the corner caught his eye. "Rebekah," he whispered. Swiftly, he made his way towards her.

Rebekah heard the call for first class passengers to pre-board, but she couldn't bring herself to move. She was still debating within herself whether she had made the right decision when she left. If only she wasn't so afraid. Sighing, she began collecting her things, deciding it was too late. She walked out on him; she couldn't go back now. She knew her heart belonged to him, but there was no way he could understand her fears and her lack of strength. She was positive she would miss him, miss what they had.

Even here, she could feel his presence; it was as if he was standing there with her. Turning around to head towards the plane, she froze in place when she realized he was.

"I'm sorry," he whispered.

"For what?" Rebekah's hands were trembling as she sat her bag down and took a tentative step towards him.

Jason ran his fingers through his hair, unsure of where to begin. "I'm sorry for that trash that was printed, I'm sorry for hurting you, but mainly I'm sorry for letting you walk away." He was ecstatic he was able to get there in time, but his heart surged with even more happiness as he saw relief flood through her eyes.

She took another step towards him, slowly closing the gap that existed between them. "You aren't responsible for what they printed. You didn't hurt me. And, most importantly, you came after me when I didn't have enough strength to stay."

No more hesitation was required. In one large step he spanned the remaining distance between them. Cupping her face in his hands, he tenderly lifted it upwards. "I love you, Rebekah Thomas," he whispered before pressing his lips against hers. Everything he wanted to say he poured into that kiss and he was surprised when she ended it so quickly.

Staring into his eyes, Rebekah lifted her hand to his face, tracing the outline of his jaw before running her fingers through his hair. "I love you too, Jason Taylor. I just need some time." She smiled as his eyes lit up with joy.

"I understand that."

"Do you?" She took his hand and led him to a seat next to hers. The clock ahead of her ensured she had time for this. "I'm not proud of the way I acted earlier."

"Bekah," he started, but she quickly cut him off.

"Let me finish," she softly demanded. He nodded his acceptance. "I tried not to fall in love with you, but it was pointless. You are my heart. But," she took a deep breath and began playing with his fingers, "I'm scared. I know I shouldn't be, but I can't help it. I want you in my life, I need you there, but I also need time. All of this has happened so fast."

"I know." He picked up her hand and brought it to his lips. "And, if you need time, if you need to slow down, then I understand. But, I need to say something too."

"What?"

"I need you to talk to me. Tell me what you are feeling and don't shut me out. I need you to know that I would do anything for you, that I would never hurt you, never betray you. I understand how difficult this is for you after losing Steve, but I'm asking you to trust this. And, know that I will always love you."

"Deal." Tears formed in her eyes and one escaped, rolling down her cheek. Before she could brush it away, Jason beat her to it, gently caressing her cheek. Leaning forward, their foreheads touched, resting against each other.

"This is the final boarding call for flight 3791 to Houston," they heard over the announcement system.

Both stood, Rebekah placing her bag on her shoulder

and grabbing her suitcase in one hand. Jason took her other hand and walked her to the gate.

"I love you," she whispered.

"I love you too."

Stepping onto the ramp, she turned one last time. She was so glad he had come after her. She didn't know what the future held, but she was positive it would include him

Jason watched her retreating form until he could no longer see her. Glancing at the ticket in his hand, he sighed, wondering if he could get a refund for it. 'Oh well,' he thought. 'At least I made it here in time.' With a smile on his face and a song in his heart, he turned to head home. He knew things would be difficult, and they still had a long way to go. But, he was sure they would be able to work something out.

Throughout her entire flight, Rebekah's mind struggled with the reality of the situation. She hadn't lied to Jason; she did love him and she wanted to be with him. However, they had to find a way to reconcile their differences. Every glance in her direction she felt was an accusatory one or a questioning sneer. She felt like wearing a sign that read, "Yes! I am the girl in the picture. No! I am not his mistress." Never had she any reason to deal with anything like this, and although she loved and trusted him, she was unsure of what awaited her when she returned home.

The airplane lurched forward as it touched to the ground, and for a moment, Rebekah resembled that uncontrollable feeling. Un-boarding the plane, she was hesitant to move forward too quickly. She knew her parents would be there, and she didn't know if she had the strength to face them. Suddenly, she realized she was in the passenger pick up area. Both of her parents stepped out of the truck with smiles on their faces.

"How was the wedding," her mother asked as her father loaded her luggage into the truck. Just being in there ripped at her heart as she thought back to her last trip in this truck.

"The wedding was beautiful," she answered honestly.

"And did you have a good weekend?"

"Until today."

"What happened?" her father asked, joining them in the truck. He glanced back towards her, worried about how tired and worn out she looked.

"You mean you haven't heard?"

"Heard what?"

Reaching into her carry-on bag, she pulled out the magazine she had unconsciously packed that afternoon. She handed it to her parents, anxiously awaiting their response. After several silent moments, her father handed the magazine back. "You looked absolutely beautiful."

"I looked beautiful?" she asked incredulously.

"I love that blue gown," her mother added.

"I don't believe this! Your daughter is sprawled out on the cover of a tabloid, and all you can talk about is how

I looked?"

"What else do you want us to say?"

"I don't know. Say something, anything. I can't believe you hadn't heard about this already."

"Rebekah," her mother turned to face her. "Does anyone else, other than Kate, know you are dating Jason?"

"No."

"Okay then, why would anyone we know give that magazine a second glance?"

"I don't know. I was just afraid someone would recognize me."

"Honey, it's the press. If you are serious about being with Jason, you are going to have to deal with them. I know you can handle it, and so do you. But, I also know you are scared. I just hope you don't use this as an excuse to run from someone you love."

"How do you know I love him?"

"Because we know you," her father broke in. "You've been happier this past month than any other time before. You talk to him constantly, and you have looked forward to this weekend for two weeks."

"That's true," she replied quietly, leaning back against the seat.

The rest of the ride home was spent in silence. By the time her parent's dropped her off at her house, she was feeling better about the entire situation. She knew her heart belonged with Jason. Now, they just had to find a way to make this work despite the thousands of miles separating them.

However, the next morning, Rebekah was no longer as sure of herself. Butterflies surged through her stomach at an alarmingly fast rate as she entered her classroom. Bracing herself, she prepared for the battery of questions that would appear at any moment. She knew her family may understand, and they were right, to a point. Many people may not take the time to look at that picture, but it only took one. The way gossip spread through the school, it wouldn't be long before everyone knew about it.

The bell to dismiss the students from the cafeteria to their first period classes rang, and Rebekah took her position in the hallway to monitor them as they headed to class. Immediately, Terri Gill, one of the other 8th grade History teachers, accosted her. "So", she began, "I guess we can assume that is whom the roses were from?"

Sighing, Rebekah turned to face her friend. Her mother was right. If she intended to stay in this relationship with Jason, she would have to get used to dealing with the ramifications of the press in her life. "Yes. We met in New York when I was there last month, and we've been dating since then."

"Why didn't you say anything?"

"What was I supposed to say? I wasn't even sure what was going to happen when I came home last month. Should I have announced it at the faculty meeting?"

"Rebekah, I don't mean it like that. I'm just curious,

and you know I'm not going to be the only one."

Wistfully, Rebekah glanced around at the now crowded hallway, knowing her friend was right. Terri Gill would not be the last person to want to know what was going on. Turning, she tried to reassure her. "I know you didn't mean it like that, I'm just not sure how to respond to any of those questions."

"Honesty always worked for you before."

"True, but this is personal. Should I stand in the front of each of my classes and announce it to them?"

"No, but I wouldn't sweep it under the carpet if they ask. You're always telling me that eighth graders want to be treated as adults, even if they are just kids. If they ask, tell them. You know as well as I do that if you don't, the rumors will only grow more and more out of control."

Just then, the warning bell rang, indicating there was only one minute left before the morning announcements began. "I wasn't the mistress. I just wanted to make sure you knew that."

Terri scoffed at Rebekah's remark. "Please! Like there was ever any doubt about that. If there is one thing I know about you Rebekah, it is that you have one of the best personal characters of anyone I've ever met. I never believed for one moment that you were the mistress, and neither will anyone else."

Turning, Rebekah entered her classroom with a general feeling of uneasiness settling around her. As the door shut, she faced the students she dearly loved and wondered which one would be the first to ask. She was granted a moment of reprieve when the morning announcements began and each of her students stood for the Pledge of Allegiance and the Pledge to the Texas Flag. During the rest of the morning announcements, Rebekah took attendance and prepared for the class to begin, almost feeling as if she was preparing to stand before the firing squad.

The morning announcements ended, and Rebekah took a slow breath, letting her mind drift to Jason and wondering how his day was going.

Unfortunately, for everyone in the studios, Jason Taylor was in a horrible mood. He had spent the first hour of his morning on the phone with the editor of the tabloid trying to get them to print a retraction. Although he had no control over what was printed in the first place, he still wanted to rectify the situation, for Rebekah's sake. Disappointingly, the editor was refusing, stating over and over that they had checked out their story before printing, and it had been confirmed that what they had was the truth. Even with the threat of a lawsuit from Jason, they still wouldn't budge. They were standing by the fact that their story had been corroborated before printing. Shaking his head, Jason tried to figure out who in the world would substantiate that story when he heard a knock on his door. "Come in!" he yelled gruffly.

"Wow! What has you in such a sour mood this morning?" the petite brunette asked, entering his dressing room with a smug look on her face. Suddenly, Jason realized the answer was staring him in the face.

"What the hell did you do Carrie?" he asked angrily.

"I don't know what you're talking about my dear." Her voice was laced with sugar as she coyly sauntered towards him. She knew she was playing with fire, but she was determined she would not be the one to get burned this time.

"You know exactly what I am talking about. Who did you talk to on Saturday night?"

"Why, I talked to just about everyone silly! Wasn't that evening beautiful? I swear Kacee looked absolutely radiant, although not as happy as I looked on our wedding day." By the time she finished speaking, she was directly behind of him, hands resting on either side of the chair he was sitting in, their eyes meeting through the mirror in front of them.

Anger blazed through his cool blue eyes as he spun around in his chair to face her. "I warned you the other night, Carrie. Stay away from Rebekah."

"Please! I didn't go anywhere near her. All I did was answer some questions one of the kind reporters there asked."

"Right and you just conveniently added in the part about her being my mistress."

"Are you going to deny that you are with her?"

"What I do and don't do with my personal life is no longer any of your concern. It stopped being your concern the moment you decided to have an affair."

"But, Jason," she practically pouted, her hand brushing against the side of his face. "I was just lonely for you. You were gone so much, and I missed you."

"So you turned to another man?"

"Okay, it was wrong, I admit that. But, things are different now. We're working together on the same show now. We're in the same storyline, loving each other. You can't deny that."

"It's a job, Carrie. Being with you is a job."

"A job you are enjoying more and more every day," she pressed.

"That's why you did this!" he said, reality suddenly hitting him.

"Did what?"

"I've been trying to figure out for weeks why you all of the sudden had the urge to act when you never before evidenced any desire to do so. You've been working this since you came on the show."

"Jason. This is our chance, our time to focus on us, to rebuild what we had. But, we can't do that as long as Ms. Goody Two Shoes is in your life. That's why I told the reporter about us. I knew she wouldn't be able to handle the burden of the press, not the way I can."

Standing abruptly, Jason forced Carrie to take a few steps backward, stumbling over her own feet. "Understand this. There is no us. We are over, and no amount of us working together is going to change that. I don't love you, Carrie, I never really did. I do, however, love Rebekah, and you need to deal with that."

"You can say that all you want, but I feel the truth every time we are together in a scene. You can't deny the passion that is there."

"Sure I can," he thundered. "There is no passion there, and if you sense any, you are making it up. Do you know how I manage to stomach the scenes we are in together? Rebekah. It is her face I picture every time I have to look at you like I want you. It's her lips I imagine every time I have to think about kissing you. It's her body I think of every time I have to touch you."

Shock and pain registered across Carrie's face as the weight of his words hit her. She had known Jason could get angry, but she had never seen that anger directed towards her. In her heart, she knew he was lying, both to himself and to her; she just needed to help him see it. "Jason," she began, but he quickly cut her off.

"I've had it Carrie. Get out! Don't come to my room again. Stay away from me, and stay away from Rebekah. In fact, get used to her being around, because I intend to have her around much more often! Now, leave."

Resignedly, Carrie walked towards the exit, turning to look at him one last time. One way or another, she would get him back in her life. Maybe she had gone about this the wrong way this time, but next time, she wouldn't be wrong. Getting rid of Mary Poppins was the way to go, that much she was sure of, and come hell or high water, she would have her husband back.

Hours later, an exhausted Rebekah rushed to grab the ringing phone as she entered her house. "Hello?"

"Bekah? A voice asked on the other end, and immediately a smile spread across her face as she recognized his voice.

"Hey you! How was your day?"

"Long," he sighed. "And yours?"

"The same. Do you want to go first?"

"Actually, yeah. I have to apologize."

"For what?"

"I spent the morning trying to get the editor to print a retraction of their statement."

"You didn't have to do that," she whispered, touched that he would even try.

"I know. I wanted to. But, he wouldn't budge. I even threatened to sue him, to no avail. He said they were standing by their story because they had it fully substantiated before they printed it."

"Substantiated? Who in the world would back up something like that?"

"I'll give you three guesses, but I can guarantee it won't even take that many."

Rebekah let out a breath as she realized he was right. There was only one person who would love to paint her as his mistress. "Carrie," she stated.

"Bingo! See why I love you? You're even smarter than me. I couldn't figure it out at first. Then, she showed up in my dressing room, and it all became suddenly clear. And, not just the newspaper, but the whole situation."

"There's more?" she asked incredulously.

"Remember when she first came onto the show? I was trying to figure out why she was so unexpectedly interested in turning to acting when she never showed an interest before. But, after this weekend and this morning I was put two and two together and now understand her motives."

"You."

"Exactly." Jason sighed, exhausted from dealing with the crap from his day and wanting nothing more than to see Rebekah's face. But, he would have to settle for listening to her voice for now. "Apparently, my ex-wife believed that by forcing her way onto the show, and acting with me, I would see the error of my ways and take her back."

"Wow, that's um…"

"Delusional," he finished for her. "Yeah, I know." Silence spanned their conversation as both became lost in their thoughts. "Anyway," Jason broke in. "She told me she thought we would have a chance if you weren't in the picture. I informed her that you being in the picture has nothing to do with it, but that she should get used to seeing you around, because I plan on having you around more often."

"You do?" she asked quietly.

"Yeah, I do."

"Good, because I plan to be around more often." Rebekah could not believe she just said that, but she knew it was the truth. And, she knew Jason could practically hear the smile in her voice.

'So, enough about my day. Tell me about yours."

Rebekah sighed, trying to decide where to begin. She had already told him the night before about the conversation she had with her parents. "Well, let's see," she began. "My day started as one of my fellow teachers confronted me with questions about you. Then, it continued on as each of my class periods seemed to want to discuss the weekend's events."

"Beck, I'm sorry. Had they all seen the paper?"

"No. Actually, very few of them had even seen the picture, and most of the students could have cared less about the 'mistress' part. In fact, that really never even came up. They were more interested in you, especially the girls." Rebekah gave a small laugh remembering some of the questions her girls asked her. "Mainly, they wanted to know if you were a good kisser."

"Get out of here; they did not!" Jason responded, shocked that such a conversation would even take place in a junior high classroom.

"Hey! I didn't say I answered them. I just said that was what they wanted to know."

Suddenly, the tone in Jason's voice changed as it dropped in volume and increased in intensity and desire. "So, if you *had* answered them..." he began.

Rebekah paused before her voice lowered as well. "I would have told them kissing you was like tasting a little bit of heaven." She had to laugh at the craziness of her answer, but she was right. At least she gave him an ego boost for the day.

"Well, I'm glad you think so too."

"What? You think your kisses taste that good, huh?" She joked.

"I meant yours do too."

"I know," she replied quietly, wishing he was here with her at that moment. She still wasn't sure what was going to happen with them, but she knew she was getting more and more to the point where she never wanted to leave him again.

Jason could sense the serious turn of the conversation, and he wasn't sure he was ready to go there after the emotionally draining weekend they just had. "Hey, I did manage to get a little good news today."

"Well then let's hear it," Rebekah practically demanded, silently relieved that their conversation had not turned deeper. She was constantly amazed that this man seemed to know exactly what she did and did not need at various times.

"Are you familiar with Fan Events?"

"You mean the things where soap stars go to places like malls and stand around for a bunch of adoring women to stand in line, scream their name, get a hug and then be on their merry way?"

"Hey now! I have some fantastic fans!" Jason chastised through barely contained laughter. She had just described the very reason he struggled with doing these things. However, his latest one had a definite plus to it.

"You described it exactly."

"So, why are you asking?"

"Well, the show and network have been after several of us to start doing some of these shows in the South. Most of our focus is typically on the East Coast, but it appears as if they fans down South are getting a little put out that no one ever comes their way. I've never wanted to go, but after my last trip down, I finally gave in and had them schedule a weekend."

"Really, Mr. Taylor? Couldn't get enough of the South, huh?"

"Actually, no. I couldn't get enough of you. My show is in Houston. Why else do you think I would have agreed to go?"

"I just figured you couldn't stand to be away from the South any longer; you had to come back," Rebekah replied with a laugh.

"Aren't you the comedian today?" he asked, laughing as well. "Anyway, I will be in Houston the last week in April."

"A whole month?"

"I know. But it will be here before we know it."

"It just seems so long," she whispered.

Jason sighed. These long stretches of time were getting harder and harder to deal with. At some point they were going to have to begin making decisions about their future. But, tonight wasn't the time to do that. "So will you come to this annoying fan event for me?"

"Hmmm. I don't know. Come to see you after being apart for a month. Gee, let me think about that."

"Again with the comedy," he broke in, laughing.

"Of course I will be there."

"Good, I can't wait."

"Neither can I. Look; I hate to do this, but…"

"I know. It's late."

"Yeah."

Silence suddenly filled their conversation as neither wanted to hang up the phone. "I love you," Jason whispered.

"I love you too." Suddenly Rebekah didn't think a month would pass quick enough.

CHAPTER 9

Several weeks later, Rebekah nervously drummed the steering wheel of her Blazer. Jason had arrived late the night before and was currently in a hotel in downtown Houston. She had wanted him to stay with her, but knew that for at least the first day of this trip, he was technically working, which meant he had to stay there. The managers of the comedy club hosting the Fan Event had scheduled two appearances for the day, one around lunch and another two hours later. She had promised Jason, when he called the night before, that she would be at the club around 10:30 so they could visit for awhile before the VIP part of the event began.

She wasn't sure why she was so nervous. Maybe nervous wasn't the right word; antsy was more like it. It had been so long since they had seen each other. Sure, they talked almost every night, but it wasn't the same thing. Plus, Jason had informed her a week ago that he would not be alone on this trip. The network decided to publicize this fan event big time, so they were bringing in some of their power players, including Danny, Nikki and Carrie. Plus, Jason had mentioned a new cast member that might be coming along as well. This was a chance for him to be introduced.

Houston traffic was as difficult as ever, and Rebekah was afraid that she wasn't going to make it in time, which only added more to her current state of mind. Just as she turned into the parking lot though, she saw the limousines come to a stop and she realized her timing had been perfect. Seeing Jason step out, she gave him a small wave as she quickly swung into a parking spot near the front of the building and proceeded to get out of her car.

"Now that's more like it," Jason stated with a smile, grabbing her to him in a tight hug.

"More like what?" She asked, hugging him back.

"The last time I saw you driving a vehicle, it was some huge 4-wheel drive diesel truck. This," he pointed to the vehicle beside them, "fits you much better."

"I'm glad you think so," Rebekah responded, pulling him into a kiss. Before either of them could pull away, the kiss deepened in intensity. Finally, they broke apart. "I'm glad you're here," she whispered quietly.

"I'm glad I'm here too," he answered back with another quick kiss. "Come on. Let's go inside."

Leading her gently into the comedy club, it wasn't long before they quickly joined the rest of the group. Nikki immediately pulled Rebekah into a hug. "It's great to see you again," she warmly greeted her friend.

"It's good to see you, too. I can't believe ya'll are here."

"I have to be honest. I can't say I ever thought I'd be in

Houston."

"And what's wrong with Houston?" Rebekah asked with a smile on her face.

"It's hot!" Nikki exclaimed.

"Hot?" Rebekah asked incredulously. "You seriously think it is hot here?"

"Absolutely," Danny chimed in. "It's easily twenty degrees higher here right now than it was when we left home.

"Please," Rebekah scoffed, waving her small hand. "You people have no idea what hot is. Hot is mid-August when it is a hundred degrees outside but the humidity and heat index make it feel like it is a hundred twenty degrees."

The rest of the group had gathered around them, enjoying the playful banter of the friendly group. All seemed to be enjoying themselves immensely, all except Carrie. A scowl spread across her face as Jason pressed in closer to Rebekah. "It doesn't matter how hot it is now," he broke into the conversation. "What matters is that the scenery around here makes things *much* hotter!"

A smile broke out across Rebekah's face as she felt Jason claim her lips with her own. Behind them, Nikki smirked as she watched Carrie roll her eyes at the scene before her. This was definitely going to be an interesting weekend.

Moments later, the host for the afternoon came by to explain to the group how things would work for the day. The people who bought VIP tickets would begin coming in around 11:00 AM. They would have thirty minutes to mingle with the fans during which time they could take pictures and sign autographs. At 11:30 AM, they would open the doors to the rest of the people and the group would go backstage. The first show would begin at noon and would last an hour. They would have a thirty minute break and the whole schedule would repeat itself, with the final show beginning at 2:30 PM.

Rebekah tuned out the manager and grimaced to herself as the schedule was laid out before them. For the next three and a half hours, Jason, as well as the rest of the group with him, would have to put up with a bunch of strangers fawning all over them. She wondered to herself how they could put up with stuff like this and because she remained lost in her thoughts, she didn't even realize when they were finished meeting.

"Hey," Jason whispered as he slipped his hands around her waist and drew her into him, smiling as he heard her sigh of relaxation.

"Hey, yourself," she replied. She had missed this so much. "So, busy day, huh?"

"Are you sorry you came?" Jason asked.

"Of course not," Rebekah answered, turning in Jason's arms to face him. "I'm just sorry that you have to put up with all these people today."

"It's all part of the job. It's really not too bad. Some of them are long time fans so we see them often." Jason shrugged nonchalantly. So, where are you going to sit this afternoon?"

"Right over there," Rebekah pointed to a table in the far left corner.

"Are you sure?"

"Positive. Let all your adoring fans sit close to you today. I get you much longer than any of them do."

"Yes, you do," he whispered back, leaning in for another kiss. Their moment was interrupted though by the one person neither of them wanted to see.

"Jase, honey. They're letting in the fans." Carrie started, smiling because she knew what she was interrupting. "It's probably best if they don't see you with her."

Rebekah couldn't miss the way Carrie said *her* in that statement, as if to imply she was just some thing that needed to be dealt with. Turning, she stifled a laugh as she saw Jason rolling his eyes. "Go, have fun."

With one last kiss gave her hand a quick squeeze and headed off in the direction of the rest of the cast. Rebekah was amazed. Within seconds, she saw Jason transform himself into Brad; that was, after all, who the fans were in love with. Leaning back in her chair, she watched the interaction of the group. She could pick out who were fans of whom just by the way they interacted with each other. There were the highly obvious "Bramy" fans, those who want Brad (Jason's character) to get together with Amy (Carrie's character). Then there were the Jason and Nikki fans "Brellen", those who wanted Brad and Ellen together. Finally, there were the die hard "Bressica" fans; this group refused to let go of the relationship their two favorites had shared over two years ago.

Rebekah laughed to herself. After she and Jason began dating, she spent quite a bit of time on the internet learning a little more about his show and his character.

There were tons of people out there who spent quite a bit of time, and money, dedicated to their favorite character, or their favorite couple. So much of the money collected was donated to charity which still amazed Rebekah. Many of these were the women who showed up here today.

Before she knew it, Jason turned and caught her attention, giving her a quick wave before heading backstage. The doors opened, and more people poured into the club; this was a sold out event. Once everyone took their seats, the host came out and introduced himself and explained to the excited crowd what would happen for the afternoon. As soon as the basics were out of the way, it was time to bring the cast out onto the stage.

One by one, he introduced each of the actors there, ending with the newest member of the cast: Nathan Scott. Rebekah was astounded at the uncanny resemblance between Jason and Nathan. She knew Jason had mentioned the newest addition of the show, but she didn't know how closely they looked like each other. Looking at his wavy light brown hair, and staring into the young man's cool blue eyes, she could have sworn she was looking at a younger brother.

Much to the excitement of the crowd, the show began. Rebekah laughed as Danny made fun of Jason's character and she listened with intrigue as each actor shared information about their personal lives. Finally, the last thirty minutes of the show began, and the crowd was on the edge of their seats; it was time for the question and answer session.

The first woman stood and Rebekah laughed as she produced a shaky hand to take the microphone. "Nathan," she asked, "how does it feel to be working with two Emmy nominated actors, and what will your story be about?"

"Well," he began, with a sheepish smile. "I'll admit that it is a little intimidating at times, but this has been a wonderful opportunity for a young actor. As for my story, you'll have to stay tuned to find out. But, I can tell you that it could include a DNA test with a shocking reveal and the possibility of a love triangle."

"Speaking of love triangles," the next woman began. "Jason, what in the world is going on with Brad and Amy? Is he going to leave Ellen?"

"You know," Danny broke in. "It must be tough having all these women throw themselves at your feet!"

"Yeah," Jason joked back. "You're just jealous that the good cop isn't getting any loving on the set lately." Picking up his glass of water, Jason took the napkin underneath and threw it at Danny. "Seriously though, in an answer to your question, I honestly don't know where this is going. It always makes a good story when there is a new love interest in the mix."

"Plus," another woman piped up. "I'm sure it doesn't hurt that one of the women is the one that you love."

Jason stole a glance in the direction of Carrie and was sickened at the smile plastered across her face. If only he could tell the woman the difficulties of having to pretend to be in love with a woman he loathed. "Actually," he began, but was unable to continue as Carrie quickly cut him off.

"It is unbelievable," she broke in, excitement in her voice. "Not many women get the privilege of working every day with the man that they love. What a wonderful opportunity to remind the man in your life how much he really loves you and how great the two of you are together!"

It was Rebekah's turn to roll her eyes. Carrie was milking the tabloid "reunion" for all that it was worth. She saw Jason turn his head in her direction and she discreetly shook her head no. She didn't want him to counter Carrie's words right now. It wasn't a battle that needed to be fought. The truth would come out soon enough. Plus, she didn't want him to have to answer any questions about where they stood when they hadn't even had that conversation themselves.

Fortunately though, someone else in the audience changed the direction of the conversation by asking Nikki a question. Surprising Rebekah, a young man stood up and asked Nikki if she would go out with him. Danny answered "no" for her which drew a laugh from the rest of the crowd. Apparently, he only watched the show and didn't realize that her real life husband was sitting next to her.

All too quickly though, for the excited crowd, the show was over. The cast posed for a few final pictures and then was ushered backstage. Rebekah watched the crowd as they left the club on a "Hollywood High"; that's what she called it whenever someone met a famous person.

Smiling she slipped out of the group and headed to the backstage area. She didn't get very far as a man stepped out from behind the curtain. "Can I help you, miss?"

"No thank you. I'm just headed backstage to see Mr. Taylor." She tried to side step the man, but he quickly countered her move.

"I'm sorry ma'am, but there are no fans allowed backstage."

"No, you don't understand," she tried to reason with him emphatically. "I'm not a fan. I'm Jason Taylor's girlfriend."

"Right, and I'm Mickey Mouse. Look, miss. If you do not leave, I'm going to have you removed from the club."

Rebekah turned angrily on her heel. She had the notion to call Jason on his cell phone and have him come out and get her, but she decided against it. Glancing at her watch, she knew they only had a few moments of peace and quiet before the next show began; they would have plenty of time together later.

Sighing, she plopped down in her seat, waiting for the next show to start. Soon enough, the door opened and the next round of VIP guests entered and the whole scenario repeated itself. Yes, it was different people, and occasionally there were some different questions. But, if Rebekah was honest with herself, she was glad when the host called for the last question from the crowd.

Suddenly, the crowd was gone and a muted silence filled the space where energetic laughter was moments ago. Jason stepped away from the group and headed over to Rebekah. "So, what did you think?"

"Me? I thought I was glad it was you up there and not me." She drew his arms around her, savoring the feel of his arms around her.

"Look, I'm sorry about that one woman's question."

"Why? Let Carrie have her last ten minutes of glory. I

told you earlier, I get you much longer."

Jason dipped his head closer to Rebekah's, placing their lips inches apart. "Much," he whispered before closing the final gap and stealing a quick kiss.

"Mmmmm," Rebekah moaned quietly as he pulled away. "I love it when you do that."

"I'm glad, because I love doing it."

"Hey, are ya'll hungry for a late lunch?"

"I know I am. What do you have in mind?" Jason responded, motioning for Danny and Nikki to join them.

"Well, if you're going to come to Texas, you have to eat some *real* Mexican food and not that watered down version you have in New York!"

"Sounds good to us," Nikki piped in, but she quickly caught her husband's gaze. "No," she stated emphatically.

"Nikki," Danny warned, but she quickly cut him off.

"No, Danny! I'm serious. He can come," she said, motioning to Nathan. "But, she can fend for herself."

Quickly, Rebekah caught on to the source of their argument, Carrie and Nathan. "It's alright, Nikki. I don't mind if they come.

"Maybe I do."

"Be nice, Nikki," Jason tried to interject.

"Why? I want nothing to do with her. There's no

reason they have to go eat with us."

"It's just dinner," Jason continued.

"Fine," she replied. "But, you are the one dealing with them," she replied as she turned in a huff and headed towards the waiting limousine outside.

Danny had already called for Nathan and Carrie to join them and everyone headed outside. Rebekah laughed softly to herself as she watched Carrie fume as Jason chose to ride with her instead of the group in the limo.

Rebekah took the group to a local restaurant that was a favorite of hers. Before long, she could tell they were enjoying the atmosphere of the place, and she had eaten Mexican food in New York enough to know that they had never really experienced the real thing there before. "Just remember," she cautioned as they all perused the menu in front of them, "the food down here is fairly close to authentic."

"Well, hello," Carrie broke in sarcastically. "We're closer to Mexico here."

"I know." Rebekah was trying to be gracious, but there were times when that woman grated on her last nerve. "I was just trying to warn ya'll that the food here is probably a little spicier than you are used to."

"I think we can handle it," Carrie retorted.

"Okay," Rebekah said, almost wishing that Carrie would order the hottest thing on the menu.

"Thanks for the warning," Nathan interjected, noting the tension between the two women. He hadn't really been around long enough to understand the undertones there, but he was fairly certain that Jason's ex-wife was still very interested in him and that she was very concerned about the woman he was with now.

"You're welcome." Rebekah replied warmly, recognizing his attempt at lightening the mood. "So, tell me about yourself, Nathan."

"There's not really much to tell. I've been acting from some time, but only minor things. This is the first time I'll be working in soaps. I've lived in California, so moving to New York will be different. Plus, I still have to find a place to live."

"I'm sure you'll adjust quickly. New York is a great place to be, and you're working with a terrific group of people." Under the table, Jason gently squeezed her knee, silently thanking her for trying to help the young man feel a part of the group.

Nikki watched Carrie as she silently seethed. Outwardly, she was conducting herself fairly well, but Nikki knew Carrie well enough to know that it was killing her inside to not only see Rebekah with Jason, but to see Nathan reacting so kindly to her as well.

Once the meals had been ordered, the conversation turned friendlier, even Carrie participated without throwing out too many stinging barbs directed towards Rebekah. That friendly banter lasted only until their discussion turned back towards Rebekah. Carrie couldn't stand to have the attention focused on her for any amount of time at all.

"What do you do?" Nathan asked Rebekah, genuinely interested in learning more about the woman who mesmerized his new co-worker.

"I'm an eighth grade U.S. History teacher," she replied.

"Which means she couldn't teach anything real," Carrie broke in.

"Carrie!" Both Jason and Nikki admonished at the same time.

'No, no, that's okay," Rebekah continued. "You'd be surprised at how often that gets said. Social Studies instruction has changed quite a bit over the past few years. With state accountability systems the way they are, people have begun to realize the importance of teaching Social Studies. Contrary to popular belief, it *is* a "real" subject." Rebekah smiled sweetly towards Carrie and laughed inwardly as she saw the expression on Carrie's face.

Jason just smiled to himself, wondering when he would learn that Rebekah didn't need him to stand up to Carrie for her; she did just fine all on her own. He sat back in his chair and watched the woman he was falling more in love with every day.

After much lingering over the end of the meal, the group realized it was getting later and later and that they soon needed to leave. Rebekah knew she and Jason had to decide what would happen next.

"What are your plans for the rest of the weekend?" She asked.

"We are supposed to have a late morning flight tomorrow. Tonight, they have us staying in the same hotel as last night."

"Are you going back with them," she asked, almost shyly.

"I don't know," Jason sauntered closer, bridging the gap between them. "You tell me."

Rebekah bit her bottom lip and as she looked up at him, Jason was almost knocked over by the love in her eyes and the innocence on her face. "Stay with me, tonight," she whispered.

"Okay." For a moment neither of them moved; it was as if time stood still around them. Nothing mattered but the two of them.

Carrie watched the exchange from afar. She knew she was close to losing Jason forever, and she knew she needed to do something soon. However, before she could even think of anything, Jason and Rebekah were in her car, driving off into the sunset. Her blood boiled and she vowed to do whatever it took to keep the two of them apart long enough for her to sweep back in.

Almost an hour later, Jason and Rebekah pulled into the driveway of her two-acre home. The sun was hanging low in the sky, just beginning to dip down into the trees, bathing the house in a beautiful glow. The huge oak trees provided a cool shade over the front of the yard and were planted in such a way that they provided a welcoming invitation to the front of the modest house. A swing hung at the end of the white front porch and rocking chairs were positioned on both sides of the centered front door.

"This is beautiful!" Jason exclaimed.

"Thank you," she replied as they got out of the car and

headed into the house. "It's not a huge house, but it works for me. We had plans to redo it one day and increase the space, but that was before Steve got sick."

"Seriously, Rebekah, this place is wonderful. I can't wait to see the rest of it."

She opened the door and led him into the interior of her home. "Rustic elegance is what we always called it," she said with a laugh.

"That's exactly what I would have called it. You know, I was never one to go for the 'cowboy' look, but I really like this."

"Well," she said, gently pulling his arm. "If you like this, you will love the look of this." She led him through the house towards the back.

Once they stepped through the back door, Jason realized he was in a huge screened in porch. He could see almost every angle of the one-acre backyard. Her rose garden stood off and to the left. It was looking a little sad at the moment, but Jason knew she was working to correct that. In the center of the porch was a table and set of chairs, and along one wall was a long couch. With the sun setting, a cool breeze began to fill the large porch. "Does it always feel like this?" He asked.

"Not hardly! Once July hits, it becomes more difficult to enjoy being out here. These," she said, pointing to the ceiling fans above her, "help quite a bit, but still, when it is 110 degrees outside, nothing makes it cool enough."

"I can imagine."

"But, this time of year is one of my favorites. You can

enjoy being out here in the evenings without the fan, and definitely without the nuisance of the mosquitoes. There are some nights I could sleep out here."

"It is relaxing," Jason agreed as she took his hand and lead him through the rest of the house, giving him the grand tour. They finished in her study. "I didn't realize you were such a computer buff," he joked as he marveled at her computer set-up. In her small room, she had a computer, scanner, photo printer, and fax machine.

"I wouldn't say I'm a buff," she joked back. "But, I do like my computer. I do quite a bit of work for school on it, and all of my pictures are digital, so I use it all the time for that. Plus," she added with a smile, "I've enjoyed spending time online lately, learning all about Jason Taylor."

"You have not!"

"Yeah, I have. I have found a whole new world in the online soap community. I've learned some pretty interesting things." She sat down in the rolling chair and clicked her computer on, giving it time to boot up before showing him some of the things she had found.

"So," he continued, kneeling beside her on one knee, letting one arm drape around the back of the chair and the other rest comfortably around her waist. "You've been checking up on me, huh?"

"I wouldn't say 'checking up', per say. I've gotten quite a kick out of the people who spend their time on these online message boards. You, my dear, are a very hot topic." She bent sideways and placed a chaste kiss on his nose before turning back to the computer and accessing the internet. After several clicks, she pulled up to the first message board. "Here you go."

Jason practically laughed out loud as she scrolled through the contents of the website which was a 'Brellen' site. He couldn't believe some of the comments he was reading. His character was greatly unloved right now because of the direction the writers had sent the storyline in. With his and Nikki's character splitting to make room for Carrie's character, his fans had gone a little crazy. He had been getting tons of mail at work, and even a few gifts from this group; in the past those gifts had been pretty nice, lately they had gotten quite ugly because they did not like what was going on.

"They've been quite unhappy lately," Rebekah said.

"Tell me about it! I've been on the receiving end of some of their unhappy fan mail."

"Well, they should be upset. You and Nikki had a pretty good storyline together."

"You didn't even watch the show then!"

"True, but I've seen quite a few screencaps and video clips of your scenes together; they were pretty darn hot!"

"Do I even want to know what a screen cap is?" he asked.

"I'll show you." Rebekah clicked on a link in a thread and immediately, several pictures popped up.

"I've never seen these pictures before. How in the world did they get these?"

"Take a picture from the television," she replied.

"You mean someone actually takes the time to not only watch the show, but to tape parts of it as well? Then, they spend hours on-line talking about it? That's crazy!"

"Hey, don't knock those fans; in fact, you need to be nicer to them! They pay your salary, buddy!" Rebekah poked Jason in the chest to emphasize her point, but she couldn't draw her hand away quick enough afterward. Jason quickly captured it is his hand as he drew her closer to him.

"I love this," he whispered quietly.

"What?"

"This. Just this. Being together and doing absolutely nothing." He reached a hand up to gently caress the side of her face and could not help but smile as she closed her eyes for a second and leaned into his touch.

"I do too," she whispered back, leaning down to place her lips against his in a sweet kiss. "Let's go outside," she whispered as they broke apart.

Together, they walked out to the screened in porch and sat down on the beige couch, letting the noise of the evening surround them. A small water feature outside the porch created the effect of rushing water. The crickets were heard in the background, and every now and then, a firefly would decorate the barely lit sky.

Jason opened his arms to Rebekah, and she adjusted so she was in his embrace. His legs extended forward onto the ground as she curled up next to him, his arms surrounding her. "I could stay like this forever," he whispered, enjoying the serenity of the moment.

"You know," she answered, without looking up at him, "you are welcome to."

"I know."

Silence surrounded them once again, until Rebekah finally had to break it. "So," she began, but did not finish.

"So, what?" he asked, knowing what she was wondering.

Turning to face him, she asked the question that had been on both of their minds. "What are we going to do, Jason? I don't know if we can keep going on like this."

A soft light illuminated her face as she looked up at him. Staring into her midnight blue eyes, he did not think he could be any more in love with her than he was at this very moment. "I know."

"Maybe we don't do anything at all," she suggested.

Incredulously, he responded, "What do you mean?"

She tightened her embrace of him. "I don't mean it like that. All I mean is nothing can really change at this point. I have my job and you have yours. I have to at least get through the end of May, and particularly our eighth grade dance."

"Eighth grade dance?" He asked curiously.

"It's the end of the year dance for our eighth graders. Each year, they vote on the theme and the decorations. This year is "Hollywood Nights". They dress up, go to dinner, and then come to the dance. It really is a big night for them."

"When is it?"

"The third Saturday in May which is the last Saturday before school is out. My kids really count on me being there."

"Okay, so we don't decide anything until after that," he suggested.

"Okay."

"You know though. That won't change my feelings about you."

"I know."

"Do you, Rebekah?" He sat up fully, turning so that they were totally facing each other. "Do you really know how I feel about you? You have become my world, and I can't imagine you not being in it."

"Jase, I feel the same way." Little by little, they inched closer to each other until their faces were barely separated.

"I love you, Rebekah Thomas," Jason whispered before leaning in for a kiss. He captured her lips and clung to her as if searching for his last breath. This kiss was different than anything they had ever experienced together. Unlike the past, this time their need for air never became a struggle as they used each other for their oxygen. Jason couldn't image heaven being much sweeter than this.

He began to nibble on her lip, keeping her there for several minutes. The moment she moaned into the kiss, he knew he had her right where he wanted her. His mouth left hers and began an assault against her neck, slowly lapping up every ounce of her he could. Her body fell back onto the couch as he gently nudged her in that direction, cradling her back. His hands pushed at the bottom of her shirt, and his warm breath tingled her senses as he whispered, "I want to make love to you."

As soon as he said the words, Jason could feel her body tighten ever so slightly. "What's wrong Rebekah?" he asked.

"Nothing," she whispered, but he could tell she wasn't being truthful.

"Beck," he pressed.

Gradually, his hold of her lessened and she stood gazing out into the sea of black that was once a dimly lit backyard. Turning to face him, she rested her hands on the rail behind her. "Do you remember what I told you before about Steve and me?"

"Yes," Jason answered, stepping towards her.

"There's a little more to it." Before he could respond though, she continued. "Steve wasn't just the first man I ever made love to; he was my husband when it happened."

Jason looked deep into her eyes, knowing what she was saying. "Okay," he responded.

"I've always believed that you don't have make love until you're married, and that was the gift I was able to give my husband on our wedding night. Even though I'm older now, and an 'experienced' woman, if you want to call it that, I still have that belief."

"So we wait." Jason closed the distance between the

two of them.

"Wait?" Rebekah asked in amazement.

"We wait. It will happen, Rebekah," he vowed emphatically.

She caught the meaning of his words, and her head began to swim as she turned in his arms, placing her back to his chest. "Why are you so good to me?" she asked.

"Because you are my world, Rebekah Thomas. I love you."

Neither said another word as they each took pleasure in the moment. Thoughts of the future drifted through each of their minds, but it was more than the immediate future. Neither thought of tomorrow morning when he would have to leave again nor even May when they would have their discussion. Both were thinking beyond that, to a time when they would be together, married, as a family.

CHAPTER 10

Jason knew. He knew the moment he left Houston that it was time. Rebekah was the woman he wanted to spend the rest of his life with, and if that meant he had to move to Texas, so be it. He didn't want to leave her any more. The longer they were together, the more difficult it became to say good bye; he was tired of saying good bye. With a bounce in his step, he entered the studio and headed straight to Danny's dressing room.

"Hey!" Danny called out as soon as he saw Jason.

"Hey. I have a question for you."

"Shoot."

"Do you have any plans for this weekend?"

"Why?" Danny asked, with a cautious tone to his voice.

"I want you to go to the City with me. There's something I need to take care of and I would like you to be there."

"I don't know, Jason. We just got back from Houston, which by the way, I thoroughly enjoyed." Danny couldn't miss the smile that immediately appeared upon Jason's face at the mention of their weekend. He knew his best friend was madly in love with Rebekah, and he couldn't be happier. "I just don't know if I'm ready to go somewhere else."

"Believe me, Danny you want to come with me."

"I don't think Nikki's going to like that idea."

"Like what idea?" Nikki asked as she sauntered into the dressing room. As usual, her timing was impeccable. She always showed up at what Jason considered the most inopportune moments. He had wanted a few minutes alone with Danny before his announcement was spread to the entire world. Now that Nikki was here, it wouldn't take long for that to happen.

"Nothing Nikki," Jason responded, trying to get Danny to answer the same thing, but it was too late. The words were already out of his mouth.

"Jason wants me to go to the City with him this weekend."

"We just got back," Nikki began to whine, casting a pouting glance to both Danny and Jason. "What are you going for anyway?"

"I don't know," Danny answered honestly. "Jason hasn't told me yet. He was about to when you so rudely interrupted our conversation!"

"Well, excuse me," she replied, feigning hurt. Turning

to face Jason, she asked, "So, what's the big deal?"

"I might as well go ahead and tell you since you will find out anyway. But, you have to promise not to mention this to anyone."

"I swear," she promised solemnly, holding three fingers up in the fashion of a Girl Scout salute.

"I'm going to the City to look for an engagement ring for Rebekah."

Jason barely got the words out of his mouth before Nikki began squealing with excitement.

"Calm down Nicole," Jason replied, pretending to be irritated, but no matter how hard he tried, he couldn't keep the smile from lighting up his face.

"Gee, what's all the excitement about?" a voice asked from the hallway. Three heads immediately turned in the direction of the voice only to be greeted by a face none of them wanted to see.

"It's none of your business Carrie," Nikki answered with venom in her voice. "Just leave now."

"I was just curious to see what happened that seemed to be making Jason so happy. That's all I want for him." Her voice was sugary sweet, masking her true feelings. She had heard every word Jason said, and she was determined that it would not happen. He may buy the ring, but if she had anything to do with it, he would never have the chance to propose. She just had to figure out how to stop it.

"Carrie," Jason sighed, rubbing his forehead in frustration of the headache that suddenly began the moment she walked into the room. "This really doesn't pertain to you. Would you mind leaving?"

A moment passed as she stared at the man her heart still belonged to. She still didn't know how things got so messed up between them. "Fine, but Jason, I want you to know something. I watched you and Rebekah this weekend. I can tell how much she means to you." Carrie just couldn't bring herself to say that Jason loved her, because she knew it couldn't be true. "I just want you to be happy." Turning quickly, she left the room, trying to hide the tears that were suddenly forming. She had to find a way for her and Jason to have more time together. If he proposed to Rebekah now, she would lose him forever.

The room remained silent as the trio watched Carrie leave. "There is something definitely off about her," Nikki said the moment she felt Carrie was out of earshot. She turned to see both Jason and Danny shaking their heads. "What? I'm serious."

"Maybe," Danny replied, kissing her playfully. "But, we have something more important to discuss." Turning to Jason, he continued. "I'm happy for you man. I really am. But, what are you going to do?"

"About what?"

"About everything. Where are you two going to live? What about the show? Have the two of you talked about any of this?"

"Not really." Jason sank onto the couch suddenly feeling like a deflated balloon.

"Look," Danny continued quickly. "I don't mean it like that. I'm just wondering what will happen."

"I don't know," Jason answered honestly. "All I know is that I love her, and I don't want to keep saying goodbye. I want to be with her for the rest of my life, and I know she feels the same way."

"Then go for it, Jase," Nikki piped in. "All of that other 'stuff' will work out." She laughed as the smile returned to her friend's face. "I've got to go. I'm shooting a few scenes shortly. You two plan your weekend. I'll stay here and let ya'll do your guy thing."

"Ya'll?" Danny asked with a smile on his face.

Nikki shrugged her shoulders and glanced towards Jason. "What can I say?" She asked. "Rebekah has rubbed off on me."

"Thank you my love," Danny called out after her as she left the dressing room heading towards the set.

Furious, Carrie leaned against the wall outside of Nikki's dressing room that was a little further down the hall, seriously contemplating entering and damaging a few things. However, the rational part of her brain soon took over, and she disregarded those thoughts. She would get back at Nikki one day soon enough, the day she and Jason got back together. She was positive Nikki was one of the reasons they split up. Yes, there was that one issue of her little indiscretion, but she knew Nikki had been poisoning Jason's mind against her long before that. Jason. Just thinking about him ignited a fire deep in her soul. They were meant to be together; she just wished she could get him to see that, to remember what they had.

The sound of a phone ringing brought her out of her daydream. Nikki's answering machine clicked on, and

Carrie, sighed, irritated at the sound of Nikki's voice. "Hi, this is Nikki. I'm on the set so leave a message." Carrie began walking away when an equally obnoxious voice rung through the air.

"Nikki, this is Rebekah. I'm sorry to bother you at work, but I figured I would have less of a chance of Jason finding out about my call if I talked to you here." That certainly piqued Carrie's interest. Rebekah was trying to hide something from Jason. She glanced down the hall in both directions and then turned the knob to the dressing room, slipping inside to hear better.

"Anyway, I'm coming to New York this weekend. Jason doesn't know, and I want to surprise him. I was just hoping you could make sure he was home on Friday night. I'll be in late, probably close to 11:00. We probably shouldn't talk much, because you know how suspicious he can be. Just give me a quick call and confirm that he will be there. Thanks!"

The beep signifying the end of the call startled Carrie. She couldn't believe her good fortune. Here she was, desperately trying to devise a way to make sure this engagement didn't happen, and Rebekah had just given her what she needed. Her mind was already concocting the details of this particular plan. A slim finger hit a button on the machine and a smile danced across her face as the machine responded. Message erased.

Rebekah was actually giddy. That was a word she hadn't thought of since she was a teenager in love, but that's how she felt at the moment. She couldn't wait to see Jason again. Their time together the weekend before had been entirely too short, so when she realized she had a three day weekend coming up, she knew exactly who she wanted to spend it with. She was able to get a great deal online on an airline ticket. Of course, she had to rent a car, and it certainly was a good thing she had a great sense of directions. Otherwise she would be lost right now.

Signaling a right, she turned the car in that direction, trying to control the lead that seemed to be forming in her right foot. She was about ten minutes away from Jason's apartment building and she couldn't wait to see the look on his face when she got there. They had such an amazing connection last weekend. It still amazed her that he was willing to wait for her. She knew he had every right to walk away from her, most grown men probably would. But not Jason, he was different.

Jason had given her his garage code the last time she was here, enabling her to enter the underground parking garage. It was dimly lit, yet Rebekah found it didn't dampen her mood. Nothing could. Finding a parking spot, she quickly exited the car and used the elevator to arrive at the lobby. The bellman found her name on the list of approved 'anytime visitors' and she made her way up to the penthouse.

Taking a deep breath, she knocked quietly on the door, anticipating his presence. Silence was her only response. She was sure he would be here; Nikki would have called if she hadn't been able to keep Jason home. Reaching out a hand, she twisted the knob, surprised to find it unlocked. Shaking her head, she chastised him in her mind on the dangers of leaving a home unsecured. Hesitantly, she entered the apartment, calling his name. Again, she received no response; however, her attention was drawn upstairs. Music filtered softly from the second floor, and Rebekah decided to go up, thinking he was in the shower.

As she reached the landing, she turned towards his bedroom and was surprised to find the dim glow of candlelight coming from the room. She never pictured Jason as the "light candles and soak in the tub" kind of guy, but he was surprising her every day. A smile crossed her face as she pictured him, but almost immediately, the smile faded. The music she had heard downstairs was growing in volume, but there was no way it could cover the other sounds that floated in her direction. Obviously, Jason wasn't expecting her; he wasn't even missing her. No wonder he could wait for her, he was getting what he needed when she wasn't around.

Hurt and anger blinded her vision as she crept closer to the room. For some sick reason, she had to know. Maybe she was wrong; maybe the sounds were something else, something other than two lovers expressing their desire for one another. But, as she peaked into the room and heard the voices on the air, she knew her hopes were in vain. Her ears confirmed what her eyes were seeing as she heard a deep voice moan, "Carrie, you are amazing!"

Immediately, Rebekah jerked away from the room, her hand stifling a gasp as she pressed her back against the wall. Tears filled her eyes as she felt her heart break into a million pieces. What a fool she had been! She trusted him. She gave him her heart and he promised he wouldn't trash it, promised he would never hurt her. And he wouldn't, not ever again. She would never give him, or any other man for that matter, the chance to make her feel like this again.

As her fingers fell from her face, they came into contact with something cool against her neck. She immediately recognized it as the necklace he had given her. She traced the engraved letters "R.T." and almost laughed out loud at the wish she had held onto for so long – the wish that those letters would be her new monogram after she and Jason married. Hastily, she ripped the offending piece of jewelry from her neck and flung it across the hall. Choking out the sobs that were forcing their way out of her throat, she ran from the apartment, slamming the door shut behind her.

In the bedroom, a male voice asked, "What was that?" He was only semi-conscious of the sounds below.

"Nothing baby," Carrie responded with an almost sinister smile on her face. "Just the sounds of me getting everything I wanted." The young man smiled up at her, obviously unaware of the fact that he was not everything she wanted.

Standing in the corridor, Rebekah waited impatiently for the elevator, terrified she would run into Nikki. Unable to control it any longer, the dam broke allowing the tears to run freely. She had never heard him speak like that; his voice sounded so different than ever before. But, she laughed sarcastically to herself, apparently she had never turned him on like that before.

"Dammit, come on!" She yelled at the invisible elevator. And, as if in answer to her unspoken prayer, it immediately dinged. To her dismay though, Nikki chose that moment to open the door and check out the cause of all the commotion.

Rebekah instantly ducked her head towards the floor. It proved to be just in time too, because apparently Nikki didn't recognize her. "May I help you?" she heard Nikki ask.

More than anything she wanted to get off that elevator and tell Nikki exactly what she thought of Jason Taylor, but she had no strength left. Quietly, almost inaudibly, she whispered, "wrong floor" before the doors shut. In that one instant, Rebekah lifted her head, and her eyes met with Nikki's.

As the elevator began its decent, Nikki wondered who the woman was. "She looked so much like Rebekah," Nikki said out loud to herself. But, she immediately corrected herself. Bekah had so much life in her eyes, and this woman had none. Besides, Rebekah was a thousand miles away. Shaking her head, she returned to her apartment with her thoughts drifting to how excited Rebekah would be once Jason came back with his surprise.

Somehow, in the daze she was in, Rebekah found herself headed back to the airport. She wasn't sure how she would get home, as her ticket wasn't good until Sunday evening, but that didn't matter now; nothing mattered now. Slowly, she sunk into a chair near the entrance. Despondency filled the air around her as she watched the passengers and their families come and go. Rebekah closed her eyes and allowed her mind to go back in time to a place she swore she would never return. In her memories, she remembered the first morning she woke up to find herself alone, the first morning that she allowed reality to sink in that she was a widow. Her world shattered at that moment and in her young life, she had never felt more pain.

Without warning though, Rebekah heard a voice she never expected to hear ask, "What are you doing here, Rebekah?"

Turning slightly, Rebekah saw the one person who was able to help her with the pain so much the last time she felt like this. Practically throwing herself into her friend's arms, Rebekah cried out, "Kate!"

"Honey, you're shaking," Kate said softly, trying to comfort her friend.

"I'm so glad you're here!"

"Sit down, sit down." Kate led Rebekah to a set of chairs against the wall. "Do you want to tell me what you are doing here?"

Rebekah took a deep breath and tried to figure out where to begin. How could she explain how stupid she had been? How could she admit that she had fallen in love only to have that love destroyed in the end? Tears pooled in her eyes and continued falling onto her face.

"Is it your parents?" Kate asked. When she received no response, she continued questioning, "Does this have something to do with Jason?"

At the mere mention of his name, Rebekah lost the last bit of strength she had been holding on to, which wasn't very much to begin with. She crumbled in her best friend's arms and clung to her.

Kate desperately tried to reach her friend, to have some confirmation that she was physically okay and still somewhat coherent. "Rebekah," she continued quietly, trying to maintain a calm voice. "Are you flying out tonight?" She immediately felt some relief when Rebekah shook her head no. "Okay then," she continued, "if you're not leaving tonight, then how about we get out of here?"

Again Rebekah shook her head yes, indicating she was okay with going. Gingerly, Kate assisted Rebekah from the seat and walked her to the car, keeping her arm around her friend the entire way. She didn't know what happened, but she promised herself she would do whatever it took to help Rebekah.

Within fifteen minutes of driving around, Kate could see Rebekah calming considerably. She knew it was a good two to three hours to get to her house, so she decided to stop at a nice hotel she had seen earlier. Kate knew Rebekah well enough to know she would eventually explain what was wrong as long as she could have a long bath and a lot of chocolate.

As they pulled into the parking lot and headed into the lobby to register, Kate was amazed at Rebekah's behavior; she was numb and just going through the motions. The last time Kate had seen her like this was when Steve died, but surely that hadn't happened to her again. Kate didn't know if her friend could take the pain of losing another man she loved. Kate knew Rebekah loved Jason; she was sure of that. And, from everything that Rebekah had told Kate, she was also sure that Jason loved her as well. But, she knew that as soon as Rebekah had a chance to relax, she would tell her what was really going on.

As soon as they had entered the room, Kate ordered Rebekah into the bathroom to relax. In the meantime, she ordered anything and everything chocolate from room service. With everything laid out, she waited patiently for Rebekah to finish. Finally, she heard the door open. "I've got chocolate," she offered, lifting a spoon full of chocolate mousse.

Rebekah plastered a wry smile on her face as she reached out for the comfort food. But she knew nothing could calm her heart; it was broken, and she had no intention of ever fixing it again. "I guess you want to know what is going on," Rebekah said, sitting on the bed.

"When you're ready."

"I'm as ready as I'll ever be, Kate."

"Okay," she responded, surprised to hear the cynicism in Rebekah's voice. "So, what happened?"

"What happened is that I was stupid, that's what happened. I don't know what I was thinking getting involved with someone like him!"

"So, this does have something to do with Jason?"

"Of course it does! I was a fool. Do you remember what I told you he said about us making love? You know, about how he said he would *wait* for me?" Rebekah asked sarcastically.

Kate nodded, not wanting to interrupt her friend.

"What a joke that turned out to be! I can't believe I actually believed him!" Silence filled the small room as tears pooled once again in Rebekah's eyes.

"Did you see him?"

"No, but I certainly heard him." Almost immediately, her voice dropped several octaves. "She was there you know."

"Who?"

"Carrie," she cried out softly. She was determined to take the upper hand here and to fight back the tears, but sometimes, it was so difficult.

"Maybe she was there, maybe they were fighting and that's what you heard."

"I'm sorry, Kate. What I heard wasn't fighting!"

Kate sighed. "I'm confused, and I'm really trying to understand. Tell me what it was that you heard."

Rebekah fell back onto the bed and stared up at the ceiling. She wanted to forget this whole night ever happened; she wanted to forget the past several months had ever happened. But, she knew that wasn't a possibility. This was as real as it got. Without looking at her friend, she continued. "I showed up at Jason's apartment to surprise him tonight, only I was the one who got the surprise. The door was open so I thought I'd go ahead and go in. I knew he wasn't expecting me, but I figured he wouldn't mind. Sounds from upstairs caught my ears, so I went on up."

Kate sensed her hesitation to relive what happened, but she also knew that talking about it would help her heal. "What happened then?"

"I heard," she started to continue, choking back sobs.

"You heard what?"

"I heard people making love, and it was very obvious it wasn't a movie. I thought, surely, I was wrong. I had to be wrong. So, I pushed the door open slightly to check. But, before I could really see anything, I heard him call out her name. Kate, he was having sex with his ex-wife.!"

"Oh, honey! Are you sure?"

"Well, I know it's been awhile, but the last time I checked, that's what sex sounded like!"

Kate didn't know what to say to comfort her friend. She had been so happy when Rebekah and Jason had gotten together, because for the first time in several years, Rebekah actually had some joy in her voice when they spoke. Now, she didn't know what would happen.

"You know what the worst part was, Kate?"

"What?"

"The way he sounded. I've heard him so often now, and yet, I've never heard him sound like that. It was almost guttural, like she was able to satisfy him in a way I never could."

"Rebekah," Kate, said, crawling on the bed beside her. "For what it's worth, I'm sorry."

"I know you are, and I don't know what I would do without you."

"It's okay to cry you know," she said, giving Rebekah a shoulder to cry on.

And she did. Rebekah cried like Kate had never seen her cry before. She knew she was mourning the loss of the new love she had found as well as the old feelings this whole situation had created. After what seemed like an eternity, the sobs soon became sniffles and Rebekah calmed her breathing down; Kate knew she would finally get the rest she deserved. She was just glad she had found her when she did.

CHAPTER 11

The next morning, Jason woke up thinking about Rebekah. He and Danny had enjoyed their drive into the City the night before, but he was ready to get down to business; the two of them were going to look for the perfect ring for her. He didn't quite know what he wanted to get her, but he knew he would know when he saw it. Stretching, he reached for his cell phone, wanting to hear her voice. However, he was surprised when all he got was her answering machine.

"Beck, hey, it's me. I just wanted to say good morning. I'm not sure where you are, but I miss you. Hope you have a good day. I love you!"

Quickly though, he tried her cell phone, thinking maybe she would have it with her if she had gone out.

Kate was abruptly woken up by the offending sound of a ringing cell phone. She surmised it was Rebekah's, and jumped to answer it before she woke up. "Rebekah's phone," she whispered.

"Hello?" a confused male voice replied, and immediately, she knew whose voice it was.

"Jason?" She asked to confirm.

"Yes. Who's this?"

Click. Instantly, Jason heard silence in his ear. He tried calling back, but it kept going straight to her voice mail. 'Oh well,' he thought. 'I'll try back later.'

"Who was that?" a groggy Rebekah asked, stretching in the bed.

"No one important," answered Kate. "How do you feel this morning?"

"Like my heart was broke in two." Rebekah could read the sympathy in Kate's eyes, but she didn't want to see it. "Seriously, Kate. I'm fine. Besides I had a revelation last night."

"You did? What was that?"

"I'm done with love."

"Done with love?"

"Yep. I've figured out that the only thing that comes out of love is pain, misery, and loneliness. I'm tired of that happening. So, I'm done."

"You can't mean that, Rebekah."

"Sure I can. I'm a strong, independent woman. I certainly do not need a man to have a happy and fulfilling life."

Kate exhaled noisily. She knew there was no sense in arguing with Rebekah. Nothing could change her mind when she acted like this. Jason could come back tomorrow with an explanation for the whole thing, and she still probably wouldn't change her mind.

"You never told me why you were at the airport yesterday."

"I had taken my niece to fly back to her parents. Because she's under ten, I was able to accompany her past security to her gate." Suddenly, an idea popped into her head. "Hey. I don't have much to do the next few weekends. Why don't I come down?"

"Sounds good to me. I've got something I have to do this next weekend, but the next one should be good."

"Don't you have your eighth grade dance coming up soon?"

"That's right. That will be the Saturday night of the second weekend. You're still welcome to come though. It'll only be a couple of hours that night."

"Okay, I'll come down in two weeks."

"Kate," Rebekah continued. "Thank you for last night. I know the hand of God was with me because I don't know what I would have done without you."

"I'm just glad I could help."

"Do you think you could do one more favor for me?"

"Sure."

"I want to get out of here and go home. Can you take me back to the airport? I'm going to try to turn my ticket in for an earlier flight."

"Are you sure?"

"Yeah. I need to be done with this place. I don't plan to come back to New York for quite some time."

"We'll leave within the hour." Rebekah stood and joined Kate by the window, one friend embracing the other.

Rebekah knew her decision to be finished with love was the right one. All she needed was friendships like this one and her family. Nothing else mattered.

"This one," Jason said as he pointed to what Danny thought was the one-hundredth ring this morning. "This is the one."

"Are you sure?" Danny asked.

"Positive. This looks just like her." Jason held the dainty engagement ring in his hand. It was a simple round cut stone with three smaller stones on each side of the larger one. Jason knew he had the money to buy her something huge and gaudy, but he also knew Rebekah well enough to know that she preferred something simple. He could imagine the look on her face when he put it on her finger and he couldn't wait to do it. But, he had promised her they wouldn't talk about anything until after her school year ended.

As he wrapped up the sale and headed outside to return to the hotel, he tried calling her again, and was frustrated to continue to reach only her voice mail. 'Oh well,' he thought to himself. 'It's not like I told her I was going to call now.' He knew he would call her later that evening.

Some time later, he and Danny were on their way back home. "See," Jason started. "Nikki will be happy. That didn't even take us all weekend."

"You know she didn't care," Danny said, quietly steering the car home.

"I know."

"She just wants you to be as happy as she and I are."

"I am, man. There is no other woman like Rebekah, and there is no way I could love her more."

"I know, Jase." Danny didn't push the rest of the conversation; he knew Jason was getting lost in his daydreams of the woman he loved.

Jason closed his eyes and let his mind wander to Rebekah, not that it was difficult for that to happen. She was always on his mind lately. He wanted to create the perfect setting when he was able to propose to her. Maybe she could come here, or he could go there. It didn't really matter though; all that mattered was that he got to spend the rest of his life with her. His mind continued to drift making plans, and before he knew it they were coming into the main street of their town.

"So, do you think my apartment is still standing?" Jason asked.

"What do you mean?"

"I told Nathan he could stay there this weekend because he is still looking for somewhere to live. Of course, he's a little younger than us, and he wants to live in the City. But, he still needed somewhere to stay."

"Man are you brave! I don't know if I'd want him in my house. Have you seen his dressing room? That thing is a pig sty!"

"That's not the only thing I've noticed about him," Jason continued.

"You're talking about Carrie."

"Of course I am. Haven't you noticed the way he looks at her?"

"Who hasn't? It's highly obvious as to how much he wants to be with her. The only thing that is more obvious is how much she still wants to be with you."

"Yeah, well, he can have her. I want nothing to do with her, and haven't for quite some time. Rebekah is the only woman I will ever want."

"Well, we're here. So why don't you go check out the condition of your apartment."

Danny shut off the car and both men grabbed their belongings, took the elevator and headed upstairs. As soon as Jason entered his apartment, he began searching for Nathan. His eyes were drawn to a note on the desk.

Picking it up, he read, '*I'll see you later! I really enjoyed last night.*' Jason rolled his eyes and wondered what kind of floozy was in his apartment the night before.

"NATHAN!" He yelled climbing the stairs. He was confused as he peered into the guest rooms and couldn't find his guest anywhere. Finally, he pushed open the door to his own room. "Ah man," he moaned, poking at his sleeping co-star. "Wake up, Nathan."

Nathan woke with a start glancing nervously around the bedroom.

"Whoever you're looking for is gone. She left a note downstairs for you.

"Hey, man," Nathan started, his voice laced with sleep. "You're home early."

"We finished our business. What are you doing in my room?" A look of disgust passed over Jason's face as he thought about what happened in his own bed the night before. He would definitely have to strip the bed and wash the sheets.

"Look, I'm sorry man. This is just where we ended up. I hope you don't mind."

Of course he minded, but Jason didn't want to pick a fight. All he wanted to do was clean this mess up and talk to Rebekah. "Just put some clothes on and go to one of the other rooms."

Nathan quickly gathered his things and headed towards the door. "By the way, Jason. Thanks for letting me stay here last night, but I think I'll stay somewhere else tonight." He couldn't wait to get out of Jason's apartment.

He had enjoyed being with Carrie so much the night before, but thought it might be a little awkward if Jason found out while he was still in Jason's house.

Jason heard the door shut behind him as he pulled his cell phone from his pocket. His irritation only increased as she didn't pick up. Again, he left a message on her home machine as well as one on her voice mail.

Sighing, he stripped the bed, carrying the soiled bed sheets across the hall to the washer and dryer. He headed back across the hall, trying to figure out how to spend the last day of his weekend. He had to do something to occupy his time until she had a chance to call back. He glanced around the hall, sensing something was off. It was as if he could smell her perfume, but that was crazy, because she hadn't been there in weeks. Grabbing his keys from his bedroom, he left the apartment, never noticing the shiny piece of jewelry on the floor.

One week later, Jason was ready to seriously injure someone. He had worked twelve hour taping sessions every day that week, including Saturday. Now, on his only day off for the week, he was more restless than ever. For whatever reason, Rebekah wasn't returning any of his calls, and he was going insane with not talking to her. He knew she said that this last month of school was extremely busy for her, but this was unusual for a couple who usually spoke to each other every night. He couldn't figure out what to make of the situation.

"Jase," he heard Nikki call from downstairs.

"I'm up here," he responded with a dull voice.

Hastily, she climbed the stairs and headed to his room. "You still haven't heard from her, huh?" She asked.

"Nope," he answered, still staring up at the ceiling. "I just can't figure this out. It isn't like her to not return any calls."

"You guys didn't have a fight did you?"

"No! That's what I don't get. When I left Houston last, we were closer than we had ever been before. It's like we went from hot to cold in just one night, and I don't know why!" He glanced up to see Nikki pulling her cell phone from her pocket and dialing it. "What are you doing?" He asked.

"Calling her from my phone."

"Why?"

He wasn't able to receive an answer though because Nikki indicated someone was picking up the phone. "Rebekah?" Nikki asked.

"Hello, Nikki," Rebekah replied with a tired, angry edge to her voice.

"You sound horrible," Nikki continued, honestly worried about her new friend.

"Yeah, well I feel horrible."

"What's going on Rebekah? Jason's worried about you."

"Like he cares. I don't want to talk to him"

"What? Why?"

Rebekah sighed. "I just want to know why, Nikki."

"Why, what?"

"Why didn't you tell me he was going to be there? Why didn't you call me like I asked?"

"Beck, I don't understand," Nikki tried to explain.

But, she didn't get very far, as Jason ripped the phone out of her hands. "Bekah," he called out into to phone.

"I told Nikki I don't want to talk to you," she spat angrily into the phone.

"I've been so worried about you. You haven't returned any of my calls this week."

"And I'm not going to return any more. Look Jason, I know the truth. I know everything. We're over."

Confusion ripped through his mind, "Honey, what happened that you aren't telling me about? You know there's nothing we can't get through if we face it together."

"And there are some things a woman can't forget. You promised me you wouldn't ever hurt me." For a moment, her voice broke and he heard her vulnerability. As quickly as he heard it though, it was gone. "Look I'm not asking you, I'm telling you," she continued. "Do not call me again. Do not come to see me. Go and live your life the way you apparently really want to, and leave me out of it!"

"Beck," he whispered, his heart breaking into a million pieces, but it was too late. She had already hung up the phone. He wilted onto the floor, the phone resonating loudly as it crashed from his hands.

Nikki had stepped out into the hallway during the phone call in an attempt to give him some privacy. Now, she peered her head back in and was surprised at what she saw. This was not the same man who sat in the room ten minutes ago; this was a broken man, a shell of the man she knew. Tears clouded his vision, but he refused to let them fall from his eyes. "What is going on, Jason?" She asked.

He shook his head in bewilderment; nothing made sense. "I don't know."

"What do you mean you don't know?"

"We're over. She said we're over."

"That doesn't make any sense."

"I know it doesn't. None of this does it. But, she's serious. She accused me of hurting her."

"She accused me of not telling her you would be home," she added, trying to create some logic of the entire situation.

"Look, Nikki. I need to be alone right now."

Nikki didn't respond; she just headed out of the room. She knew he needed to figure out what was going on, and she certainly wasn't helping things. As she stepped into the hallway though, a gleam caught her eye. Bending down, she picked it up and interrupted Jason's train of thought. "Jase," she asked. "What is this?"

Standing, he all but yanked the chain from her hands. "This is the chain and locket I gave to Rebekah for her birthday. Where did you find it?"

"It was on the floor outside your bedroom door. Do you think she left it when she was here for the wedding?"

"No, I'm positive she had it on when we were in Houston two weeks ago."

"So, how did it get here?"

"I don't know, I don't know, Nikki!" Jason practically yelled. Nothing made sense in his mind right now, and he needed some peace and quiet to sort things out. "Just leave me alone," he requested.

Rebekah felt as if her heart stopped beating the moment that she heard his voice. He sounded so dejected when she would not speak to him; it only made her that much more impressed with his acting abilities. Absentmindedly, she reached her hand up to play with the necklace he had given her, as she had so often in the past few weeks. As her hand came in contact with only her bare skin though, she became reminded that she had hastily discarded it that night in his apartment. For a moment, she wished she had it back, but she quickly surmised that was a silly wish. Why should she want something that would be a constant reminder of so much pain?

Walking through her house, she let her eyes linger on the couch that sat on the back porch. That night had been so special for her, almost magical. Although they had not made love that evening, she felt like they had made a silent commitment to each other. Her heart ached as she realized the only person that commitment meant anything to was her. How could she have been so naïve?

Part of her wanted nothing more than to confront both he and Carrie about their illicit affair, but who was she kidding? She was the one who was having an 'affair'. True, both Jason and Carrie were divorced from each other, and she technically was never the other woman; but, apparently, Jason had never gotten Carrie out of his heart. Rebekah was nothing but a replacement, a fill in. Confronting both of them would not accomplish a single thing, and she refused to give him the satisfaction of seeing how much his actions had hurt her.

Sighing, she opened the door to the back porch and sat down on the couch. She refused to let her memories of him and their time together ruin her enjoyment of her home. She would reclaim her home, she would reclaim her life, and she would reclaim her heart.

She only had to figure out a way to forget him.

Nothing made sense to Jason, and the longer he thought about it, the more frustrated he actually became. 'How could things have become so screwed up?' He wondered to himself. When he had been in Houston with Rebekah, he had felt closer to her than ever before. Now, she refused to talk to him. After that afternoon in his bedroom when Nikki had called Rebekah, he had tried a few more times to call her back. Each time, she refused to answer the phone. He had thought about sending her flowers, but was afraid of what she might do to them. So, he sat there, alone in his apartment, and continued to try and figure out where they had gone so wrong. He twirled the engagement ring he had spent so many hours trying to find between his fingers, feeling the cold metal against his skin and fantasizing about how special the moment would have been as he put the ring on her finger. That ring fell to the ground and clattered though as he heard a knock on the door.

"Jason?" He heard from the hallway.

Sighing heavily, he closed his eyes and pressed his fists into them almost as if he was willing the person away. "What do you want, Carrie?" He asked in a gruff tone.

"I just wanted to check on you," she called back through the door. "Can I come in?"

'No!' Jason screamed in his mind; however, his body betrayed him as he stood and walked towards the door, opening it to reveal her in his hallway. He could tell by the way she was dressed that she wanted to do more than just check on him. She had on a short skirt that mimicked the one Rebekah had on a few weeks ago when they were in Houston. The top was also a cheap imitation of the one that Rebekah had worn and Carrie's petite body could simply not pull off the outfit the way that Rebekah's had. On Rebekah, he had found the outfit appealing; on Carrie, he just found it trashy.

Carrie took his silence as he stood at the door to be a hopeful sign and she brushed past him to enter the house. "I've been worried about you."

"You shouldn't be," he replied, slamming the door behind him as he walked past her. "I'm fine."

"I heard that you and Rebekah had a fight."

"We didn't fight." It was the truth; they did not have a

fight, she just would not talk to him.

Carrie took in his current physical state and knew immediately that he was lying. Although he was dressed very well, it was clear that he had not shaved in several days, and his hair was completely disheveled. "Come on, Jase. I was married to you; I know your habits."

"You don't know me, Carrie, and you never really did."

"That's not true," she proclaimed, trying to get closer to him. "I know you better than anyone else, including her."

Her. 'Is that all she will be from now on?' Jason wondered to himself. She felt like so much more. She was not just a 'her' to him. But before he could drown himself in his thoughts of her, he heard Carrie continue.

"I don't know what she did to you," Carrie walked closer to Jason, placing her hand on his forearm, "but it doesn't matter. What matters is that you and I are here now, together, and we have the rest of our lives in front of us." The distance between them was miniscule now, and Carrie knew if she could just be alone with Jason a few more minutes, she could forever wipe away Rebekah from his mind.

Jason's mind was reeling. The woman he wanted refused to be a part of his life, and the woman he couldn't stand to be around was offering herself to him again.

"I love you, Jason, and I know that you love me."

"The hell he does!" A voice exclaimed from the hallway. Both Jason and Carried turned around to see a furious Nikki standing in the doorway. "Jason doesn't love you any more now than he ever did, Carrie. When are you going to learn that? He mistook his fondness for you as love, and it cost him several years of his life. Now that he has tasted the real thing, do you seriously think he would ever go back?"

"If he had the real thing, don't you think she would be here now and wouldn't leave him alone like this?" Carrie asked. "Stay out of this, Nikki. It has nothing to do with you."

"It has everything to do with me, because I refuse to have you treat him like this again."

"Nikki," Carrie began in an effort to regain control of the situation, but that control was already lost and she knew it the moment she heard Jason's voice.

"She is right, Carrie." Jason said behind her.

Turning, she looked him straight in the eyes. "How can you say that?"

"I can say it because it's the truth. I don't want to hurt you, Carrie, but I am not in love with you. I never have been, and I never will be. I'm in love with Rebekah, and come hell or high water, I will figure out a way to fix whatever this is that has happened between us. For a moment, Jason was perplexed as he saw a look of panic and fear cross through Carrie's eyes. As soon as he saw it though, it was gone. Shaking his head, he continued, "Please leave."

Carrie knew better than to continue arguing with him. She would have her time with him again, but she was afraid that if she pushed it too far today, he would begin figuring out what really happened. She did not want him knowing before she had the chance to wrap him around her fingers again. Glaring at Nikki, she grabbed her purse from the couch and stormed out of the Penthouse.

"I'm glad she's gone," Nikki said loudly as she was shutting the door. "Why was she in here anyway?'

"She said she came to check on me." Jason shrugged his shoulders a pressed his fingers into his eyes.

"Whatever," Nikki scoffed. "She came here to try and win you back. It's a good thing I got here in time."

"I am a big boy, Nikki, and I can take care of myself. She wouldn't have been here much longer anyways. There's no woman I love, or will ever love, like Rebekah."

"I know Jase," Nikki fell beside him on the couch. 'Have you figured out what to do?"

"I can't figure out what to do because I don't know what happened."

"I know." Silence surrounded the two friends as they sat there together. "You know," Nikki continued after a moment. "I wouldn't be surprised if Carrie did something."

"She couldn't have. There is no way that she could have gotten to her."

"True." Standing, Nikki turned to head back to her own Penthouse. "Are you going to be okay?" she asked.

"I'll be fine. Seriously. I'll see you at work tomorrow."

"Okay. If you need anything, let me know."

Jason fell back against the couch as she left his home. He had to figure out what happened, because if he realized anything with Carrie standing in his apartment a few moments ago, it was that Rebekah was the only woman he would ever love, and he refused to go on without her.

True to his word, Jason showed up for work the next morning, looking worse than he had the day before. Danny caught him before he could go in too much farther. "Hey, man, are you okay?"

"I'm sure Nikki told you," he replied sullenly.

"Yes, she did. But, it still doesn't tell me how you are." The two men started walking in the direction of the dressing rooms.

"I'm confused as hell, Danny. Everything she said last night just doesn't add up. I find her necklace on her floor, and I'm positive she had it when we were in Houston. I just can't figure this out."

"Can't figure what out," they heard from behind them.

"Nathan, hey," Jason said as he and Danny turned around. For the first time in a week, Jason actually had a half smile on his face. For someone who looked so polished on the screen and at public events, he sure looked like a mess. His dirty blonde hair was sticking up in every possible direction and his un-tucked shirt was mistakenly buttoned. "We're just working on something from the script," he answered the young man, not wanting to get into the sordid details of his life.

"Anything I can help with?"

Before Jason could respond though, he realized the reason for Nathan's appearance. Carrie walked out of his dressing room door and turned the other direction before she could realize they were so near. Suddenly things began to fall into place in his mind. "Nathan," he asked with a sudden sense of urgency, "who were you with that night at my apartment?"

"What does it matter, Jase?" Danny broke in, sensing how nervous the young man was.

"It matters, believe me, it matters." Turning back to the young man in front of him, Jason basically pleaded with him. "Please, if it is who I think it is, I promise I won't be angry. I don't even care. But, I need to know."

Without lifting his gaze from the floor, Nathan answered. "Carrie."

"I knew it!" Jason shouted.

"Knew what?" Danny asked.

"I knew something was off about the whole thing. Think about it. I found Nathan in my bed, where he and she had obviously had sex the night before. Nikki found Rebekah's necklace outside my bedroom door.' He could see the light dawning in Danny's eyes. "I would almost guarantee you that she came by to surprise me and she saw them in my bed. She thinks I was making love to my ex-wife!"

"You know," Nathan broke in. "I don't know if this helps, but the door was not locked that night, and I did hear something unusual."

"What was it?"

"I don't know. I asked Carrie about it, but she brushed it off, and honestly we were in a position that I really didn't care that much."

"It's not your fault, man," Jason reassured. "Look, thanks for your help, but Danny and I need to take care of something."

"It's no big deal," Nathan shrugged. "I just hope I didn't cause any problems."

"You weren't the one who did. But, do me a favor and don't mention any of this to Carrie."

"Sure," Nathan replied, turning and heading back down to his dressing room. He was shaking his head, wondering what kind of woman he had gotten involved with.

"What do you think?" Jason asked Danny as they both watched the young man walk down the hall.

"I think it's a possibility. But, I think you're going to have a hard time proving it to Rebekah. Right now, it is your word against what her brain thinks she saw."

"I know, but I have to try. I won't lose her, Danny."

"I get that. But, you can't just go charging down there. You need a plan."

"Agreed, and you and I know just the right person to help."

Heading down the corridor, the two quickly found Nikki and caught her up to speed. As they both suspected, she was appalled. "Even I didn't think she could be that vicious, and I can't stand her," Nikki said with a look of shock on her face. Silence filled the small dressing room as the two men let their revelation seep in. However, that silence was altered when Nikki cried out, "Oh my gosh!"

"What," Danny asked.

"I saw her," she answered.

"Saw who?" Jason joined in, still as confused as Danny was.

"Rebekah. I saw her that night."

"What do you mean, you saw her? How could you have seen her and not recognized her?"

"Jase," she tried to explain. "It was late that night. You two were out of town, and I was half asleep on the couch, no contacts in I might add, when I heard someone cry out in the hallway. I opened the door and asked the woman in the hall if she needed any help. Her head was down and she muttered some response to me. It wasn't until the doors were closing that she looked up. Her eyes looked so lifeless, but I only saw them for a split second, if even that long. I know it's stupid," she continued, looking at Jason as if she were pleading forgiveness from him. "If I would have paid more attention, I could have stopped all of this."

"It's not your fault, Nikki," Jason assured her.

"I know, but still, I feel partially responsible. It's no wonder she reacted to me the way she did on the phone yesterday. Speaking of phones though," she said as she stood quickly and walked over to the phone on the side table by her dressing area. She began frantically pushing the buttons on her phone until Danny and Jason heard her exclaim quietly, "here it is."

"Here what is?" Jason asked.

Turning the phone to face him, she showed him a series of numbers he instantly recognized. "Her phone number," Nikki answered. "She called me here a few weeks ago. That must have been what she was referring to when she asked me why I didn't tell her. It didn't make sense at the time. This must be how Carrie knew she was going to be here."

"But why was Carrie in your dressing room?" Jason asked.

Danny finally chimed into the conversation, instructing both of them to look at the time and date.

"Yeah?" Nikki questioned.

"That's the Monday we got back from Houston."

"What's your point," she continued asking.

The light bulb went on in Jason's head for the second time that day. "That's the day I told the two of you about my decision to propose to Rebekah."

"We were in Danny's dressing room and Carrie came in," Nikki continued. "She was so sugary sweet about you and Rebekah, too sweet if I remember correctly."

Danny continued. "She must have left and heard Rebekah's message, and then deleted it."

"That's how she knew how to set everything up," Jason

said, the final pieces of the puzzle fitting together in his mind. He couldn't believe how manipulative Carrie had turned out to be. Even if he had ever been considering getting back together with her, which he hadn't been, there was no way he would now.

"There's one thing we don't know for sure," Jason heard Danny say, breaking him from his thoughts.

"What's that?" he asked.

"We don't know if this is really what happened."

"What do you mean?" asked Nikki.

"Well, this is our theory of what happened," he began and continued quickly before Nikki could interrupt, "and it is a good theory. But, we don't know for sure if that is what happened."

"I can find out," she stated simply.

"I don't want you to call Rebekah," Jason requested.

"I don't plan to."

"Then how are you going to find out for sure?"

"Kate," she answered simply.

"Kate – as in Rebekah's best friend Kate? How in the world are you going to get in touch with her?"

"I got her number the weekend that Rebekah was here for your sister's wedding."

"Do I even want to know how?" Danny asked.

"Hey," Nikki replied, feigning hurt. "I'm not that bad! Seriously!" She picked up a pillow and threw it at her husband as he stood there and laughed at her. "Rebekah asked to borrow my phone that weekend and she called Kate. Later that evening, I decided to store the number in case something ever happened and we needed to get in touch with someone who knew Rebekah. See what a genius I am?" she smirked to the two men standing in front of her. She never got enough credit around here.

"That could work," Jason replied. "But, I don't want her mentioning anything about this to Rebekah."

"If things happened the way we think they did, I'll bet Kate will be as eager to help us plan a resolution to this as we are." Scrolling through the stored numbers on her cell phone, Nikki quickly pressed the send button and waited with baited breath for her to pick up. Much to everyone's relief, they didn't have to wait long. "Kate?" Nikki asked as someone answered the phone.

"Speaking. May I help you?" she asked, curious as to who was calling her phone at this time of the morning.

"I certainly hope so. I'm not sure if she ever mentioned me, but my name is Nikki Camarelli, and I am a friend of Rebekah's."

"I know who you are," Kate replied with concern laced in her voice. "Why are you calling?"

"I need to know what happened two weeks ago."

"Why don't you ask Jason? He can certainly fill in the blanks."

"That's just it, Kate," Nikki tried to explain, waving off Jason's attempt to take the phone from her. "If what we think happened is true, Jason can't explain anything. He wasn't even home."

"What do you mean he wasn't home? If he wasn't home, then who did Rebekah see that night?"

Immediately, a smile spread across Nikki's face. "I knew it!" she exclaimed.

"Knew what?" Kate asked, thoroughly confused.

"Rebekah thinks that Jason was making love to his ex-wife, doesn't she?"

"She doesn't just think it, Nikki. She saw it."

"That's the thing though, she didn't." When she heard Kate preparing to interrupt, she quickly continued. "I promise you. Jason was in the City with my husband that Friday night. He let our newest cast member stay at his apartment while he was gone, and Carrie seduced him. She knew Rebekah was going to be in town."

Silence filled the air waves as Kate processed everything Nikki had just said. "That explains why she didn't recognize his voice," Kate replied, all of the pieces falling together in her mind.

"What do you mean?" Nikki asked, still trying to fend off Jason. He was absolutely dying to know what was going on. Nikki was trying to let him know without actually talking to him, and it wasn't working.

"Rebekah said that when she heard him calling out Carrie's name, he sounded like he had never sounded before, like Carrie satisfied him in a way Rebekah never could."

"Hah!" Nikki laughed outloud. "Carrie only wishes that was her reality." Not able to fend off Jason any longer, she knew she had to finish the call. "Look, Kate. I have Jason standing here with me, and he is dying to figure all of this out. I'm going to need to go and fill him in."

"Wait! What are we going to do?"

"We?"

"I may not know you very well, Nikki, but I do know Rebekah. And, I know that she's been the happiest she's been in a long time with Jason. I won't let her lose that."

"Well, I feel the same way about Jason, and I know he feels the same way about her."

"Good. So, what are we going to do?"

"That's what we need to figure out. It's going to be everything I can do to keep him from heading down there right now."

"He can't," Kate insisted.

"Why not?"

"She is in a very strange state of mind right now. She thinks she saw him with his ex-wife, and it devastated her. He has to have a plan instead of just charging down there."

"I knew I was going to like you," Nikki smiled. "What do you have in mind?"

"Well, I'm going down there this weekend. Why don't you put Jason on the phone, and we can all work something out."

Nikki turned to face Jason who was nervously drumming his fingers on the table. "We were right," she whispered as she handed him the phone. "Here, she wants to help you plan what to do next."

On Saturday morning, Rebekah was glad to have a reprieve from her life. Kate should be in any moment, and she couldn't wait to see her. Listening to Jason earlier in the week had been so painful. He had been so uncaring, so cruel, acting like nothing had even happened. She never imagined that he could be like that.

With relief though, she heard her friend knocking on the door. With a rush, she threw the door open and embraced her friend. "It's so good to see you," exclaimed Rebekah.

"It's good to see you to," replied Kate.

"Come in. Do you remember where the guest rooms are?"

"Yeah, I do." Kate headed to the room she had stayed in the last time she was here.

"I didn't plan too much for dinner," Rebekah said as Kate came back into the living room.

"That's okay. I'm just glad I could be here. Are you sure you're doing alright?"

"I won't lie," Rebekah admitted. "It does hurt some. And, hearing his voice earlier this week was not easy. I still can't believe he would be so cold as to act like none of this was any big deal."

"I still don't know what to say, Beck. Every time I saw him that weekend in New York, he seemed so sincere, like he really was in love with you."

"Well, he *is* an actor. I'm sure it was pretty easy for him to fake."

"So," Kate said, trying to change the direction of the conversation, "are you still going to your dance tonight?"

"Sure am. Do you want to go too?"

"You know, I think I will."

"Good. It's going to be hard enough to be there. Having you with me will help."

"Why will it be hard?"

"Remember I told you the theme was 'Hollywood Nights'?" Kate nodded her head yes, praying she knew exactly where Rebekah was going with everything, in fact, she was counting on it. "Well," Rebekah continued. "They are going to be using movie posters and pictures of actors and actresses."

"Right."

"I can almost guarantee you that there will be pictures

of Jason all over the place particularly since most people around here know we were seeing each other."

"Probably," Kate agreed, knowing there would be. "Look, we'll deal with all of that tonight. Let's just enjoy our afternoon now."

"Okay," Rebekah agreed, knowing her friend was right. Why dwell on something she couldn't control?

For the rest of the afternoon, both women relaxed and spent time visiting and catching up. By late afternoon, it was time for them to head to the school. Rebekah had promised she would help set up and get the kids checked into the dance, and that was always a long process. Once they were in for the night, they couldn't leave until the dance was over.

The Eighth Grade Parents had done an outstanding job on the decorations. A red carpet ran from the parent drop-off area to the inside of the cafeteria and gym. White lights twinkled all over the place and stars hung from the high ceiling. The walls were decked with pictures of real Hollywood stars. For a moment, Rebekah allowed herself to get lost in what her life could have been like. She was drawn out of her reverie though as her teaching partner came up to her.

"Too bad your boyfriend couldn't have been here," Terri commented. "The kids would have loved it."

"Yeah," she replied absentmindedly. "The kids would have enjoyed that."

Rebekah was thankful that before too many more questions could be asked, the kids started unloading. The teachers and parents spent the next hour helping the kids get checked in. Once that was over, she headed inside to mingle and watch her kids have a good time. They had their whole lives ahead of them, and she loved that for them.

Before long though, an exciting buzz could be heard. The kids were wound up about something, but before she could leave to find out what it was, she heard it. "Jason Taylor is here!"

Rebekah looked for a place to hide. Anger surged through her body. How dare he come here and cause a scene? Just as she turned to find him and give him a piece of her mind, he was standing in front of her, wearing a tuxedo.

"What are you doing here?" she asked angrily through clenched teeth, glancing towards Kate who had a strange smile on her face. 'Did she know about this?' Rebekah wondered.

"I'm here because I love you."

"Bull!" She was trying to keep her voice quiet, but it was becoming more and more difficult. "You don't care about me, and your actions made that perfectly clear a few weeks ago."

"Listen, I know you aren't going to believe this, but that wasn't me."

"You're right, she scoffed. "I don't believe you."

By now, a large group of students had crowded around them much more interested in the love life of one of their teachers and a Hollywood star than their own dance.

"He's telling the truth honey," she heard behind her. She was surprised to turn around and find her father there.

Turning back towards Jason she continued, "I can't believe you would stoop so low as to bring my father into this."

"I had to. It was the right thing to do." He saw her roll her eyes, and he knew he had to convince her fast. "Look. I know you came to New York several weeks ago, and I know you saw something that would throw anyone for a loop. What you don't know is that the man you saw wasn't me but Nathan, the new co-star that looks so much like me. Carrie knew you were coming, and she set that up."

Rebekah was trying to take it all in, and her head was swimming. He could see that, but he knew he had to keep going.

"He's telling the truth," a voice said as Rebekah tried to process who was stepping around Jason's strong form. In the dark of the room, Jason's on-screen brother stepped closer towards her. "I was the one in his apartment that night," Nathan continued. He was glad he had been able to arrange the trip to help Jason out.

Kate also stepped closer to the situation to provide her friend with some much needed assistance. "Nikki and I talked," she whispered. "We all figured out what happened. I promise you, he's telling you the truth."

"I wasn't even in town that night, Rebekah," Jason continued. "I had taken Danny with me to the City to buy something for you." Reaching into his pocket, he drew out a small velvet box and she gasped, along with most of the other eighth grade girls around her. "Beck, say something," he prodded.

"I don't need you to take care of me," she whispered. "I can take care of myself." She had decided to give up on love, but she felt her resolve fading fast. If she was honest with herself, she would admit that she didn't want to spend her life without him.

"Beck," he continued, moving closer. "I don't want to take care of you. I want us to take care of each other forever." He could see that he was winning her over.

Danny and Nikki stepped forward too and many of the girls got even more excited. "He's telling the truth." Nikki said. "We cornered Carrie, and she finally admitted to everything. She broke into my dressing room when you were leaving your message and deleted it. Then, she set everything up so you would find them there."

Rebekah glanced at Jason and could read the hope in his eyes. He hadn't betrayed her! She saw him reading her eyes as well and smiled as he got down on one knee. "Rebekah Thomas, I love you with everything that I have. I promise to love you for the rest of my life. Will you do me the honor of being my wife?"

Silence filled the gym as every student there waited in anticipation for her answer. This was every young girls dream and they all wanted to know how it would turn out. Finally, one of them broke through the silence by asking, "What's your answer, miss?"

"Yes," she whispered, looking deep into his eyes. "Yes, I'll marry you!"

Jason slipped the ring on her finger and jumped up, picking her up and swinging her around. "I love you, always and forever." Placing her on the ground, he kept his arms around her as they began swaying to the music.

The kids turned back to their dancing still humming with an excited buzz. Rebekah smiled to herself as she and Jason heard one of the girls comment to the guys around her, "see, I told you that sometimes love is enough!"

"Yeah, it is," Rebekah whispered to him before he captured her lips in a kiss.

CHAPTER 12

Six weeks later, Jason sat in his dressing room contemplating how much had changed in his life over the past few weeks. He still couldn't believe how close he had come to losing Rebekah, and he was extremely glad he had been able to keep her in his life, permanently. Now it was time for the final piece of the puzzle to be dealt with, Carrie. This woman, in her zest to reunite them, had almost completely sabotaged his relationship with Rebekah, and although he believed in forgiveness, he knew it was going to be very difficult in this case.

He knew Carrie had been wondering where he had been. Fortunately, while in Houston, he had been able to call the Executive Producer and explain what was going on; he had some vacation time, and they assured him that as long as he came in the first week, he could take the next five in vacation, and it would fit fine in the storyline. His character was going to be going on a business trip anyway, so there was no need for him to be onscreen. During the week he came back, with the added bonus that Carrie was on her scheduled vacation that week, he had been able to tape so many of his scenes in advance that he was only going to be off-screen for about two weeks. And he had thoroughly enjoyed those weeks that he had been off; they had been a time he would never forget.

Jason knew Carrie had to be extremely nervous. He knew that Danny and Nikki had refused to say anything to her after they initially cornered her. She had asked them where he had been when she came back from her vacation, but of course, they never shared the information, knowing that Jason and Rebekah wanted to confront her together. But, before he knew it Carrie sauntered into his dressing room.

"Hey, stranger," she said calmly, even though she was extremely stressed inside. She was positive Danny and Nikki had filled him in, but when he didn't confront her right away, she began to hope for the best. Maybe he finally realized that she did what she did because she loved him and they could go on with their lives, together.

"Hi, Carrie," he replied, just as calmly. He wanted to keep her in here, at least for a little while, giving Rebekah time to get there.

"You've been gone awhile. Did you enjoy your vacation?"

"More than you know," Jason responded. "And you?" he continued, trying to be civil.

"It wasn't as long as yours, but it was good."

Jason simply nodded his head in response knowing she was absolutely right. There was no way her vacation could ever measure up to the time he had off. So much had changed for him and Rebekah in such a short amount of time.

But, before he could get lost in his thoughts of the past few weeks, Carrie continued. "Look, Jason, about before," she began, feeling it would be best to discuss everything now instead of waiting any longer.

"It's in the past, Carrie. I know why you did it," Jason broke in, biting his tongue on everything else he wanted to say. 'Where is Rebekah?' he continued silently wondering.

"You're not mad?" Carrie asked incredulously. Carrie was dumbfounded. She couldn't believe her good fortune. Miss Goodie-Two-Shoes was gone and Jason was acting like it was no big deal. Maybe if she was lucky enough, she could be moving back into his, their, Penthouse by the end of the week.

"I wouldn't say he's not angry," a voice spoke from the doorway. Immediately, Carrie whipped her head around and a sharp intake of air was heard as she realized who was now in the room. Quickly, Rebekah continued, "I would just say that he doesn't really care anymore."

"Carrie," Jason broke in as he stood and reached out a hand to draw Rebekah into the room. "I believe you know Rebekah, my wife."

Silence filled the room as Carrie tried to process everything that was swirling around in her brain. "That's where you've been," she whispered, still shell-shocked.

"We were married five weeks ago, the weekend after her school let out for the year," Jason answered, drawing Rebekah closer to him and noticing she had the papers behind her back.

"So what now?" Carrie asked, almost angrily. The shock had worn off and she was furious that she hadn't run off Rebekah after all.

"I'm moving to Texas," Jason answered simply.

"Well that's about the stupidest thing I've ever heard of," Carrie continued her tirade. "You work here. What the hell are you going to do, fly in every day?"

"Correction," Rebekah cut in. "He used to work here." Pulling the papers from behind her back, she handed a copy each to Jason and Carrie. "These are the script changes. They were just delivered while I was down in Nikki's dressing room. I knew you would want to see them, so I took your copies for you."

Rebekah smiled sweetly as Carrie ripped her copy from her hands. "What do you mean script changes," she asked.

"I told you," Jason answered, flipping through the pages and glancing over them to see if all of the changes had been made. "I'm moving to Texas, which means I'm leaving the show. I've got the money set aside, and I don't need to be here any longer. Because of the success of my last movie, I've accepted two other offers. One actually films in Texas, the other in several other countries."

"Some marriage that'll be. I give it a year tops," Carrie scoffed.

"My marriage is none of your concern," Jason retorted.

"Fine, go. At least I won't have to pretend to enjoy working with you anymore."

"Actually, you're right, especially since you won't be working here at all any longer."

"What the hell did you do Jason Taylor?" Carrie practically screamed.

"It's not what I did, Carrie, it's what you did. You are responsible for every one of your actions. I just made sure the execs knew what occurred."

"Please, like they care about your love life."

"You're right; they could care less about my love life. However, they do care about why they are losing one of their longest running actors and why their newest young male actor, who has the potential to bring home an Emmy this year, is off his game. You are too big of a risk to them, too big of a liability. So, you're gone too."

"So, why didn't they tell me anything?" she asked.

"Gordon's a friend of mine; he saved the moment for me. If you don't believe me, go upstairs and ask them. But, Carrie, I'm telling you now, the answer will be the same."

"So this is what the changes say?" she asked, glancing at the papers in her hand.

"Read the last few pages and see for yourself. You and I will be in a car wreck; we tumble off a cliff. Your body will be found, but mine won't be."

"They left you the room to come back that you asked for," Rebekah said quietly. She had never been one to gloat, and she didn't want to start now. Even though the woman in front of her caused her an almost endless amount of pain, she knew Carrie was hurting, and she didn't see a need to cause any more pain.

Carrie, however, felt differently. "How dare you!" she screamed, almost launching herself at Rebekah, turning her anger in the one place she felt it belonged. "You did this. You caused all of this, simply because you couldn't keep your hands off of my husband!"

Immediately, Jason turned and tried to intercept Carrie, but Rebekah just placed a hand on his arm, gently stopping him. "He's my husband," she stated simply. Carrie stopped dead in her tracks as she watched Jason's protectiveness over Rebekah. Never had she seen him act that way regarding her. Quickly, Rebekah continued. "Look Carrie, I know that you are hurting right now, but it's over."

"The hell it is. You will hear from my lawyer," she pointed a bony finger towards Jason.

"For what, doing what I warned you I would do?" Jason broke in. "I told you to stay away from Rebekah, but you couldn't resist. You are the one who lied to the press. You are the one that had someone else impersonate me. If anything, I have more cause to contact a lawyer, but I won't. And if you're smart, you won't either."

"This isn't over," Carrie whispered, fighting to continue putting on a strong front, but quickly losing that battle.

"Yeah, it is," Jason replied. "Everything is over. You're finished working here. You're finished with your non-existent relationship with Nathan because he smartened up and wants nothing to do with you. And, just like I've been telling you for months now, you're finished with both me and Rebekah."

Nothing was spoken as Carrie watched the two people in front of her as they held hands and flaunted their 'relationship' in front of her. There was nothing left to say. "Enjoy your sham of a marriage," she said, turning on her heel to leave. "May it fall apart soon." Carrie stormed out of the dressing room, grabbing the door and slamming it behind her.

Jason and Rebekah watched her leave and the moment the door slammed shut, Jason sank into his chair, pulling Rebekah down with him and settling her on his lap. "I am so glad that's over," Rebekah sighed.

"I know; me too. Now, we can focus on the rest of our lives."

Happiness radiated from Rebekah. "Are you sure you want to do this?"

"Do what?"

"Walk away from this? You know you don't have to. You know I can always teach here because I don't want this to ruin your career."

"Rebekah, we already talked about this. This is what's best for my career right now. Think about it. I've got two movies coming up, both of which have the potential to be blockbusters. You're happy in Texas, and I love being where you are happy." Jason quickly quieted any further arguments she could have had by kissing her passionately.

Minutes later, the breathless couple pulled apart. "Mmmm," she whispered quietly. "I love it when you do that."

"I know."

"You know, huh?"

"Yeah. You only told me about a hundred times on our honeymoon."

Rebekah smiled slightly, raising an eyebrow at him playfully. "I wouldn't remember. I was more involved in other things."

"Really?" Jason asked almost seductively. His hot breath tingled against Rebekah's neck as he began at her jaw and kissed his way down to her shoulder.

Rebekah closed her eyes and got lost in the emotions his touch elicited. Images raced through her mind in no particular order. She remembered watching him as she walked down the make-shift aisle in the sand, her parents and their closest friends surrounding them as the sun touched the waves of the ocean and they said their vows to one another, dancing under the stars with only the music of the waves and their hearts to guide them, making love for the first time. 'When had her dream life become her reality?' She wondered to herself.

Jason could feel her drift off, even with the passion of the moment. "Where did you go?" he asked.

"I was just wondering when all my dreams became my reality," she answered, smiling as Jason's own smile reached his eyes.

"I love you," he whispered. "Nothing could be more perfect than this."

"I disagree," she said, smiling as if she had something

to hide. "I have a surprise that will make this day even better." Rebekah stood from his lap and headed over to the purse she had dropped on the floor earlier.

"What are you up to?" Jason asked.

"Patience my dear husband," she replied. "You know I took a later flight down here because I said I had to take care of a few things at work?"

'Right," Jason answered hesitantly, unsure of where she was heading with this.

"Well, I had a few other things to take care of too."

"Okay."

Taking a piece of paper out of her purse, Rebekah sauntered back over to him, wondering how much longer she could keep him in suspense. "I know it's early, but I wanted to be sure before I told you."

"Told me what, Beck?" he asked, clearly getting slightly agitated.

Rebekah stopped in front of him, wedging herself between his legs, staring into his eyes. "I'm pregnant," she whispered.

A stunned silence filled the room as Rebekah watched Jason's eyes fill with joy. "Are you sure?" he whispered back.

"I'm sure. With all the infertility stuff I had before, I called to make an appointment with my doctor the moment I suspected. She did a blood test this morning to confirm it and put a rush on it. I guess that's the benefit of having such a good relationship with your doctor. She knew how devastated I'd been by everything in the past, and I think she was hoping this was as real as I was hoping it was. I'm only five weeks along, but the blood test confirmed it."

Jason reached his hand up in amazement and gently caressed her stomach. Tears filled Rebekah's eyes at his tender action. "So," he said. "I guess we're having a honeymoon baby, huh?"

Rebekah didn't even have a chance to answer him before he stood up, grabbed her to him, and swung her around. The sound of their laughter surrounded them. As he placed her on the ground, her hands went to his face. "I love you, Jason Taylor."

"I love you too, Rebekah Taylor. Always. Forever." Jason bent his head down kissing his wife gently on the lips. 'Yeah,' he thought to himself, answering his question from so many months ago. 'Love is definitely enough.'

EPILOGUE

"Mrs. Taylor," the nurse implored again. "You have to relax. It is almost time for you to push and the more you relax, the quicker we can get this baby out."

"No! We're not ready. I'm not ready. I refuse to have this baby without Jason here." Rebekah practically screamed, visibly exhausted. "You have to slow this labor down," she continued breathlessly. "I can't," she tried to continue but couldn't as another contraction hit her. "Ow, ow, ow, ow! Get this baby out of me now!"

Nurse Hawthorne shook her head and laughed. "That's what we're trying to do, honey."

Rebekah Taylor had been in labor for six hours, but it had only been in the last hour that she alternated between aching to deliver the child and begging for her labor to stop.

"Where's my husband?" Rebekah asked, slowly coming back from the edge of pain from her last contraction. "He was supposed to be here hours ago. I just don't understand where he is." Rebekah was near tears as she realized that their baby might be born without his father present. Everything about this seemed so unfair.

"He's right here," Jason proclaimed, crashing through the door. "I'm right here." He smiled to himself as he realized he could actually see the relief flooding through his wife's body.

"You almost missed it," she whispered, tears clouding her eyes as she desperately clung on to his hand.

"But, I didn't. I promised you I would be here, and I am." Jason brushed the damp hair of her forehead as he placed a sweet kiss thee.

"What took you so long? You were supposed to…" Rebekah once again tried to continue but was unable because of the force of the contraction that hit her.

"Shh," Jason broke in, squeezing her hand. "We have more important things to worry about, like you relaxing enough about me to allow this precious baby of ours to be born."

"I just wish…"

"I know, Bekah," Jason placed a kiss on her hand as the numbers on the monitor evaluating the contractions began to climb, indicating another contraction.

"It's almost time," Nurse Hawthorne said quietly as she stepped closer to the couple. "You have a great effect on her, Dad."

Jason broke out into a huge smile at the truth of her

statement. He knew he had a good effect on Rebekah because she did the same for him. At the same time, he knew how difficult this delivery was for her. For the first time in her life, her mother couldn't be there for her, and he knew it was killing both of them. In a way, he felt like it was his fault; that's why he had been so late today. He knew that he had to do something to try and make this whole situation better.

Rebekah had been feeling so well, and although her doctor had a few reservations, she had allowed Rebekah to fly to New York to accompany Jason; he had agreed to come back to the studio to tape some flashback scenes.

That was three months ago.

While she and Nikki had been shopping one afternoon, Rebekah had collapsed. Her blood pressure was off the charts, and she was complaining of difficulty with her breathing. Jason still remembered how bleak his world had become for the first few moments after he received Nikki's call; he was terrified that he would lose both Rebekah and the baby. But, the doctors had determined that while the situation was precarious, Rebekah was still in good shape. Apparently, the asthma she struggled with as a child and teenager had come back in full force; she was not getting enough air for both herself and the baby and when she collapsed, they baby was trying to figure out a way to get his own air. The doctors ordered Rebekah on complete bed rest, and she was instructed in no uncertain terms, that she was to remain in New York. She was not allowed to fly as it could pose to be too much of a risk for both she and the baby.

Naturally, Rebekah balked at the doctors' orders; she was not the type of person who could easily be so idle, particularly when she had a classroom full of students she felt needed her undivided attention.

"Okay, Mrs. Taylor," the nurse continued. "Dr. Cantrell is on her way. We're going to get you situated to begin pushing."

"Are you ready sweetheart?" Jason asked.

"Absolutely!" Rebekah asserted. "I just want to hold this little precious baby boy as I walk around."

Jason laughed at Rebekah's eagerness. He knew she was anxious about this birth and also ready to be able to get out of her bed for the first time in months. Her life, their life, had been put on hold throughout the last trimester of this pregnancy. They had to stay in New York permanently, abandoning their life in Texas. He was just as ready for this to be over as she was.

"I understand this baby is ready to meet Mommy and Daddy," Dr. Cantrell said as she walked into the room, fully gowned and ready to deliver the baby.

"Not near as ready as I am to meet him," Rebekah said with a half smile. She threw her head back on the pillow, preparing for the exhausting work she had ahead of her.

"All right," the doctor said as she began walking toward the new parents. "Rebekah, I'm going to need your full cooperation. When you feel the need to push, push with everything you have. Jason, you will need to help her out some. If I tell you to rest and stop pushing, make sure that you do just that."

"Okay," Rebekah whispered feeling the onset of another contraction. She felt Jason grab a hold of one leg and the nurse grab the other as she bore down to push.

She couldn't keep track of the number of pushes she had; at times it seemed like she had been laboring for an eternity, at other times, it seemed to go by too quick.

"The head is finally out," Dr.Cantrell exclaimed. "One more push, Mrs. Taylor, and you will be able to hold your beautiful new baby."

Before Rebekah could even process the doctor's statement she again felt the urge to push again and almost immediately, her baby was born. Quickly, the doctor cleared the baby's throat and a small cry filled the air. "You have a beautiful baby girl," the doctor announced as she placed her in her mothers arms.

"A girl?" Jason asked. "We thought it was supposed to be a boy."

"Who cares," an exhausted Rebekah broke in with a smile on her face. "Just look at her. She is beautiful."

"Yes, she is," Jason agreed as he placed a gentle kiss on his daughter's forehead. "She's almost as beautiful as her mother." He placed a kiss on her head as well. "You did great, Mom."

"I love you," she whispered.

"I love you too."

Both Jason and Rebekah watched their daughter in amazement for several minutes before the nurse took her to clean and swaddle her. Rebekah leaned her head back against the pillow watching the nurse and her daughter. She knew it would be a few minutes before she would be able to hold her again, but already her arms ached from missing her angel. The only thing that could make this day more perfect,' she thought to herself, 'would be having the rest of her family here to meet her.' She barely had time to focus on that though before the nurse was bringing her daughter back to her.

"I'll let your family know they can come in now," the nurse said as she left the room.

"But we don't have anyone here," she stated in confusion.

"I called Danny and Nikki earlier. They were on their way the last time I spoke to them"

"That's sweet of them to come," she whispered softly before turning back all of her attention to the precious baby in her arms. "You know," she continued. "We're going to have to think of a new name. I don't think that Jason Junior is going to work for her."

"We could always go with Rebekah Junior," he teased, running his thumb across the soft skin of the baby's forehead.

"You are so not funny, Mr. Taylor," she chided playfully.

"What? It could work."

"What about Elizabeth?" Both Jason and Rebekah immediately turned their heads to the sound of the voice in the doorway.

"Mom!" Rebekah exclaimed. "How did you know? When did you get here?"

"Slow down, Rebekah," her mother ordered. "Your

husband can answer all those questions. Right now, I want to see my granddaughter."

Rebekah turned to face her husband. "What did you do?"

"It was no big deal." He shrugged his shoulders. "I knew how much you wanted your family to be here, so I had them flown in this morning. You know there's nothing I wouldn't do for you."

"I know, and I love you for it." Before she could stretch up to give him a kiss, she felt the baby stir in her arms. "Okay, angel baby, there is someone here you need to meet."

"Actually," her grandmother whispered. "You have several people here you need to meet."

"Who else is here?' Rebekah asked. But, before her mother could answer the question, the door slammed open and a flash of red rushed by.

"Is he here? Is he here?" A small voice asked as Jason scooped her up.

"Is who here?" He asked with a smile.

"Is my baby brother here?"

"Actually, pumpkin, your baby brother is a baby sister instead."

"A sister?" She asked excitedly. "I have a sister? Can I see her?"

"Here she is," Rebekah whispered as she choked back a

sob, looking up at her husband and her three year old daughter. Jason had accomplished the impossible. Not only had he flown out her parents, but their precious Emily as well. She had missed having her daughter with her every day while she had been confined to New York. Her mother had come up a few times and brought Emily with her, but it wasn't the same as when they were all together at home.

"Can I hold her and dress her up?" Emily asked.

"Not right now, pumpkin," Jason replied. "Right now, Mommy is going to feed your sister and then they are both going to take a nap."

"I don't like naps," she said, looking at him very seriously.

"I know," he replied with a laugh. "That's why you are going to go with Nana and Papa. But, Mommy and your sister need one."

"Why?"

"Well, being born is hard work, and they both need to sleep."

"Is Mommy going to come back home now?"

"I am," Rebekah replied, silently glad that her daughter had missed her at least a little bit.

"Does the baby get to come home too?"

"She does." Jason kissed her on the nose. "But, not for a few days, and definitely not until we let both of them rest."

"I love you, Mommy," Emily practically shouted in her three-year old excitement as she was passed back into her Papa's arms. "And, I love you too, baby."

"We love you, Emily," Rebekah whispered back, fighting back tears as the room began to clear out.

"Danny and Nikki are in the waiting room and said they would come by later. They know how tired you are." Rebekah's mother said as she kissed her daughter on the forehead. "I'll be by later too. Right now, the three of you need some quiet time."

"I love you, Mom," said Rebekah.

"I know, honey." Her mother turned and walked out of the room, shutting the door behind her and leaving the small family to themselves.

"And, I love you, Mr. Taylor," she continued, staring adoringly up at her husband. "I love you more and more every day."

"I know. And, I love you too."

"Thank you, Jason."

"For what?" He asked as he moved a chair closer to the bed so he could admire both his wife and his new daughter.

"For everything: for bringing Emily and my parents here, for being here for me and with me, for loving me."

"That last part is easy."

"For me too."

Jason leaned forward and softly kissed Rebekah on the lips. When they broke apart, he placed his hand on his daughter's head and gently stroked the fine hair there. "Are you disappointed?" He heard his wife ask.

"Why in the world would I be disappointed?"

"Well, she's not the son you were planning for."

"Maybe not, but she's one of the most beautiful ladies in my life. I could never be disappointed with the blessing that God has given us."

"I'm glad, because I'd have to hurt you if you suggested she needed to go back in and keep 'cooking' for a while."

"Yeah, I kind of sensed that," he joked back. "Seriously though, I have everything I need, and definitely more than I ever planned on. You have given me so much, Rebekah. You've given me a place to call home, two beautiful children, a family, and most importantly, you've given me your love."

"You'll always have that, Jase." Silence filled the small hospital room as their daughter gazed up at her two parents.

"I know. So, what do you think of Elizabeth?"

"I think it's as perfect as she is. We'll have an Emily and an Elizabeth."

"Then, Elizabeth it is." Jason leaned forward to place another sweet kiss on her forehead. "Hi, Elizabeth. I'm your Daddy. And, this," he continued, pointing to

Rebekah, "this is your Mommy."

"We love you very much," Rebekah finished for him.

"And if there is one thing that being a part of this family will teach you." Jason broke in, "It's that our love is enough to accomplish anything!"

"Yeah, it is. Our love is definitely enough. Five years later, I think that we finally get that." Rebekah said that last part directed more towards Jason than their daughter.

"I'm so glad I met you, Mrs. Taylor." Jason whispered before placing his forehead against hers.

"Me too, Mr. Taylor." Almost a decade ago, she had thought her life was over; her heart had been broken. Now, she knew, her life had gone on and her heart was not only healed, but overflowing.

ABOUT THE AUTHOR

Marisa Adams is an avid reader with an immense passion for great love stories. She is an educator, wife, and mother but always finds the time to squeeze in a little time to get lost in the worlds of her characters. She has been writing for years and has published several short stories before branching into the world of novels.

Marisa believes in love at first sight and happy endings. Each of her books will remind you that romance and true love still exist even in today's fast paced world.

Made in the USA
San Bernardino, CA
11 February 2016